The Language of Silence

by Merilyn Moos

The Language of Silence

by

Merilyn Moos

Copyright © 2010 by Merilyn Moos

ISBN: 978-0-9566467-005

Published by Cressida Press in conjunction with Writersworld Ltd

Copy edited by Sue Croft

Cover design by Charles Leveroni

Printed and bound by www.printondemand-worldwide.com

www.writersworld.co.uk

WRITERSWORLD
2 Bear Close
Woodstock
Oxfordshire
OX20 1JX
England

The text pages of this book are produced via an independent certification process than ensures the trees from which the paper is produced come from well managed sources that exclude the risk of using illegally logged timber while leaving options to use post-consumer recycled paper as well.

For

Josh Moos

ACKNOWLEDGEMENTS

I wrote this novel to lift the weight of secrets from which my parents had hoped to protect me. You may accuse me of having written a work of non-fiction, thinking you recognise characters and places in the text from real life. But be assured that this is a story. It is true that it draws on my experience of being a member of a 'second generation', whose parents had to make a life in a foreign land, and some of this is in the book - but I am not. It is a story of painful otherness, of persecution and exile, which flows down through the arteries of generations and which so many millions will unfortunately recognise.

Many people helped me in the process of writing. My special thanks to Richard Kirkwood, political and historical detective extraordinaire, to Annie Duarte whose editorial skills and literary flair have no match, to Kate Hughes for her final editorial polish, to Lucie Kinchin for her ultimate sub-copy editing, to Wendy Harris, Chouchou Crawley and Veronika Krapf, for their translations of often difficult texts, and to Christine Jackson for her invaluable financial, literary and moral support, without whom this novel would not have been published. Barry McCloughlin set me off on the protracted hunt for my mother's past, which inspired this novel, and I would recommend his *Left to the Wolves* to anybody interested in the fate of Irish Communists in the USSR in the late 1930s. I also want to thank Tessa de Carlo, Peter Church, Dan Goldberg, Dawn Gill, Ginger Hjelmaa, Gerry Lander, Kathy Leander, Hannorah Lee, Cathy Levy, Rosie Slay and Sarah Thomas for their comments and support. My thanks go also to Graham Cook from Writersworld, Sue Croft, copy editor and Charles Leveroni, cover designer, for their dedicated work on my behalf.

I remember my father, Siegi Moos, who fought till his death against want and superstition, and for equality and justice, and who loved the song of the lark, and my mother, Lotte Moos, who, as she lay close to death, opened wide her eyes to the strains of Mozart's Piano Concerto No. 21 and raised her clenched fist in salute as we sang her the Internationale.

Merilyn Moos was born to refugee parents in Oxford, grew up in Durham, graduated from Oxford University, obtained an MA in Contemporary Cultural Studies, and became an FE and HE lecturer and enthusiastic political activist. She now lives in north London.

Merilyn Moos has been writing stories since she was a child. She is the author of numerous academic articles, mostly on educational policy and the increasing segmentation for post-16s, and a couple of biographical articles, all written over the last thirty years. She has also appeared in two television documentaries on the effects of displacement.

The Language of Silence is Merilyn Moos's first novel. Already in her fifties, she started the perilous journey of discovery into her parents' hidden pasts, and this encouraged her to write *The Language of Silence*.

Part I

Chapter 1

Hundreds of demonstrators are blockaded in the underpass, police pushing us from the further end of the tunnel, and police preventing us exiting at the other end.

'It's safer if you stand with your back against the wall,' I shout to Sam. He has the advantage of being tall for his age and, even in the crush, I can spot him, his head wrapped in his red scarf.

So many people are squeezed together. Rolls of sound bounce off the walls of the tunnel as demonstrators yell to each other to stay calm.

'We're moving, Mum,' says Sam, at last at my side. And for the first time in many years, he takes hold of my hand and starts to pull me through the crowd. We move towards the exit and sunlight.

As we emerge, he puts his arm through mine.

'Let's get to a cafe,' I suggest. 'I need to recover.'

'Mum, you know I've got my politics homework to do.'

'The one that was due in last Friday?'

'What d'you know about a comparison between Nazism and Stalinism?'

But before I've time to respond, to argue that such comparisons are usually facile, my mobile rings.

'Leave it,' Sam instructs me.

But I can't.

When I arrive at the hospital, my mother is sitting propped up in bed. She looks frail, though her eyes maintain their cornflower blue gaze. She shouts at me as soon as she notices me: 'This is an asylum! They're going to kill me. Just look what you've done to me. You'll be sorry.'

1

'This is a hospital,' I try to reassure her.

An asylum: such an old-fashioned word.

'You said we were going to visit a friend and instead you leave me here. You're going to kill me.'

Unable to calm her, I go to find a doctor.

'Your mother will be fine,' the doctor tells me. 'There was a concern about her breathing.'

I escape home. Sam is waiting for me.

I return the next day. My mother lies, propped up by pillows, deathly pale, her cheeks shrunken down to her gums, her skin a parchment yellow, her eyes, which had burned with the memory of past struggles, opaque.

I reach between the bars on the side of her bed, raised because the nurses fear she could roll out, and take her hand. I do not want to. She pulls her hand away.

'What about me?' I want to yell. 'You never held my hand when I was ill.'

She could soon be dead. Is this not the time to tell her I love her?

'You are beautiful,' she announces, looking at me.

I shake my head, taken aback by the unfamiliarity of the intimacy. Is she bidding me farewell? I do not want my mother to die. I do not want my past to disappear.

'The sculpture you're doing in your evening class is wonderful.'

Why is she telling me this? She does not like me to lay claim to success.

'It may not be wonderful, but it's good,' she continues, nodding at me, as if to emphasise this diminution of praise.

I nod back, silent.

'I had a fall,' she tells me. 'Just a fall. A little bruise. You brought me here just for that? What a pity. All I did was stub my toe.'

She pushes her foot out from under the blankets for me to examine its unblemished state.

Then she reaches out and takes my hand and squeezing it, announces: 'Lovely to see you.'

On my next visit I take in a slice of home-made chocolate cake baked specially for her. She glares at me as I offer her a slice, then grudgingly opens her mouth, and, lifting her hand, points into it with her finger. I raise the cake to her lips and she takes a bite.

'Nice?' I ask.

She points to her mouth again.

'Why don't you feed yourself?'

'I don't want it now,' she informs me.

My mother recovers. I knew she would when she announced: 'Lenin's a good man. Not like that bastard Stalin. He killed Lenin. Did you know that?'

Unexpectedly, we laugh.

'I met Stalin. You didn't know that, did you?'

I shake my head.

She looks coy. 'In Moscow. In 1936.'

'You're sure?'

'I was at a meeting,' she whispers.

'What were you doing there?' I ask, puzzled.

My parents had poured an undiluted hatred of Stalin down me, along with the daily pint of milk. She had never before mentioned that she had ever been to the USSR.

She pinches her lips tight, as if they were super-glued together, and turns away, her face towards the window. I kiss her gingerly on the back of her head.

Their eyes questioning, the hospital staff have told me I am the only person who ever visits her. 'There is nobody else,' I snap, unwilling to explain.

Despite my fears that she is no longer able to look after herself, the hospital declare her fit to return home.

3

Chapter 2

Mine had been a childhood of silences. Where other children boasted grandparents, aunts and uncles, I had none. No photos adorned our mantelpiece, no photo albums appeared out of drawers.

My parents never talked about their parents or their families. Instead, ghosts filled the spaces, peering down from over the doorways in our neglected Victorian house. They were everywhere, down the worn stone stairs leading to the basement, dancing in the fireplaces, present in every breath and word spoken by my parents. Later, I was to decide it had been Death who was in attendance. Not that anybody had died, for there were no relatives to die.

I tried to ask my father, when I was about three or four, about his family. The storm clouds of disapproval and aggravated emotion settled heavily over him and I fled into my bedroom and silence. I learnt early that talking was dangerous.

I tried my mother. 'Did you have any brothers or sisters?' I had enquired tentatively.

'Why are you asking? What's it got to do with you?'

If I wanted my parents to love me, there were questions it was wiser not to ask. Whatever it was they were protecting me from, it was dangerous. If I wanted to survive, it was best left alone.

The house in my childhood had not felt like a home. There was my parents' bedroom; my bedroom, so tiny that there was space only for my bed and a chest of drawers; the upstairs drawing room, which I could only enter after an adult had invited me; my father's office downstairs, which was permanently off-limits; a tiny kitchen, and the front room. This room was our hub, if such a thing existed. Here we ate our meals, my mother and I did the ironing, and here, crammed into the drawer of a chest, were my books, a few toys, and my paints and pencils. It was also where, on a few evenings, my mother played the piano, appearing with old, battered, bound volumes of Mozart and Bach, the music echoing with laments.

Our street teemed with the neighbourhood's children but my parents found something wrong with all of them. My first friend was Michael. He lived a few doors down the road from us. We were both aged five when he - or rather his university parents - invited me round. I was filled with the thrill of friendship and happy to be invited for a second visit. Michael took me down into the basement, which was a converted old kitchen, filled a bucket half full with water and swung it around so fast that nothing spilled. I was so excited, I told my father. He banned me from visiting Michael ever again. There might be an accident, he told me, but he looked angry. Why was I being punished? I suspected it must have had something to do with going into the basement.

'I've told them you don't want to play with him again,' my father informed me, 'because you were frightened.'

I was too young to understand that my father's objection was to Michael's being a boy. Uncomprehending, I felt forlorn and diminished. I never went over to Michael's again.

Then there was Janice, who lived in the next road. The same age, I had met her at the regulatory birthday parties which my parents, knowing her parents, had to allow me to attend. She looked like a bean pole, even by Durham standards, topped with a sharp chin and a sharper voice. 'I don't like your house,' I remember her telling me. But fortunately my parents decided that the family were stuck up. Janice went to a private school, and she was therefore an unsuitable friend.

I would never have dared aspire to become friends with Mary, one year above me at primary school. My parents had declared her off-limits, even though she lived opposite us, because she was obviously too old for me.

There was the girl next door but one, but I never even found out her name. 'Common,' said my father. Once, I had managed to escape through the old wooden door which led from the bottom of our garden into the back street. As this was forbidden, I slipped out without informing either parent, weighed down with anxiety over this minor transgression. I only dared to hang around briefly, envying the little group of friends as they played tag and chatted away to each other, yards from my house. My parents noticed I was not at home.

'Anna!' I heard my mother shout. 'Your father wants to talk to you.'

I had to knock on the door of my father's office before he would call out 'Come in,' and there I stood before his desk as he sat in his large chair opposite me, explaining my brief moment of illicit freedom.

'You don't want to be like them, do you?' he scolded. But I heard a discrepant note of despair.

'No, Papa, no.'

I was too young to comprehend that he feared for me, feared that I would be waylaid in the long slog up the foothills to the class securities he aspired to for me. But I did understand I had done something very wrong, without quite knowing why.

I made do with an imaginary sister, Jo, whom my parents had locked up in the fearsome dark cellar in the house. I called her after Jo in *Little Women*. Jo, entombed in the darkness, was largely beyond my reach, but I lay in bed and imagined whispering to her about how unbearable my life was. I never wanted to grow up, I told her.

Here I sat, my back as close to the large anthracite stove as I could get it, for this was before central heating and the northern climes were cold for much of the year in those pre-global warming days. I didn't know what to do with myself. Too often, there was nothing I wanted to do. I pulled out a book. Books were my childhood friends. I got out my water-colour paints, but I understood I wouldn't be able to turn out anything worthwhile. Mostly, I stared out of the large Victorian window onto our little garden and felt isolated, as if I were in a large floating balloon. There was nowhere I felt 'at home.'

Chapter 3

Memories of childhood are sticky. Not that I remember most of my childhood, but I cannot pull myself free from its glue. Childhood is a bit like a volcano. You never know when it's going to erupt.

There were good things. Did I not grow up in a super-stable nuclear family, cared for by devoted parents, my father with his prestigious job, my mother the stay-at-home 1950s housewife? They even sent me to the Church of England primary school. That's how 'normal' we were.

The first day I was at school, sitting on a long wooden bench waiting for our 'dinner' to be served, the little girl next to me wet herself. I watched as the warm liquid splashed on to the floor and curled into a small pool under the table. Nobody noticed. 'Nobody cared,' I reported back to my parents that evening, though I did not like to shame the girl. I caught a look of misery passing between them.

'The school is so convenient,' my mother said.

'Such a good reputation,' my father agreed, but he did not sound convinced. 'The headmistress likes you.'

She did, too. She was the only one.

Twice a week, we crocodile-filed to the local chapel. I loved the walk from the school to the chapel, along a quiet lane, lined with trees. This was where I learnt how sticky buds miraculously swell and then unfurl, the fresh green leaf twisting out, and later, fading into the autumn.

I liked the quiet of the church, the high carved wooden ceiling, and the large stained-glass windows, which, when we were good and lucky, the sun poured through, splattering us in its light. I swelled with the organ's howling accompaniment to our hymns. After the hymns we prayed, and I was swathed in the sound of the voice of God. I squeezed my eyes tight shut when we knelt down on our hassocks. With an innocence beyond my years, I bathed in the glistening words about Christ and how he performed miracles to help the sick and the needy.

How long was it before I took a peek? It was the rustling that did it. I could hear the other children fidgeting round me. At first, I found them lacking in a desirable piety and not behaving as good children should. But one day, overcome by what I might be missing, I dared open an eye just a little bit. Might as well have been a mile. 'Hear, oh Israel, the voice of the Lord, thy God.' I was not hearing the voice of God but of our headmistress, Miss Aspen. I had made a mistake. She was reading, not speaking. She was not expressing God's wishes. I cannot have been more than six, but I now realise this revelation set me on my path to atheism.

As we grew older, our class in Junior school was a frequent stopping-off point for missionaries, who wished to save us from ourselves. We were, on the whole, part of the great unwashed and, when they were not preaching to us about saving the souls of babies in Africa, they were trying to save ours, and, no doubt, their own at the same time.

I refused to bring in money for starving black babies. Even when I was told I could theoretically adopt one and give it a name, and wouldn't that make me proud, I smelt condescension and contempt.

I refused to take the pledge and commit myself forever to forsake the pleasures of alcohol. I was too young to make a binding promise for the rest of my life. Those who took the pledge were allowed, for a price, to pin a badge to their clothes to show everybody they were set upon the road of righteousness. I rejected this privilege.

I refused, and this was even more serious, to join the Christian Union. The missionary arrived to persuade us to follow in Christ's path. If we joined up, we would then be given cards, which we had to fill in daily to show we had read the appropriate section of the Bible.

Dubious about what we were being asked to do, I stuck up my hand.

'Yes?'

'What if we were lost somewhere?'

'You could read it when you got home.'

'But what if I was stuck in a bear pit or something?'

I was the only child in the whole year to refuse to sign. I was not going to lie by committing myself to something I knew I would not fulfil. I was proud of standing up for myself, but nervous. I told my parents what had happened that evening. We were sitting around the rich mahogany table over our supper, which we always ate together. That look again passed between them. They said nothing. Remembering, I feel such sadness for them. It would have been so different if their daughter had been in a German school, as they had. But there was nothing to be done. My parents had been defeated and there was no changing the past.

My punishment in school was swift. Five or six of my classmates surrounded me the next day.

'Doubting Thomas!' they screamed repeatedly at me.

'What?'

'Yer know.'

'No.' Unlike these children I had never heard of Doubting Thomas.

'What d'yer learn at Sunday School, then?'

But I had never attended Sunday School.

'Thomas who didn't believe that Jesus was dead till he had stuck his fist into the gash in our Lord's side,' one of my tormentors explained to me.

'You don't believe that.'

'Heathen! Heathen!'

From then till I left primary school, Doubting Thomas was who I became. I did not wear this name with pride.

The teacher was little better. After another talk about the need to save up our pocket money so we could pay for missionaries to rescue poor African babies' souls, pocket money I did not have, I asked her: 'Are you saying that if somebody has not heard the word of Christ, they will burn forever in Hell?'

Which is where, I felt, she would have sent me straight away, given half a chance.

Secondary school services were a deep disappointment. Instead of a walk to a chapel and the accompaniment of a real live organ, we squashed ourselves daily into the assembly hall, so packed in, it was impossible to even scratch an itch. Then we sang our hymns to an old upright, and listened to the Headmistress praying to the Lord to clear us of our sins, and forgive others as we wished them to forgive us. Amen. I had my eyes wide open now. So why were the Catholics not allowed in? Presumably, they were not to be forgiven. Every day, after the service, the doors were opened, and we all watched the handful of Catholics apologetically file in. We were, it seems, Church of England, so we were all right. Even then, I was aware of the hypocrisy.

A handful of my schoolmates took pleasure in asking me what church I went to. Faltering under the persistence of the attack, I became somewhat economical with the truth. 'Of course I go, but I don't remember the name,' became my retort, knowing they knew it was a lie.

Hoping for some way out of this mess, I asked my mother what religion we were. She told me, looking uncomfortable, that she had been a Lutheran, my father a Catholic. Indeed, my father used to chant parts of the Liturgy at me in Latin. But, he informed me, he hated the Catholic Church because it encouraged guilt. 'Mea culpa, mea culpa,' and he would pretend to beat his chest. He used to say you could always tell when somebody had been brought up as a Catholic. You could see it in their eyes.

My mother must have told him about our conversation. If you want to go to any Church at all, you go, he comforted me, assuring me that he would come too. God forbid.

I was a master at guilt. I had no need of Catholicism. When I was still quite little, I would lie in the bath, wondering why Christ had been crucified and fearing that somehow I could be responsible.

'I have sinned,' I confessed to my mother. It pulled at my guts to tell her.

My mother had come in to check how I was managing in the bath and whether I had dried myself properly. I always hated being alone in the bathroom, an add-on to the house, which felt as if it were likely to fall off again every time the wind shook and howled through its slanted roof, which it did often.

'What have you done?' my mother asked me. She sounded amused. But to me, this was no laughing matter.

'I can't remember,' I told her. She laughed.

But I knew I was bad. The whole world had started to spin out of control. I was sure there was nothing I did not know about sin and the Devil.

How often I thought of Christ, with the Devil whispering sweet nothings in his ear, as he stood high up on the hill, with the whole world at his feet. How strong he must have been to resist. How strong not to be tempted to worship the Devil if he could possess all the kingdoms of the earth. Yet we killed him. Why did he let it happen?

It was the religious affairs teacher at secondary school who finally persuaded me that God could not exist. The four Gospels of the New Testament, with their message of hope and salvation, at least for the righteous, was far too liberal for her. Twice a week, we were hurled into Revelations and the Horsemen of the Apocalypse. Bunyan was our light relief. So I learnt that I was going to be damned and sent into the fires of Hell, where I would burn in agony for the rest of time. If this was the case, why bother with believing in the first place?

Chapter 4

My parents had landed in Durham after Durham university had offered my father a lecturing job. With poignant hindsight, I now realise my father was also drawn there because the Durham hills reminded him of the Bavarian mountains of his childhood home.

My father was always busy: lecturing, speaking at meetings, or active in local politics. Being with him was always a treat, at least while I stayed a little girl. These were rare idyllic moments, freeze-dried in time.

He would potter around in the garden, asking me to help him. The only plant that flourished was the Russian vine, with which he fought a losing battle, as his pruning appeared to give it strength. I would pick up its decapitated tendrils and carry them to the bonfire that he lovingly built and rebuilt at the bottom of our tiny garden. Thus he attempted to reassure me that all was normal in our lives.

It was the holidays. I did not like holidays. I did not like school either, but school got me out of the house. I used to think that being alive was vastly overrated.

My father arrived home early one day. He came in, switched on the wireless, sank down into one of the armchairs opposite where I was sitting, and started to cry.

'What's wrong, Papa?' I had never before seen my father weep.

'The King has died.'

I regarded him, puzzled.

'I shall take the day off work, in respect,' he continued.

I did not like seeing my father so upset and was astonished that he was taking time off from the university. Even when he worked from home, he would never emerge from his study till my mother presented supper.

'He was a good King. He helped keep Britain safe. Not like his brother. *He* sympathised with the Nazis,' my father whispered.

'What?'

'We were made welcome here.'

My father did not respond to my further probing. I left him alone in the room.

He threw himself into mourning. He put on his dark suit and black tie. He assiduously polished and brushed his best leather shoes. Later, he attended both the university and city services held in Durham Cathedral. My mother rolled her eyes.

'It was a beautiful service,' he told us after one of them, eyes glistening.

The subsequent coronation passed without further upset, except that I refused to buy a coronation mug at school. Why pay all that money for an ordinary mug with the Queen's picture on it? Almost all the other children brought in their precious pocket money or asked their parents for money to purchase a mug. For those who could not afford a mug, there were small boxes which contained three pencils with rubbers at the end, and the details of the Coronation carved into the side. I failed to understand why my class was getting so excited.

But my nascent republicanism was no doubt facilitated by my parents' refusal to give me pocket money. 'When you are older,' was all my father would say when I would tentatively let him know how incredibly rich the other children were. All I wanted was to buy one of those modern ice lollies at the end of the school day, like the other children did. I would never have gone through the agony of asking my father for money, which he would certainly have refused, for something as trivial as a Coronation mug.

My father, an avid newspaper reader, discovered that the newly-crowned Queen Elizabeth was to do a celebratory tour of Newcastle. He wanted the three of us to go to see her. My mother did not come.

So it was my father and I who took the twenty-minute train journey to Newcastle. Going anywhere with my father was special. Thousands of people lined both sides of the road. We were nowhere near the edge of the pavement, our view obstructed by lines of even earlier devotees. It must have been one of the few days in the year when the sun shone on this northern town, but as the hours of waiting passed, I felt increasingly hot and bored. In the end, there were shouts that her coach was about to come round the corner, and the crowd started to push forward. My father and I jostled on the pavement so that we would get a view. My father hoisted me up in his arms so I could see. Her coach passed in a second and I could only pretend to my father to having seen a glimpse of Her Majesty.

I came home from school a few days later. It was my father who, unusually, opened the door to my insistent knocking. He smiled at me, which was reassuring, and led me into the front room. There he gave me a cardboard cut-out of the Queen's carriage and horses. I rarely received presents. My parents did not believe in spoiling me. I enjoyed cutting and assembling the golden carriage, the frisky horses with their tails which had to be cut around with such care, and, of course, the Queen herself, with a magnificent, jewel-studded, crenellated crown, which defeated even the most careful hand.

I could not interpret the class's gaze when I reported my weekend's activities the following Monday. I had assumed that they and their families would also have been lining up along the Queen's route, but I had been the only one.

'Yer talk funny,' they told me soon afterwards in the playground.

'No, I don't.'

'Yer do.'

I started to walk away.

'Where d'yer come from, then?'

'I live here.'

'Yer talk funny,' the children repeated. And there was a wave of laughter.

I did not tell my father.

I did not hear my parents' German accents. Their English was fluent and elegant, far more so than anybody else with whom I came into contact. How painful this is, even now, to remember that my middle-class vowels compounded the buried twang of a foreign tongue. I may have thought I was as English as the next person, but no, the other children had spotted me for the alien they knew I was. Even today, strangers sniff and scratch around the way I speak, trying to divine the stuff I'm made of.

14

There was one other excursion my father and I took together, in those brief childhood days before the protuberances of pubescence drove us apart. Durham was at the centre of a mining area, now long gone. One summer day, there was my father telling me to come with him to town. Perhaps I was nearer puberty than I now remember, for I replied: 'I don't want to.'

'You'll enjoy it when you get there.'

'What is it?'

'It's a march.'

'I'm tired.'

'You won't be tired when you get there.'

So here I was, running down the hill, towards the beat of the drums and the rhythmic boom and squeak of the brass bands and the accordions. I carry those sounds in me still. How I loved it, as the miners from pit after pit came marching past the bottom of our road, bearing their union banners high. So many banners were draped in black. Too many deaths from accidents in the mines. It was like a medieval carnival - a great annual celebration of survival against the odds - high odds when you're a miner. The men were wearing their Sunday suits, the women their best dresses.

We pushed our way through the crowds down to the racecourse by the river where the meetings were being held. Here hundreds and hundreds of people stood and listened to Hugh Gaitskell, the leader of the Labour Party which was in opposition. Gaitskell, who looked taut and worn, was beaming.

'Look at you all!' he proclaimed. 'Look at all the colours of your clothes, the ribbons in your hair. I don't need to tell you how different from a few years ago.'

The war was still in everybody's memories.

When a trade-union bureaucrat stood up to speak, corpulent neck in stiff, starched white collar, my father insisted we move on to the next platform.

'Why?' I asked.

'You'll find out,' he responded.

But I already half knew. The daughter of the trade-union officer for the local miners went to my school. She lived in the largest house in Durham, with a well-tended garden overlooking the River Wear. And she made sure we all knew

15

it. How very different from my school friend Val's council house, which overlooked the pit. How unfair, I had insisted to Val all those years ago, that the man who represented her mining father should be so much better off than him. Val had shrugged. But it did not escape me even then, that this trade-union bureaucrat did not stand shoulder to shoulder with his men.

Standing next to my father, in a thinner crowd than around the official platform, I heard Lord Wedgwood, now Tony Benn, declaring his wish to give up his inherited place in the Lords and stand for the Commons, which I somehow knew to be right, and so I clapped him, as did my father.

I observed the power of Aneurin Bevan, but cannot remember a word he said. Strange men - but no women - rose to speak, and though I did not understand the details, I understood their message - that the newly nationalised coal mines were betraying their hope. Much later, I was to read about how the miners, triumphant and hopeful of a greater level of workers' control, returning to their pits the day after nationalisation, were met by the same manager, now an employee of the nationalised coal industry, but with the same politics and preferences as before.

My father stood there, at Platform 2, smiling, his beloved worker's cap pulled down firmly over his head. I had no idea why, but I too was happy. This was my second lesson in belonging to the 'father land'.

Chapter 5

My mother could not cage her fears as I was growing up. I had asked her permission to bring home my only secondary school friend, Val. Not only had my mother agreed, but she had laid on a wonderful, I now suspect intimidating, spread of pumpernickel, salami and smelly cheese for our tea.

I should have guessed where this would lead.

'Val is too worldly, with her talk of nylon stockings and men,' she told me afterwards.

Val could not come to our house again. But Val was my best friend. Wasn't my mother pleased that I had somebody to bring home? It was useless to protest. She must know something I did not. Clearly I had to keep watch for the wolves wandering in the shadows.

My mother watched my body as I developed breasts. How I hated her stare and her touch when she insisted she come into the bathroom. It was in the bathroom that my awareness of the carnality of my existence arose. What was she doing in there with me? I found it mortifying. She was certainly not embracing me into the sisterhood.

My nakedness was repugnant. Indeed, I knew that to reveal any flesh was sinful. I could not bear to look upon or touch any part of my body. I refused the gaze of the mirror and always looked away when I got in or out of the bath. Even in the bedroom I undressed and dressed myself beneath my nightdress. This was what decent girls did. I had the added misfortune that my 'chest' began not to bud but to bulge at what was, in those days, an unusually young age.

I was mortified too as the first trickle of warm blood stained my knickers. What was I to tell my mother? I hid my knickers at the back of a drawer. But then it happened again. I had to face her. She went out and bought me a huge packet of large coarse sanitary towels, and explained to me how to loop them over a belt that I had to wear round my waist. I was sitting on my bed when, without knocking, she opened the door and just stood there. Then she had said, 'You know what to do now?' I did not dare tell her I didn't know which side was up, which down. 'You will need these once a month.' I was horrified. Was there something wrong with me? But my mother was too embarrassed to explain about menstrual cycles, never mind their biological purpose. My puberty had probably taken her by surprise. She did not rejoice in my womanhood. I was appalled and ashamed.

It was obvious that I had to hide what was happening from my father. I cannot now remember how I reached this conclusion, though I knew it to be right. I knew about shame and the importance of purity.

My mother explained I had to wrap the used towels in old newspaper and deposit them in the bin in the kitchen. This was an impossible task. How to get the paper without asking for it from my father, the Cerberus of everything in print, get downstairs without any risk of running into him, and place it in the small bin in such a way that he, who was the family's bin disposer, would not notice it? The solution was to hide the towels. Which I did, at the back of the drawer. I discovered that, in no time at all, the blood dried and ceased to smell, especially if I kept the window open. I built up a significant collection. But I was horrified at what I was doing. There is no forgiving the corporeality of the body.

Every month my mother delivered a packet of enormous towels, which she left on the edge of my bed. Nothing was said.

I look at myself in the few photos of me from this time. I am a contemplative-looking child whom nobody would bother to call pretty. But, I was growing curves. This was the dream of most of my classmates, but it was not mine. I did not aspire to look like Marilyn Monroe. All I wanted was to stay flat-chested and tubby. But my body had other plans, and beneath my old-before-its-time face there developed a more fleshy version of an hourglass figure.

Things were getting worse between my mother and me. She may well have envied me the freshness of youth, suspicious that I might start pulling boys. Maybe she feared that my father would pay me more attention than he did her. I had started trying to avoid my father, though at the time I knew not why. 'What are you two talking about?' I would hear my mother cry out from some other part of the house, when I inevitably bumped into him on the stairs and we passed the

18

time of day. Then she would appear, looking flustered.

She need not have worried about boys. They were an alien species. Of course, I had to be careful of men. Mustn't sit on their laps. I was a touch sceptical about that one. How could I get pregnant when the man was wearing trousers? But apparently, newspapers between the man and myself would do the trick. That's what the girls said, as I eavesdropped on their chat one day during the school break. Not that I knew much about the male physiognomy, even at fourteen. Still, as I had not so much as held a man's hand, I knew I could not conceive. Not so poor Shirley, who, pregnant at fifteen, was thrown out of the school. It gave the headmistress material for her sermons for weeks to come.

One unusually bright summer's day, when I was about seventeen, my mother informed me she had been standing on the steps of the house when she saw me kissing a boy, right in front of her.

'Such bad manners. Such impudence. Your father and I won't stand for it.'

'Stand for what?'

'You were kissing him. Shamelessly.'

'Whom?'

'I told you to come in at once but you ignored me and just continued.'

'That's rubbish,' I screamed at her. I had not yet kissed any boy. Anyway, I would die rather than show an interest in a boy where my parents could spy on me.

She knew that was a lie, she told me. I was always lying to her about men.

Furious at her for her untruths, I nevertheless felt accused.

She did not speak to me for almost a week after that. When I'd been little, she would refuse to speak to me for a few hours, but her silences had grown longer as I had grown older. Not for her the raised voice as a sign of disaffection. Silence, as I gradually came to realise, was her weapon, her way of showing me how bad I had been.

After a day of silence, when younger, I would wait, wounded, till she emerged out of her bedroom, and appeal to her to tell me what I had done wrong.

'Please tell me what I have done. Please.'

'Not done, you mean.'

'What have I not done?'

'You can work it out for yourself.'

We three would sit down together at meal times, my mother refusing to address me, except through my father.

This time, however, I had had enough. There had not been a boy. There had not been a kiss. In my turn, I refused to speak to her. Days passed.

One day when I was working in the room downstairs, my mother came in and spoke: 'Move your homework from the table. I've made supper.'

My mother knew language to be dangerous. But it was the last time she used silence to reduce me.

And here is a puzzle. I had used the weapon of silence back against my mother. I had finally fought and I had won. And yet I knew I was in the wrong.

Chapter 6

My mother had a hard time of it in Durham. This was the 1950s and mothers, certainly if they were also the wives of university lecturers, did not go out to work. Mothers kept house. But my mother had other ideas and did not partake in the joys of housewifery or the limited opportunities that Durham offered.

Mothers were supposed to put regular meals on the table. But not mine. She shut herself away in her bedroom. My mother would appear when she was ready, and, if I were really lucky, would prepare the lunch or supper before I started to feel giddy and sick with hunger. She did not appear to enjoy the mothering side of things.

'The sun is out.' This was a risky thing to say.

She understood this code. 'Where is there to go?'

'Wharton Park.' This took courage.

'You don't want to go there.'

'You never go out.'

'I take you to school.'

'No, you don't. I always take myself,' I retort.

'Of course I do. I wait for you at the school gates.' She lets out one of her laughs.

I accepted my imprisonment, and, as so many hostages do, identified with my captors.

But I adored my father. He was tall, good-looking and very intelligent. When I was little, I'd loved his telling me stories about my much-loved soft toys at bed time. He'd stand at a discreet distance, while I lay covered up by a mountain of heavy blankets - the only way of keeping warm at that time - which rubbed my chin. My parents, and here I point my finger firmly at my father, wanted me in bed - and out of the way - at 6pm (this was stretched to 7pm when I became eleven). But what made it all right was that, as long as I was good, my father on most nights spun a web of words around the two of us.

My favourite animal had been Pandy, a small bear which had all but lost its head to my mongrel dog, Tiddy (an unexpected and much-loved present from my father). Then there was Blue Doggy, who provided inspiration for many a story, and an unhappy, hand-knitted grey animal with dangling arms and legs, unfairly cast in the role of Jailor. Dolls, with their shiny faces and regular hard bodies were of no interest. Every night, my father collected the animals together and told me the next adventure they had got up to, which regularly ended up with one of the poor creatures being sent for punishment by Jailor to the prison, which we pretended lay behind the small airshaft grill above my bedroom door. Everything ended 'happily ever after', though it sometimes took a few days for catharsis before the naughty one was released. But there was many a night when, sleepless, I stared up at that grill and was afraid of what lay beneath. Now, I guess that my father had also been seeking release.

My father would suggest a walk. 'Do you want to come?' he sometimes asked my mother, but she almost invariably refused. 'I don't have time for walks. I have a meal to cook.' So my father would usher me out of the back door, and out onto the green hill which was still untouched by the suburban sprawl which was soon to infect its sparse beauty. There was a wood over the crest and he would walk me there, pointing out the plants and birds. The lark was his favourite.

My mother would emerge from her isolation to stare at us from the kitchen window as we set merrily off. I felt something was wrong with what I was doing, but I couldn't put my finger on it.

My father strode fast, and taught me to walk from the hip. I used to love trying to go faster than him. He used to march me to the bus stop, but even then would remind me to remember always to walk as far from the kerb as possible, because men in cars might snatch me and do unspeakable things.

Puffing up the hill together one day, my father told me about his escape from Germany. 'It was so far, I wore out my pair of shoes,' he informed me, looking down at his beautifully-polished, brown leather shoes, which were getting muddy as we clambered up the slippery green hill opposite our house.

22

So he began this story, a story about a life left behind, so I would not be scared.

'Why did you leave?' I had asked him. He told me, in a matter of fact sort of way, that the Nazis had come to power in January 1933. 'And?' I had demanded. My father hesitated, brushing back his thinning hair. He had, he said, been active in organising resistance against the Nazis and therefore had to get out. He fled the night that the Parliament building, the Reichstag, had been set alight. 'You know what that is?' he had asked, and I had nodded, though I didn't. He knew the Nazis would blame the Communists. But, mark my words, they did it themselves, he told me.

I felt so proud.

It was all downhill once I left primary school. The older I grew, the closer to womanhood I became, the more difficult my father seemed to find me. What made this process of growing up even trickier was that my mother also became increasingly hostile.

Once, aged thirteen, I burst unbidden into my father's study. I had learnt, before I could even talk, never to reveal emotion. But this time I had had enough. My mother had, for reasons long forgotten, yet again refused to speak to me. I entered my father's study without knocking.

'I hate my mother!' I shouted.

My father looked pained.

'I can't stand the way she treats me.'

He instructed me to get out of his study immediately. The next day he left me a letter. I took it out into the garden and tore open the envelope as far as possible from the house, standing at the top of the stairs that led down to the back alley. I read: 'If you ever upset me like that again, you will kill me.'

That was the last time I hoped my father would take my side.

But it was over my body that the most bitter battles were fought. I had learnt very early that bodies should be concealed, not that my blue dress did much revealing, it hung so loose.

My mother had instructed me, 'Do not show your chest,'

23

though she had meant 'breasts'. And I had said, 'Why is that?' And she had replied, 'Your father said so.' I nearly died of mortification that she had discussed such intimate details of my body with my father.

So here I was in my loose, demure party dress, even though it was blue, a colour I detested. I had protested, in a way still foreign to me, how much I had wanted a dress, for I had few clothes and none remotely suitable for 'going out'. I was beginning to want to look good. After much parental stalling, I was finally rewarded with a visit to the shops - with my father. He had stood stiffly by as I nervously searched the pokey shop for a dress he would consider suitable. I finally found one I liked enough, in which I would not be too embarrassed to show myself to him. He looked me over when I tried it on, and, strangely proud, gave his consent.

My mother, for the first time, agreed to my meeting up with other pupils from school, to go to the local Saturday 'hop'. 'I'll be back by 10pm,' I had promised, desperate to be allowed out. Elvis Presley would be strutting his stuff.

I emerged from my bedroom. There, at the bottom of the stairs, stood my mother and father, blocking my route to the front door. I was not to leave the house. They had decided. I was not old enough.

I did not go out that night. Neither did I question why my father was so diligent in 'protecting' me.

Soon after, my father took to locking me in the downstairs room with him and turning the key in the lock behind him. I was not prepared the first time. Leaning over the other side of the table where I was sitting, he lectured me on the dangers of men. One thing led to another, he explained. I must never let them lay a finger on me. I did understand that, didn't I? It was for my own good. It would damage my reputation.

He stood over me, lecturing me.

'You are too young to go out with boys. Where will it lead? Don't you realise how you could damage my reputation?'

I try to argue. 'I have done nothing wrong. What's so bad about talking to boys?'

'You've done more than that.'

'No, I haven't.'

'Don't lie to me.'

'I'm not lying.'

He unlocked the door and left the room without a backward glance. A couple of hours later, it was time for the family evening meal. I had to sit inches from him. Nobody spoke. I wanted to run away.

My father repeated this performance one more time before I met Alan. Maybe he had perceived something in me I knew nothing of, for a few weeks after my first incarceration, I slipped out of the house one unusually warm Saturday afternoon and went up to Wharton Park to have a look at the Women's Rally, which had been organised by the local Labour Party. Only a few minutes from our house, I hoped my parents would be their usual preoccupied selves and I could get to the park and be back so quickly that my absence might pass unnoticed. I hated them so much, it fuelled my courage to escape.

My friends sometimes tell me how lucky I was to have had left-wing parents. But my gravitation to the left was less easily explained. Politics was never discussed in my presence, and, on the rare occasions I expressed a radical thought, I would be told to keep quiet. 'You have verbal diarrhoea,' they both repeatedly told me. My parents, as I realised much later, had not learnt that silence is a tool of survival to have this strategy destroyed by an articulate daughter.

So, here I am at a Labour Party Women's rally. I sat on the grass and listened again to a young Tony Wedgewood Benn declare he would continue to fight till he had the right to give up his peerage, and I was enthralled. I observed how different the audience was from the one at the Miners' Gala. One thing Durham provided was a fast route to understanding social stratification. It was not just that the audience was mostly women; they looked so much more middle-class: no turbans, so many tweed suits and so deeply and boringly respectable.

I was just thinking it was time to head home, when a gentle-looking, round young man came and sat down next to me. 'I recognise you,' he told me as I stared at him, dumbstruck.

25

'I was just about to go,' I informed him, scrabbling to get up in my haste. I squinted sideways at him on my hands and knees, noticing how old he was, his tummy which had grown over-fond of beer, and his sweet smile. He was seated on the grass right next to where I'd been sitting.

Plopping myself back down onto the ground, I shake his outstretched hand. 'I'm Alan,' he says.

'Anna.' I'm so unused to saying my own name, the sound seems to get stuck in my mouth.

'I thought I'd come and count heads,' he says, in answer to my unspoken question as to what a man was doing at a Women's rally. 'The Labour Party can still get the old dears out.'

I fail to take him up on his sexist turn of phrase, and instead say: 'I prefer the Miners' Gala.'

Why is he laughing?

'I've really got to go,' I repeat, this time managing to stand upright.

'I'd like to see you again.'

'I don't know who you are,' I tell him seriously, not yet quite aware that I have started to feel my first stirrings of desire.

'I thought you knew.' He appears to be reaching for my hand. 'I'm a mature student. On a trade-union scholarship. At your father's college.'

'Oh dear.' His information had not calmed me, as I guess he had anticipated.

He kissed me ever so quickly on my cheek. 'I will see you outside Woolworths at 3pm next Saturday,' he called after me as I started to run down the hill.

Thus I came to ignore my father's 'advice'. Alan became the first man I ever went out with. The reasons I gave for getting out of the house, I now realise, were small-scale lies. I was going for a walk, I was going to the library.

Alan and I talked about the everyday things of life. He told me all about how he had been a shipwright, and an active trade-unionist, about how he was the first person in his whole family to get to university. What do you believe in, he had wanted to know. I told him I was a socialist but thought the local Labour Party was corrupt and I would never support them. He was delighted. But he did persuade me to go canvassing with him in a by-election, early training in the fastest way of stuffing leaflets through letterboxes. We discussed the Algerian war of Independence and Camus, apartheid and the Sharpeville Massacre. He asked me to marry him. I told him not to be so silly, I was off to university soon. Our meetings took place in parks and coffee bars, and a few times I dared to enter his digs, where, once, after a cup of proper coffee, we fell together onto his bed. But, despite his pleading, I refused all entreaties to remove my clothes or open any hooks or zips.

But, wonderful though it was, I was left with a profound sense of my own wrongdoing and inadequacy. How could this man fancy me? Should I have believed him when he told me I was the most beautiful girl he'd ever seen? He even appeared to find what I had to say interesting. 'Well, I'd never have thought of that,' he told me, and he actually seemed to mean it. But I hadn't learnt about men for nothing. He wanted something. I must beware.

I needn't have worried. Though I took great care never to demonstrate any sign of affection, never mind hold Alan's hand in public, the relationship was doomed. My fears were well founded.

The next time my father entered the downstairs room, I jumped up, in an unsuccessful attempt to reach the door before it was locked. He walked up and down, while I stood opposite him, defiant.

'Sit down. You're disturbing me. How can I talk to you when I can't concentrate?'

I sat down. He had seen me holding hands in the street. Did I not understand how disrespectful this was to him? He didn't want me to go out any more.

'I knew you were lying,' my father began.

I started to shout: 'Yes! Yes. I went to Alan's room. Nothing happened. We had a cup of coffee together. That's all.' This had the irrelevant merit of truth.

'You did, did you? How dare you do that to me.'

'It has nothing to do with you.'

'I forbid you to go there again.'

'I'll go if I want to.'

'It's for your own good.'

'Let me out!' I screamed.

That night, I slipped out after my parents had gone to bed and walked a long time to where the cars streaming along the A1 created an arc of flowing light. I wanted to stick out my thumb and hitch south.

I hated my father and did not want to be in the same house as him. Miraculously, I had got into Oxford to study Philosophy, Politics and Economics. I had thought it a mistake when the letter arrived informing me I had a place. I had never thought of myself as especially bright, but loneliness had made a bookworm of me and I bubbled with the excitement of ideas. It had been my father's idea I apply to Oxford and I had done so because acquiescence was easier than opposition. But Oxford had one big advantage. It was a long way away. When I left for university, I knew I was leaving home. I knew when I stood on the curved stone platform of the railway station for my first journey down to Oxford University that I did not ever want to see my father again.

I did not understand my father's fears or know how to untangle the knots. That was not to come till much later. What I did take in was how perilous life was. My father had built us a home, but it was floating on a very thin raft of being. How easy it would have been for the world to knock us all off into the waters that could rise over us at any time.

As for my mother, how could I have comprehended her apparent lack of concern at my father's eccentric behaviour, her failure to protect me, to utter one word in my defence? It was not a good lesson in sisterhood. I still wonder whether she knew what my father had been up to. It is only now that I can glimpse the grief that she so actively buried, depressing all other emotions, including her capacity to love.

It took me a long time to come out from behind the cloud of my childhood. But childhood lay in another time, viewed from a long way off. All my life I had felt I was losing time. When the Mad Hatter in *Alice in Wonderland* talked about beating time, I was right there with him. Time got lost if you weren't watching it carefully, and it got lost even when you did.

Chapter 7

Escape to university did not dilute the hostility between my parents and me. I remember telling John, as we were having our first-ever proper conversation, walking down the sweeping red-carpeted stairs of the Oxford Union, that I wanted nothing – ever - to do with my parents.

I had met John when I attended my first meeting of the Oxford University Socialist Society. For me, this was an act of belief, but also rebellion. I would have dismissed as idiots anyone who had suggested at the time that my parents were socialists.

John was unmissable. Small, with dark shoulder-length hair which shook in time with the emphasis of his rhetoric, he would not stop talking or moving. Why, during that first encounter in my first week at university, in some dismal and dark room, amongst the arcane and incomprehensible arguments about whether the USSR was a workers' state, he should have spotted me, I've never understood.

'Can I walk you home?' he asked at the end of the meeting, fidgeting, his weathered grey flannel trousers held up by the tight clasp of his belt. He had large brown eyes, an open expression and a hopeful smile. I agreed.

Always an early riser, I would finish off five hours' work by lunchtime and meet John, with much secret excitement, in the bar of the Oxford Union (at least after he signed me in, as women could not then be full members). A third-year student, also studying PPE and expected to get a First, he introduced me to his Oxford. We strolled along the river, disregarding the damp mists which so often clung to the Oxford countryside, chatted our way around Christ Church gardens, drank cider - a wonderful discovery - in the pub opposite the Bodleian Library and attended endless meetings and debates on subjects from public transport to abortion. John always had a point to make. I was happy to stay quiet.

John and I began to swim together in the buzz and thrill of Oxford University left-wing politics. The imbalance of male and female students - one woman to every seven men, mostly from public school - gave much of the university the feel of the old boys' club of a public school. John, from a northern

Direct-Grant Grammar School, with a father active in the Cooperative movement, was almost as out-of-place there as I was.

Sexual inequality was insidious, institutionalised but not spoken out loud. Many nights I climbed the high wall out of my all-girls college (to protect the weaker sex from their rapacious brothers) as 'we girls' were not allowed out after 11pm, (a restriction which was not applied in men's colleges), to fall gladly into John's embrace as he waited for me on the forbidden side of the wall.

A few months later, my tutor called me into her office. Unaware of what I could have done wrong, I sat nervously down in front of her desk. Did I know a student called John?

'Yes.'

In a matter-of-fact, but enquiring sort of way, she read me a letter, signed by both my parents. I still remember parts of it:

Our daughter is now in your care. We have good reason to believe that the student, John Church, is intent on her exploitation, which she is far too young to understand. We hold you responsible for ensuring that she does not see him again.

'Do you know Mr Church?'

'John's my boyfriend.'

'I assume there's a problem.'

'My parents are always doing this sort of thing,' I assured the tutor, furious.

She appeared surprised, looking at me from over the half-moon spectacles which Oxford dons appeared to wear as some sort of status symbol.

'I won't pay any attention,' I told her, and in the silence, I stood up and left her office.

I did go home for as short a time as I could manage during those brief stop-offs when the university accommodation was closed during the vacations. My mother took to wrenching the phone out of my hand when John phoned me, or removing the receiver from its cradle and hiding it somewhere so it would not ring. Prohibited from using the phone myself, I got distraught when John apparently failed to call.

'He isn't suitable for you,' my mother told me. 'You are too young.'

When I finally introduced John to my parents, my mother announced, as soon as he had left the drawing room: 'He's a spy. The only reason he would go out with you is to spy on us.'

'So what kind of spy is he?' Though I knew this was nonsense, a grain of doubt was sown, to grow, unobserved, in its own time.

'What does it matter? He'll be a spy for the CIA or KGB. It makes no difference.'

'You've forgotten MI5. He's English.' I enjoyed the sarcasm.

'He could also be from an old Nazi intelligence unit,' she continued.

'They don't exist any more.'

She regarded me as if I were some sort of idiot and ordered John out of the house.

So great was my fury with them, it did not cross my mind to wonder what had caused such paranoia.

I could never do the right thing, especially when it came to men. Men inhabited a forbidden land which I must never enter on pain of hurting, or maybe killing, my parents. Not that I consciously accepted a word spoken to me by either my mother or father. But their anxieties and petty jealousies took up residence in my soul.

I strode out into the big wide world, refusing to see my mother and father, except rarely, for the next twenty years, assuming that I was leaving them, their silences, paranoias and insecurities behind.

Part 2

Chapter 8

Sam has come home triumphant from a 'Reclaim the Streets' action, dumping his bike as per normal in the hall.

'Move your bike, Sam.'

Sam glares at me.

'I'm proud of you,' I tell him hurriedly. 'You're like your granddad.'

Sam had been force-fed on stories about my parents.

'How d'you mean?'

'Your granddad also believed in putting right the wrongs of the world.'

'Good for him! But Nazism was in your face. The problem with global warming is that it isn't visible. The tactics of the 1930s are no use now.'

'But spontaneous bike rides don't challenge capitalist power. That's what lies at the root of global warming.'

Sam, I notice, is pulling a face. 'Demonstrations won't get us anywhere. Did the two-million march stop Britain going to war against Iraq? We have to act more directly to stop global warming. There isn't time for all that mass mobilisation. We'll all be dead soon if we follow those methods.'

'Your grandfather also took to the streets.'

Sam suddenly looks pleased.

'See. Anyway, his methods weren't too successful. I don't notice the left stopped the Nazis. Ahha, Ahha.'

'The left were split,' I start to explain.

'See!' Sam sounds exultant. 'That would never happen to us.'

Sam's birth had rescued my father and me, healing the

rift between us after so many years of silence. My father was overjoyed, writing a poem for the newborn. It told how Sam's birth alone would have made his life worthwhile.

Sam had been born only in the nick of time. One year later, my father was dead.

He had had the good manners to die suddenly. I'd rung my parents' home one morning, to be informed by my mother that my father had lost his footing and been taken to hospital. I picked up my coat and ran. There was no time to find out more.

He had lain in Intensive Care, shafted with tubes coming from places painfully intimate for such a private man, while I sang him the Internationale and he waggled his toes to the beat. That is my last memory of him.

The nurses had asked me to hush. 'Are you not aware there are other patients?' But I had not cared. It was my father I was there for, my father whom I had needed to say goodbye to. I understood the truth of his dying. 'I will carry on the fight,' I had whispered to him, leaning over him, choking on my tears, a promise I cannot ignore. For me, he would forever be a fighter, not the sick man that the hospital had transformed him into.

After I'd left my parents' home, the night of my father's death was the only night I was to spend with my mother. She asked me to stay with her and I did, though I loathed being near her. It was the only night that I did not spend with my infant son.

My mother refused my attempts to get involved in the funeral arrangements. Even in death, my father belonged to her alone. The hearse was late and my mother cursed, her tears still-born. Later, she took the urn of his ashes and put it by her pillow, where it remained. She had kidnapped my father and there was no place for me to mourn.

I grieve for him still.

'I'm hungry,' declares Sam. 'I haven't eaten all day.'

I fry up my standard English breakfast of eggs, bacon, tomatoes and baked beans, even if it is 4pm. It does not take long to cook and is large and tasty. Sam disappears one moment before it is ready.

I shout up the stairs.

'I'm having a bath. I won't be a minute.'

He finally reappears, to state: 'The toast is cold.'

'Make some yourself, then!'

Finally, he sits down, the dog lying under the table, between us. I'd decided on a dog when Sam was little. If he couldn't have a father, he could have a dog.

'I wish I'd known my granddad,' Sam suddenly announces.

'You were only little when he died. D'you remember him at all?'

Sam shakes his head. I observe my son's green-grey eyes, his glowing cascade of hair, his dark arching eyebrows, the high cheekbones that I like to believe he got from me.

'It was because of you he and I started talking to each other again,' I tell him. 'He was so happy when I was pregnant that I forgave him for lots of things from the past.' I hurry on. 'He was so lovely when I told him that your father and I were no longer together. I'd expected him to be censorious but I was wrong. We were sitting on a bench in the park. He said: 'Being a single parent isn't such a bad thing, you know', but he looked so sad.' I turn my head away from Sam, so he doesn't see my tears. 'He visited me almost every day in the hospital after you'd been born. He would appear the minute visiting hours began, so I was never alone. I could see his smile almost before I saw him.'

Sam is regarding me seriously. 'Was Grandma pleased that you were expecting me?' he asks.

But I don't want to tell him that when I informed my parents that I was pregnant, my mother's response was: 'Oh, it's such a rainy day.' How I'd rushed out of the house, crying. How my father had followed me and rubbed my back, comforting me. How it was the first time I could remember him touching me.

I say to Sam: 'She wasn't over the moon, not like your granddad.'

I had delayed informing my parents that I was pregnant, correctly fearful that my mother would see me as her rival for attention and take offence. I had guessed she would not appreciate this display of my successful sexuality.

'Old ladies don't like their babies growing up,' Sam concluded, nodding.

Sam's birth had been a miracle. I had felt the idea of motherhood unappealing until almost the last tick of the biological clock. I had been so miserable in my own childhood that any responsibility for the birth of another who could experience equivalent pain, was unthinkable. Any nascent desire to have a child was well and truly turned off. But I was lucky. A man came along who took me and shook me by my emotional collar. A child was conceived.

Sam arrived in the world as he meant to continue, causing trouble. Why should he be born when he was perfectly content where he was? One caesarean later, and there I was, holding my baby boy.

Unable to bear his crying whenever I put him down, I became happily welded together with him for large parts of the day and night. In the end, I was weaned, though not completely. I still recollect the down on the cheek, the trust in the eyes, and Sam's unconditional love. Now I hear him upstairs, playing his loud music and singing in his deep grown-up voice, and fear my love affair is ending.

Chapter 9

My mother's return home from hospital does not go well. She locks the world out, shooting both the top and bottom bolts. The front door key is therefore useless, unless she is able to come to the door herself. I incapacitate the bolts but my mother then leaves the key in the lock on the inside, blocking access. The carers, sent daily in a council hospital package, are regularly unable to gain entry.

Occasionally, my mother does let them in.

'Mrs Weilheimer accused today's carer of stealing her money. She threw the contents of her purse down onto the table and told the lady that she had stolen £10,' the council organiser informs me over the phone.

'Do you have somebody else?'

'We're running out of people we haven't tried already.'

The next carer is finally despatched.

My mobile rings. The organiser is pleasant. 'Mrs Weilheimer had an accident on the floor and told the carer to clear it up. When the carer bent over, Mrs Weilheimer attempted to hit her over the head with a hammer.'

'My mother is a published playwright and poet,' I almost sob down the phone. 'She's just a bit paranoid.'

'We do understand,' replies the voice, 'but we may not be able to continue sending carers if she is going to behave like this. Could you perhaps come over more often? That might be a solution.'

'I'm not coping as it is. I'm a single mother and teach.'

'Could she move in with you?'

I'm shaking.

'My mother and I have never got on.'

I can hear that he believes he has my measure. An undutiful daughter. 'Well, you should visit whenever you can. She is calmer after you've visited her.'

Guilty, I phone my mother.

'Hello. It's me.'

'Who is 'me'?'

'Me. Anna.'

'How strange. Kay phoned me and said 'Hello, it's me', too.'

'That's what people say.'

'No, it isn't. It's too much of a coincidence. What are you concealing from me?'

'I thought you'd recognise my voice.'

'You mustn't suppose anything of the sort.'

Silence.

'How are you?' I ask her.

'Could be better, could be worse.'

'How is your son?' she now asks me.

She cannot remember his name again.

As I am emerging from a lecture, on my way to my next class, my mobile judders. I get myself near to a window in the corridor to improve the poor reception, as the students jostle and chatter around me. The care organiser is telling me that they have not been able to gain entry for two days now and are most concerned. Nor has my mother answered the phone when I have rung her. Flinging useless excuses behind me, I rush off, push my way down the stairs, drive all the way over and hammer at her door. There is no response.

I'm familiar with her refusal to respond to the phone or to open the door. I have tried to organise an alarm for her, but she has rejected it.

'What do I need with that? There's nothing wrong with me. It's just a device for the police to listen in to what I'm doing.'

I call the police. This could be another false alarm but there is no way of knowing. She has played these 'hide and seek' games for many years but I can never know whether she is, as she has been before, close to becoming unconscious. I no longer have to introduce myself when I ring the police, but they are always courteous.

As the police are about to charge the door, she opens up. The police have smashed in her front door before. Now she locks herself into her bedroom, screaming, 'Get out! Get out!'

I apologise to the police, who reassure me that I did the right thing.

When I finally manage to push open the bedroom door, dislodging the chair which she has managed to ram up against the handle, I discover my mother huddled in a foetal ball on the bed, her soaked nightdress bunched under her hips. The blankets lie on the floor. She has been shredding books. The contents of the cupboard and the chest of drawers have been emptied over the floor. Only the urn containing my father's ashes, next to her pillow, is untouched.

'Burglars!' my mother screams, observing my shock at the destruction. 'I've had burglars!'

That evening I sit with my friend, Aphro, over a glass of wine, at my kitchen table.

'Don't go,' she suggests, when I discuss the problem of my mother with her. 'Call her bluff.'

'But it may not be bluff. I can't win. If I don't go, I worry. If I do, I get abused.'

'You've to stop her getting to you.' Aphro can be unbearable. She is pulling a face at me and stroking her short, No. 2 head of greying hair.

'But I'm scared.'

Aphro gives me a curious and not entirely sympathetic glance.

Chapter 10

My mother has moments of lucidity.

'Tell me about your family,' I urge her. She is lying on her enormous lumpy Victorian sofa, and I perch on an armchair near enough for her to hear me but not touch me.

'You don't want to hear about that,' she replies, as she has always done before.

'But I do.' It is only now that I dare to push her to talk about the past. I have previously been too frightened of opening up the box of death.

'Have I told you about Uncle Paul?' she asks.

I shake my head vigorously and untruthfully. This is the one story she has been able to tell me.

'Uncle Paul was such a lovely man. But that idiot went and volunteered to fight for Germany in the First World War. Got his head blown off. Anyway, he never came back. His wife didn't believe he was dead because they didn't find the body.'

I decide to risk asking her for the names of her parents.

'I can't remember.'

She has never told me their names. 'Who cares about family?' she used to say.

'Do you have any living relatives?'

'You'll thank me for not introducing you.' She pulls a face at me as if at a co-conspirator.

'I'd like to find out about other members of our family.' I surprise myself by my insistence.

'No, you wouldn't.'

A few days later, my mother is back in hospital. I call the ambulance within minutes of arriving at her home. She had been a parchment yellow. Quite the wrong colour.

The hospital establishes that she has another chest infection. I arrive the next day to find my mother caged, the bars on either side of the bed raised to their full height.

'Get me out! Get me out!' she is screaming at the medical staff.

'How are you?' I lean over the bars to talk to her, as she lies, propped on her pillows.

She becomes quiet, turning her head dramatically away from me.

'What has happened to your face? You're bruised.'

Silence.

I chase through room after room, lined with beds, crammed in along both walls, in an attempt to track down a nurse.

'Why are you imprisoning my mother?' I demand.

'She is getting out of bed and peeing on the floor,' the nurse explains. 'And then she slips and falls.'

'Have the bars stopped her?'

'No. She crawls to the bottom of the bed and falls off.'

'I don't want the bars raised so high.'

'I'd like you to talk with the doctor.'

The doctor phones me as I'm driving to work. I stop and park on a double-yellow line. Why does he have to phone now? I am thinking about my lecture. And I hate being late for the students.

'We think it is necessary to sedate your mother.'

'Why?'

'She is a danger to herself.'

'And what else?' I sense he hasn't told me the full story.

'The nurses have said they will no longer treat her. She is abusive to them.'

'I don't want her drugged. Aren't your staff trained to handle confused old people? Or do you drug them all?'

'Your mother has scratched one of my staff so badly that the nurse has had to receive treatment herself.'

'Oh. Did you not cut my mother's nails?'

'We have now. Your mother is also trying to bite my staff. And she pulled out so much hair yesterday that one of the nurses has a small bald patch.'

I feel a combination of pride and horror.

'Only start with the minimum amount. Otherwise I won't agree.'

'Yes, yes,' I hear the doctor say. As I push my way through the traffic to get to my lecture on time, I try to calm myself.

When I see her the next day, the woman who was my mother no longer exists. Her head is thrown back, eyes half-closed and glazed, arms so limp she is unable to raise them.

She is dribbling from her mouth. I mop at the wet with a tissue. I remember how I felt when I was ill. She never touched me then. I do not want to touch her now.

I storm up to a nurse who is standing behind the nurses' station, staring down at something on her side of the partition. I may not have got on with my mother but I cannot bear to see how she has been destroyed and taken away from me.

'I'm busy,' the nurse states, without looking up.

'I want to see a doctor *now*.' I keep tight control of my voice.

'There is no doctor available.' She still does not look up at me.

'Call one.'

'It's the weekend. I can call the sister.'

'Please.'

'It's a round change. It'll take a few moments.' She glances up, as our negotiations are completed.

Half an hour later, I intercept the sister as she is about to leave.

'What has happened to my mother?'

'We sedated her, as you asked.'

'I only agreed to a minimum dose.'

'That isn't what we were told.' She sounds indifferent.

'How much have you given her?'

The sister looks annoyed. She moves over to the rack of medical records and starts to flick through them rapidly. Then she announces: 'I'm afraid her records are not available at the moment.'

'Where are they?'

She almost smiles: 'The files are constantly being used.'

Apoplectic, I insist that a doctor phones me.

I am rushing to pick up Sam when my mobile rings. I draw up in a bus bay, knowing full well this will mean a ticket.

'This is Dr Harris. I believe you wanted to discuss your mother's treatment.'

'I'd like to meet you in person.'

'I'm not your mother's designated doctor, but you're welcome to tell me what the problem is.'

'You have turned my mother into a zombie.'

Dr Harris knows exactly what I'm talking about.

'On some rare occasions, the patient can develop

41

contraindications,' he agreed.

'What medication did you give her?'

'Diazepam.'

'How much?'

'200milligrams.'

'That is a large dose for an old person.' I have done my homework, searching out reliable medical information on the Net.

'It's normal.'

'Not for an old person. There is a known association amongst the elderly between that level of medication and semi-paralysis.'

'She is likely to improve with time.'

Dr Harris, I note, is no longer disagreeing with my analysis. I say: 'Only *likely*? I warned you to start off with only a small dosage. How come I have a better knowledge of the side-effects of the drug than you?'

'We treated her to the best of our ability.'

This is exactly what worries me. She has been reduced to being another statistic, not worth the time for the doctor to do more than spend one minute consulting with me on the phone. How inconvenient for them that she persists in living. All I say is: 'I want all medication stopped.'

'It already has been,' Dr Harris tells me, and hangs up without bothering with the niceties of the normal goodbye.

I am considering bringing a case of negligence.

What am I to do with my mother? She can no longer live at home as she is not capable of doing anything for herself.

She has also stopped speaking.

I mourn for memories, which will now never be mine. I want my mother to speak to me, as she has never spoken before, to tell me the stories of her childhood, to tell me about her parents, to tell me about her life. I want to know something of her; I want to know myself.

Dr Harris phones me again. 'We want to put your mother into a psychiatric ward.'

'I want to meet to discuss this.'

Why does he go so quiet? I add: 'Why can't she stay where she is?'

'There's nothing wrong with her any more that we can medically treat. It's no longer possible to keep the long-term sick in general wards in this hospital.'

He does not mention that the government is targeting 'bed-blocking'.

'So, after turning her into a vegetable, you thought you'd resolve what to do about her by dumping her in a psychiatric unit.'

'It's attached to this hospital and very pleasant.'

I wonder if he would have described the old mental institutions in a similar vein.

'Where is she now?' But I have already guessed.

'She was moved earlier today.'

'Without consulting me!' I hiss

'You were not available. The unit is part of the same hospital. This is a courtesy call.'

'She won't like being in a psychiatric ward. She'll think she's in a lunatic asylum, being lined up for the fatal shot.'

'I'm sorry. I don't understand you.'

I have got so sick over the years of trying to explain to ignorant doctors that having to flee Nazism is not good for one's mental health, and that for my mother, a hospital has meanings the doctors cannot not even dream of.

43

Chapter 11

As the light prematurely fades early one evening, I collapse onto my bed to watch TV, ignoring the cats and unsorted clothes. I scramble for the phone when it rings, finding it just in time under the duvet.

'It's Ruben.'

I find myself pressing the receiver hard to my ear, my heartbeat speeding up.

'My God! My God! I thought you might be dead.'

'Oh no! And how are you?'

'How did you get my number?' I am squeezing my eyes tight shut. The world is swinging around me.

'You're in the phone book. Same surname.'

'Didn't change it. And you?'

'Would you like to meet?'

We fix to see each other in a few days at the café on the hill. I sit very still till my body stops shivering and the dots clear before my eyes. The taste of youth, when the male body was beautiful and all life was in the future tense, grows large inside me.

I make sure to arrive a little late for my meeting with Ruben, but he's not there and I sit down on a bench outside the café in the sunshine.

I remember how Ruben and I had first met at Oxford. I'd been spending many evenings thudding the staircases of the male colleges to persuade their largely public-school-educated inhabitants how nice it would be if they supported the proposal that Oxford women be allowed to vote in the University Student Union, which, at that point, women were not allowed to do, a policy of exclusion which many of these boys still took as natural. One day, I was paired with Aphro, the organisers insisting on safety in numbers. After canvassing the allotted college, I went with her to meet her friend, Ruben, a will-o-the-wisp man with a halo of curls and bright, seductive green eyes, whom I'd instantly fancied.

'Where did you find him?' I remember whispering to Aphro. I'd once asked Aphro about her name. She'd explained that her mother, an enthusiastic Bohemian, and her father, just released from the Forces at the end of the war, had met while studying Classics at Oxford, and wanted to celebrate both their personal rapture and the beginning of a new and better world. Her mother had taken her Finals six months pregnant, concealing this offence, for which she would have been expelled, by wearing a particularly voluminous gown. They had called their daughter Aphrodite, which Aphro had quickly learnt to abbreviate.

Later, Ruben and I had found ourselves taking the same lecture course, programmed for 9am. There was hardly anybody there, and we spotted each other in the lecture hall without difficulty. He moved to sit next to me. The prospect of seeing him, and, if I were really lucky, going off to his lodgings afterwards, provided a powerful incentive to get up early on a Monday morning. But the past lies behind unassailable fortifications. It is hard to touch what might have been.

I recognise Ruben, sauntering round the corner of the café. Who folds whom in their arms? I find my body dissolving of its own accord and want to cry.

We queue up without speaking and finally order a cup of tea and a slice of chocolate cake with two forks, just like we used to do. Carrying the cups and plate outside, we sit down opposite each other at a trestle table.

'You haven't changed. Small and perfectly formed,' Ruben murmurs.

'You mean I'm plump.'

'You were never skinny. I like it.' He is grinning his lopsided smile. 'And your hair is different. Like a zebra, only the stripes are red.'

'At least I've got hair. What happened to your curls?' I lean over without meaning to, to stroke his head. He moves, as if unintentionally, out of my reach.

'You are married?' I ask, drawing back.

'Another time.'

'Children?'

'You'll have to give me more time before I can talk about these things. What about you?'

'Job; ex-husband; single parent of one child,' I summarise.

'How old?'

'Seventeen. A boy.'

'Congratulations. John's?'

He hasn't forgotten. 'No. In the end, the relationship didn't work. I killed it by accident.'

Pause.

'You're no longer living in America?' I bend towards him again.

'Time for a new start.'

'But you'd been there since your twenties. What happened?'

Ruben does not reply. We sit in silence. I try to sip my tea.

'Are you still on the left?' Ruben finds it easier to ask questions than answer them, I notice. Never mind. Just sitting here talking to him is lovely.

'Armchair socialist. What I vowed I would never become. I call it 'BS' and 'AS'. Before Sam and After Sam.

Ruben is frowning, but I ignore this.

'BS', I was a leading member of the union, of the rank and file, and an anti-racist campaigner.'

'I remember you coming from a German socialist family.'

'Sure, though my father didn't want me involved in left-wing politics. D'you remember, he even banned me from joining CND.'

I recall standing by the piano reading the 'Join Now' CND recruitment leaflet I had sent for. Those were the days when the government told us to seal off our windows with brown paper in the event of a USSR nuclear attack.

'You can't Join CND,' my socialist father instructed me, instantly appreciating the situation as he walked into the room. No need for him to knock.

'I'm going to.'

'You'll ruin your chances of a career in the Civil Service.'

'I don't want to be a Civil Servant.'

'How can you possibly know what you will want to do at your age? You'll damage your prospects of any respectable job.'

How full of contradictions my father was.

'But you did join?' Ruben is asking me.

I nod. 'At university, so my father never knew.'

46

'It's so strange that they didn't want you involved in left wing activities.' Then he adds: 'So tell me, what have you have been up to 'After Sam'?'

'These days, I only come out on demos.'

'Better than me, then. Is that it?'

'Teaching. Looking after my mother. Keeping sane. All the thrills and spills of looking after a child by myself.' I don't tell him how I have only just managed to wave through the storms.

For some reason, Ruben suddenly seems upset. He sits staring at his empty cup.

'I've got to go. I'll ring you. We'll meet again soon,' he tells me.

I wrap up my half of the cake and walk slowly home. It is still light but I run myself a bath, and lying in the very hot water, try to work out what just went wrong.

Chapter 12

'I want to take some of my mother's papers out of her home, but is that the right thing to do? My mother may go back.' I've rung John, in the hope he will shed some light on what to do. If there is one person who will be interested in revelations about my parents' pasts, it will be John. One divorce later, we still hope to keep each other from drowning.

'You must take their valuables for safe keeping,' John replies.

'Of course. But that's not what I'm asking.'

With my mother away, for the first time in my life I have the chance to discover what secrets lie in my parents' home of forty years. It isn't the gold and silver that concern me.

'You can't take stuff out of the house unless you can return it in the same state.' John is adamant.

'Why do you always defend my mother?' I shout. I had wanted the answer, 'It's OK to go ahead.'

'Your mother and I got on,' John reminds me.

'Not when she threw you out of the house.'

'That was early on.'

'Oh yes, after we were married she used to flirt with you, while you both argued about the Right Opposition to Stalin, and I felt like an invisible wallflower.'

'Should we get back to the point?' John's deep voice sounds amused. It had been the sound of his voice as much as the tumbling flow of his words that had attracted me. I still find it appealing.

'She doesn't even know what she's got.' I argue.

'That's irrelevant.'

We are unable to agree.

I go downstairs into the room where my mother used to sit, bars at the windows and a smell of dust that I do not want to disturb.

You may not come in here. I am entering where I fear to tread.

The first package of secrets is easy to spot. Two large, battered brown envelopes lie on my mother's desk, next to her beloved, silent typewriter, specially purchased in Paris. I look in, expecting my mother's jottings. Instead, inside the first envelope are hundreds of ancient, tissue-thin sheets of paper. I can see German writing on them. I try to unfold them. They are all creased up together. I don't want to tear them. I push them all back into the first envelope and open the second. More letters. Who are they from? The secrets of my family's past are about to engulf me. I am terrified.

I have been into this room regularly and these envelopes were not on the desk or evident anywhere else in the room. My mother could have retrieved them from their hiding place and then forgotten that they were now visible. Maybe she started to connect to submerged memories of her past and wanted the papers next to her. But what, I muse, if she had left them here for me to find?

I place the envelopes beside me on the front seat of my car, covering them with the car's usual detritus. I am carrying stolen treasure. Once home, I conceal them in my desk. They feel like a nuclear device, which will explode on approach.

It is late in the evening, and I've given up trying to sleep. Even a large glass of red wine didn't do the trick. I ring John, who never sleeps, from my bed.

'I found two envelopes, stuffed full with letters, all written in German.'

'Where were they?' He sounds remote.

'They were just sitting on her desk.'

'You've got to look after them.'

'What the hell do you think I'm going to do with them!'

'Have you put them somewhere safe? I must see them.'

'I'm frightened of them.'

'You've always wanted to find out about your parents.'

'A part of me wants to let sleeping dogs lie. My parents' pasts belong to the past. Why don't I leave it that way?'

'Because there are so many secrets . . . I'm so sorry, Anna, but I do have to go. It's after 11pm and we still haven't eaten. Some other time?'

'I'm afraid of what those letters will do to me.'

'At least you'll understand your hinterland better.'

I lie in bed and remember the moment I decided that my

parents were probably right about John. He and I were walking down St Giles together. As ever, John wasn't listening to a word I was saying. I was even worse then than now at negotiating my way through disagreements with others. But John was young also: he couldn't appreciate how upset I was getting. Whatever were we talking about? I suddenly decided: my parents were right. This man did not suit me. I didn't understand then, as I do now, that my father was jealous of there being a man other than him in my life, and my mother was jealous because I was on the cusp of adulthood and romance.

Nor did I interrupt John to tell him: 'I want to say something.' Instead, I marched off, as I had done before, leaving John standing at the kerb, shouting after me. I was sure he would follow me. Still young enough to assume the eternity of youth and of life, I tossed my head and disappeared round the corner. But he didn't follow me. He didn't even phone me. Not this time. Instead, he took up with somebody else.

After we'd both departed Oxford, John and I did get back together. But we viewed each other with suspicion. He had confirmed that he would leave me. I knew he would. That he protested, shaking with feeling, that it was me he wanted, made no difference. I needed more certainty of somebody's love than it was possible for him or anybody else to give me. Even if he did love me, he would not continue to love me. He would surely find out how unlovable I truly was. I had always known how worthless I was, but, in the clear light of the relationship, this normally hidden rotten core would be revealed. John would turn away from me. So I knew he would leave me and told him so. Persistently. In the end, he did.

Chapter 13

The usual assortment of flyers, bills and letters are lying on the mat by the front door when I get back from work. Over the essential cup of tea, curled into the sofa downstairs, I first open the envelope from the USA.

The letter informs me, in clipped academic tones:

I am researching Louise Weilheimer. Married a comrade, Dennis Fitzgerald, born in Dublin. In the USSR in 1936. You have the same surname. Would you happen to know where I could find her?

Signed, Seamus Arbouth.

Shaking, I sip my cold tea. I knew my mother had married my father in 1932. Laughing, she had informed me that my father was late for his own wedding. But she had told me with a fury buried in her voice, which I'd not understood. Had she been lying to me? How otherwise could she have married somebody else in 1936?

I am intimate with paranoia. I grew up with it, as if it had been a sibling. I don't want Seamus Arbouth's letter to be true. A mistake. I start to shake, my stomach to convulse.

I want my parents to have always loved each other. Other people's parents have marital problems, but mine were as if concreted together. They were devoted to each other. Couldn't stick a cigarette paper between them.

Sam, returning late from football practice at school, finds me sobbing, hidden away in my bedroom.

'What's the matter now?' he asks.

'Nothing.'

'Have it your own way.'

I ring John later that evening.

'I need your help,' I begin.

'God speaking. What can I do for you, my child?' he replies.

I explain about the letter. John promises to find out who Seamus Arbouth is.

'He's one of us,' he informs me, a few days later, delighted to have done his research with such excellent results and such speed. John loves the intrigue of politics, the web that holds us in its historical weave.

'*You* can contact him, as you're so excited about it,' I hiss.

A few days later, John phones me just as I am about to go to bed. 'I've got news.' Pause.

Why does he have to give this such a build-up?

'Yes?'

'Seamus is really keen to interview Louise. He'll come over specially to London if she agrees to see him.'

'But did you find out why he's so interested?'

'Ah, yes. He was born in New York in what he called 'Little Ireland'. His father fled Ireland during the earlier troubles, and then married an Irish girl. Seamus was brought up in the best of left-wing Catholic households.'

There is a pause while I laugh appropriately. 'But why does he want to interview my mum?'

'He's some sort of lecturer in New York. I didn't find out everything, you know. Has books already published. Does research into Irish history. You know the sort of thing.'

No, I don't. I make appropriate grunting noises down the phone.

'He's writing a book about Irish Communists. He's been allowed into the Moscow archives. Quite fascinating. They won't stay open for long. I must ask him about the Stalinist show trials.'

'Yes, John.'

'That must be where he got the information about your mother marrying Dennis,' John decides.

'I don't believe it. Especially if it's from the Stalinist files and after 1933. My mother was already married.' I am indignant.

'That's the wrong approach. The question is, what does it mean in terms of your mother? And, if we assume there's some truth to the records, what was she doing in Moscow?'

My mother looks alert when I arrive; mornings seem to suit her better. I tell her about Seamus Arbouth. Arbouth and I are now corresponding via email. He had told me he had written to her.

'What does he want with me?'

'Did you get his letter?'

'No.'

The nurse who had been sitting next to her gives me a little secret poke. My mother, she later informs me, had torn up a letter from the USA and tried unsuccessfully to flush the bits down the loo.

'He only wants to talk to you.'

'What about?'

'I thought you might know.' She hates my knowing anything about her. As though I am stealing something from her.

'If you don't know, I won't talk to him.'

'People will be able to read about you when you were young.'

'I'm still young.'

'Of course you are.'

Then, finally, she agrees. I inform Seamus Arbouth that Louise has finally said she will see him. He phones me a few days later from the airport.

'Do you want me to come with you?' I ask.

We agree I'll keep in the background. We meet in the hospital foyer, introduce ourselves and shake hands. To my surprise, he has an Irish accent. He seems a solid fifty, wearing brogues and a heavy tweed suit. Surely, this is not typical New York apparel?

My mother looks so small, sitting propped up in the armchair, next to her bed, when we arrive. The staff have dressed her up for our visit. She is wearing a wonderful red hair band.

I introduce her to Seamus. My mother nods her head at him. She appears to be smirking. I remind her that he is here to talk about Dennis.

'Who?' she asks.

Seamus leans over her: 'Dennis,' he shouts into her ear. 'The man you were with in Moscow.'

'I've never been to Moscow.'

Do I imagine that she is batting her eyelids at him?

'Yes. In 1936.'

She is shaking her head, smiling: 'I would know if I'd been to Moscow,' she admonishes him.

'You remember Dennis. You first met him here in London.'

But she keeps on shaking her head. At one point, she remembers that I'm in the room and, turning slightly, smiles conspiratorially at me. But she does not answer any more questions. I am almost relieved.

I make sure to visit her the next day. I ask her why she refused to talk to Seamus Arbouth.

'Who?'

'The man who came to see you about Dennis Fitzgerald.'

'Who?'

'The American who visited you yesterday.' My voice is rising.

She shakes her head at me, her look expressing sympathy for my ignorance and idiocy.

'Nobody has visited me for weeks.'

'Did you ever know somebody called Dennis Fitzgerald?'

Again, that shake. She has turned her face away from mine.

Chapter 14

I put my hand into the thicker of the two envelopes and draw out a jumble of paper. The flimsy folds have a faintly acidic smell, as if from over-ripe perfume. I want to put the sheets into some sort of chronological order but many of the sheets are not dated. Others have had their tops torn off, removing the date and address of the sender. Other letters end without a name or a signature.

It takes weeks, sifting sheets so fragile they feel as if they could dissolve into dust. My fingers tremble. I sit at my oak kitchen table, the papers before me, and stare out of the patio doors onto the pots of red geraniums. I can only work for short stretches at a time. Finally, the papers are in a rough order.

They start in 1936, sent from Nazi Germany. After my parents had arrived in Britain. I stare at the almost indecipherable signatures: Vater. Mutti. Are these my mother's parents? I feel the walls of the room receding.

I track down a translator, Chris, the cousin of a friend, who'd been born in Germany. She arrives to take a look at the documents. 'You understand that much of this is written in archaic German handwriting,' she explains to me. 'I will do the translation for you as long as we can agree a rate. This is not easy work.' Her meaning hangs over us.

So it was that a few days later, the postman knocks at the front door and hands me a bulky envelope. I tuck it away in the depths of my desk. A couple of weeks later, stomach in knots, when the sun is filtering in through the doors of the kitchen, I sit down on the warmed kitchen chair and open the envelope carefully. Inside the bubble-wrap I find a single sheet. A small note is stuck onto the paper: 'Rather than taking the risk with the post, I'll give you back the originals when we meet. This is only the translations of the 1936 letters. I will give you time to breath before sending 1937.'

It is easier reading the translations on a crisp white sheet of paper. It distances me from the originals.

17.January.1936

We do not have the document you require. Nor the clothing you requested for Frieda .We would like to see Frieda again. We wish you all the best for your crossing, should that still be possible.

Vater, Mutti

Is my mother living with a woman, Frieda?

11.April.1936

My dear boy,

At the moment I am in the office, after I have wandered, full of admiration, through the exhibition in the German Museum. I wish one could meet this perfection in all fields of life!
Louise called on the evening of Easter from Wien.
I sent you only the 10 marks at the end of March because the 10 marks sent at the beginning of March were almost fatal for my trip to Bremen. You never know what the moment will bring. Stay well.

V

V must be short for Vater. He must be sending his daughter, and 'my dear boy', money. What put him in such danger? I imagine him going to the bank, holding tightly onto his old briefcase.

'That's a Jew,' the small group of young men, idling at the street corner, start to whisper to each other. Look at his shoes. Real leather. And so polished. They don't need more. So what if it isn't true. One of the lads pushes himself up to Vater. If Vater crosses the road, he betrays his fear; if he *walks on, he risks his life. 'Where do you think you're going?' the thug asks. Before he can think of an answer, Vater is on the pavement, tripped over by the man's foot. He licks the blood on his lip, hears their laughter echoing in his ears. 'Where are all your things?' is how Mutti greets him as he returns, so quietly, to their Berlin apartment, late that day.*

7.12.1936

It's your birthday, dear Louise. We waited a long time for you. We were so glad you were born. We miss you, our daughter. And we miss Frieda.

Uncle gave us a little Honoecker joy.

Fritz

What a tender embrace across the breadth of Europe. But surely Honoecker is a Jewish festival. I fear what I am about to find. And who is Fritz?

The next bit of translation has a note typed above it: 'I can't be sure who this is from. It's a carbon copy, unlike the other letters, and it has no date, address or signature. The first sentence below is from a fragment of German text, which you'd placed with the following sheet, though neither is dated or signed.'

Just a few years, Mother, Father. This will blow over. We'll be back before you know it.

Darling daughter, come back to us. We think of you always.

These letters concern people whom I knew nothing of and knew never to ask about. No grandparents had ever crossed the lintel of memory when I was a child. Yet here they are. What do they have to do with me?

I imagine Vater drawing the curtains to their apartment.

No eyes can glimpse him now. Only a chink of light illuminates where he sits at his desk. He fills his favourite fountain pen and, when all is quiet, composes a letter to his far-away daughter. It conceals more than it reveals.

Imagining them hurts my head. Thank goodness the letters only start in 1936, not 1933 when my parents left Germany. Fewer letters to burn myself reading. I guess my mother can't have saved the earlier letters. Didn't predict that she was leaving her parents forever. That the letters were all that was left. Didn't you tell me, Mum, that you had thought Hitler was an idiot? Wouldn't last more than a few years?

I return the sheet to its envelope. I don't want to read any more.

Chapter 15

'Show us your pass, or we will have to get somebody to vouch for you.'

The security guards, who have watched me entering and leaving the university for years, have stopped me.

'You look awful!' Pat tells me, chancing on me as she goes through the gates. Pat, now safely on the other side of the turnstile, taps at their office window.

'I'll vouch for her.'

'You should fasten the pass to your clothes, like everybody else. That's what the clip is for,' states the top security man, growing very tall, before letting me in.

I glare.

Pat laughs. 'The most important thing in a place like this,' she informs me as we wait for the lift, 'is to make friends with the security personnel.'

I nod. I am coughing fit to burst, fishing for the tissues which I've just bought. The stairs are too much of a challenge. The lift doors fail to close, till Pat kicks them hard. The students with us in the lift start to giggle.

'Why did you come in?'

'I can't afford not to. If you're part-time, you only get paid if you come in.'

'Cup of coffee? I've got a kettle in my office.'

I had noticed Pat at a staff meeting where she and I were both arguing fiercely for the importance of teaching theory. Pat now hands me a hot dark drink in a much-used mug.

'Everything OK?'

'Sorting out my parents' papers.'

From the recesses of my bag, I fish for one of my favourite lipsticks. It has just the right amount of shine and I apply it generously, hoping this will help me feel better.

The seminar is part of a sociological module on the role of the family. I sit on the table, my legs casually swung over the edge, hoping to break down the stiff, staff-student boundaries, a late exhibition of my 1960s' anti-authoritarianism. This gets more difficult as student numbers in the classes keep going up and up. There are over thirty students sitting there in front of me. This is our first proper session together, so I shouldn't break them up into groups for a bit.

'How many of you have children?' I ask.

I watch as the students glance around nervously at each other. Almost half the class, mostly women, put up their hands.

'Must be difficult to do a degree and look after kids.'

A soft rumble of assent.

'And how many of you have to work?'

Virtually the whole class sticks up their hands, more confident now.

Some of the students start to tell their stories. One has to work thirty hours a week to support herself and her two children. Another works five nights a week at a petrol station. He comes to class straight from work. 'How do you keep awake when you get here?' I ask him. If he's lucky, he sleeps on the job.

'Who looks after your children while you're working or at uni?' I prompt the class.

It is always the same. Occasionally, a father features, but usually, the students talk about the women in their families looking after the children.

Their mothers are often aged around forty. It is their grandmothers, their children's great-grandparents, who are about sixty, like I am. My son is a mere teenager. I tell them that my grandparents were born in the mid-nineteenth century. They gaze at me as if I were a friendly but alien species.

I'm always amazed by how different their lives are from mine. I envy them their families, the rolls of names, of mothers, grandmothers, sisters and cousins, which pour out as they explain their complex childcare and living arrangements. Their lives are made up of the stories of their parents and their parents before them, passed on from one generation to the next, the very tissue of existence which they have lived and breathed. Despite their immense financial and logistical problems, I envy them their lives.

It is the end of the teaching day. Pat is already outside,

leaning up against her bike, smoking.

'You're still here, then,' Pat remarks. 'How did it go?'

'The students are as lovely as ever. But it's hard when you know that almost half of them won't finish their degrees, through no fault of their own.'

'We do our best.'

'They need smaller classes and more individual attention.'

'For that you need an old university, more middle-class students and more money.'

'I think the staff-student ratio is awful just about everywhere these days.'

Pat laughs. 'Ah, but would you want your son to come here?'

'I talked to one of the students at the end of the class. He was a Nigerian who had fled for political reasons. Had to leave his wife and baby behind and hasn't a clue if he'll see them again. You know Nigeria is on the government's 'white' list as a 'safe' country, so he hasn't managed to get refugee status or rights of residence. He's always afraid, and the sort of jobs he gets have to be in the unofficial economy.'

'I sometimes think the university's main function is as a refuge for the world's great unwashed.'

'If only. I had to tell him that, if he goes on working his present hours, he may find finishing his degree very difficult.'

'And?'

'And he asked how else could he survive? I had no solution. I couldn't help thinking of my parents. They were the great unwashed too. But at least there was some sympathy for left-wing intellectuals fleeing Nazism. For him, it's out of the frying pan into the fire.'

Time to go. Blowing my nose, I say goodbye. I need my bed.

Chapter 16

The train travels through an urban landscape of grey-tiled roofs and windows, high above the ground. I peep into others' lives. I am on my way to the Public Records Office at Kew.

It has taken me the better part of my adult life to find the courage to start excavating my parents' political pasts. A friend, dedicated to historical research into revolutionary movements, discovered that my father might have worked for the Comintern. I had protested that this was not possible, that my father would never have worked for the Third Communist International, charged with spreading world revolution, but increasingly Stalinised. Try the M15 records in Kew, if you want to find out, he had suggested.

That had been a few years back. I had prevaricated. My father had told me about his escape from Germany and his work for the Free French. But I had always suspected that my father had a political past that he had not told me about. My mother, I had supposed, did not merit much attention. Unlike my father, she had been of so little interest to the Gestapo that she had been able to catch a train out of Germany. Little did I know.

I had wanted my freedom from my parents' paranoia and over-possessiveness. Hunting their pasts was no escape at all.

Seamus Arbouth must be wrong, but I need the proof. The possibility that this aspersion is true, rattles me. It isn't every day that a daughter discovers her mother 'in flagrante'.

M15 has finally agreed to open my parents' records. The train shudders to a halt at Kew station.

At the Public Records Office I have to establish my identity. Then a pleasant-mannered man, dressed in the uniform of well-fitted suit and polished black shoes, collects me from Reception and ushers me into a large office, crowded with dark desks. I am shown to a chair.

'You know you can only use pencil in here?' he asks
I nod.
'Just tell me if you need anything.'

He sits down quietly at the table next to mine. The sunlight through the deep windows illuminates the swirling wisps of dust.

Nervous, I tell him: 'I first need the Ladies.'

Again, he nods with the politeness born of centuries of public school and Oxbridge moulding. Instead of pointing out to me where to go, he escorts me there himself. He does not leave my side for the next six hours

Instead of the thin folder on my father which I'd expected, including details such as when he first came to Britain and his naturalisation papers, in front of me on the table lie two extremely thick, battered files on Louise Weilheimer.

I find it hard to focus. 'Louise Weilheimer, née Zweig', reads the front sheet. These cannot be about my mother, who cooked meals badly, braided my plaits every day before school, and hid herself away in her bedroom for days at a time. The words swim about in front of me.

'What about my father, Emil Weilheimer?' I ask my minder.

'No other files,' he informs me.

I do not believe him.

Feeling nauseous, I open the files. There is an initial page which lists the addresses of my parents in the 1930s. Why did MI5 care where my parents lived? Surely MI5 would not have the manpower to watch all refugees like this? Each inscription had been written at the time, in different people's hands, pushed between lines and stuck in margins. It is not in a clear sequential order.

I try writing down the addresses but cannot understand why there are so many between 1936 and 1938. They are all in NW3, but there are too many of them. I'm finding it hard to focus. It seems that Louise and Emil were not living at the same addresses. In an attempt to bring some order to these incongruities, I start to write down the months, then the days, for the MI5 scribes are precise in their transcriptions,

I think I am going to faint and place my head on the desk in front of me, resting on my arms. The minder comes over. I get the impression he is not surprised.

'I want to have the files photocopied,' I explain. 'For my personal use only.' I have to get out of here.

He explains the procedure slowly to me. To my surprise,

it is quite simple; there is no real problem.

Fearing I will fall, I walk down the sweeping stairs towards the front door and fresh air.

Two fat, A3 envelopes of photocopied papers arrive within the week.

It seems my mother's relationship with my father was far from the simple loving relationship I had thought. I am aghast, as my reality dissolves before me. They lived at different addresses in London for much of the 1930s.

Almost at the beginning of the file I notice the references in the MI5 papers to Louise Weilheimer's taking a trip to the USSR in 1936. They flag her up, in a hand-written initialled note in the margin, as 'somebody to be kept an eye on', though she had a relatively low security rating. What on earth was she doing in the USSR? 1936 was the year leading up to the mass trials and executions. Hardly a good time for a tourist trip. Was it something to do with Dennis after all? Maybe Seamus Arbouth was not so far off the mark, and not the charlatan I had first taken him for.

I go into a state of decline.

Chapter 17

March.22.1937

I am planning to come to London. Uncle has paid for the trip. Father has booked the ticket. I have documentation for Customs but no official invitation, which is cause for concern. I don't like leaving Father for Seder night.

Don't make any special preparations. All I want is to find you healthy.

Greetings and kisses from all.

Mutti

28.April.1937

My dearest,

Arrived home after an unpleasant journey, and was greeted by father. I keep telling him about you and the pleasant young man who put himself untiringly at my disposal. I returned with the impression of having seen a happy married couple. So pleased to have been with you.

Vater of course pleased I have returned safely. I am sad that I could not say my goodbyes to you properly, but am so glad I have been to visit you.

Has the Frenchman turned up?

My heartfelt thanks for your great love and goodness.

A thousand greetings and kisses.

From Mutti

Chapter 18

'It's a gamble telling Social Services my mother comes from a culturally Jewish background,' I confess to John on the phone. It's late afternoon, darkness taking gulps out of the sky.

'She's going to have to go to some sort of Home when she leaves hospital,' John replies.

'I could be making a big mistake.'

I am stretched out on the chaise longue, bought long ago with John, with much excitement, in a flea market. I have squeezed it under the bedroom window so it gets maximum light. I had claimed it in the marital break-up. I come here when I need quiet.

'I asked her whether she was Jewish the other day, and she asked me whether I had seen her in a synagogue,' I continue.

'That's Louise!' John is chortling. 'But why are you trying to get her into a Jewish care home anyway?'

'A hunch. The letters.'

'I've always suspected that your family had some Jewish antecedents.'

'But can I ascribe to her a state of being she denies?' I can hear John slurping away at his wine. Is he listening to me?

'We know your mother could be a touch economical with the truth. But if you're right, you'll be doing her a favour. She could well feel more at home in an ambience which reminds her of her childhood. You remember that time we visited last month in the hospital, how much more child-like she'd become? That's what happens with some old people.'

'But if we were to accept that my mother was brought up in some form of Jewish household, there must have been a very strong reason why she then denied it.'

John laughs: 'It's called socialism.'

I had feared that at least some of my family had disappeared into the camps. Where else were they? They cannot all have died young from natural causes, even though this is what my mother had tried to persuade me to believe. If

I'd accepted what she told me - my mother's and father's families had been particularly unlucky in their health.

I'd assumed that the Nazi's insane 'scientific' fractional divisions, which claimed that anybody with one Jewish grandmother was themselves Jewish, even though the rest of their ancestors were as 'Aryan' as could be, might have lain behind the disappearances of at least some of my mother's family. My father had been a Catholic, and fled Germany because he was an active anti-Nazi, so that sorted that. My mother had left to be with him. Nothing Jewish about it. If my parents said they weren't Jewish, that would do for me.

And yet, I find the whole topic makes me anxious and unhappy. Have I refused to see the truth of what was going on? When I'd asked, before I knew better, about having grandparents, I was told that they had all died from a combination of deadly diseases. But, when I tried to find out more, my parents were wont to turn around and leave the room, in my mother's case first saying: 'Why are you asking me that?' in a taut, flat voice. I rapidly learnt never to talk of the past, for fear I would destroy them. But I too became afraid of what I might hear. I colluded in the silence. Could I have helped release them from their pasts, if I too had not become so afraid of the ghosts?

'Ethnicity has to be lived,' John is telling me, but I'm not really listening.

'I suppose as the Nazis increasingly targeted the Jews, my mother's parents would have been 'encouraged' to define themselves as Jewish.'

'Identity is not a fixed thing.'

'My mother's mother was a socialist. They were left-wing enough to call Louise after a female French revolutionary. A left-wing family stretching back to at least the early 1800s! That's my tradition, not the Judaic bit.'

'People can embrace more than one definition.'

'Do you think my mother believed she was Jewish? If she says she is not Jewish, can she be Jewish? My parents rejected all the Jewish rituals and customs. We celebrated Christmas. We ate a pork joint on Sundays, with apple compote. She made good crackling.'

'She was a lousy cook.'

'She told me that the Jews didn't fight back against the Nazis. That there was even collaboration with the Third Reich.'

67

'That's a very sectarian reading of history.'
'She didn't encourage me to think she was Jewish!'
'What matters is that she survived.'
'To die in a Jewish Home? Am I betraying her to put her there now?'

Chapter 19

26.12.36

We visited M yesterday. The nurses tell us she is much better and is often very reasonable.

Do write to your sister.

From V

3.2.37

We visited M. She is well and her condition bearable.

Can M really be my mother's sister? Once, when still little and unable to sleep, I'd sat on the stairs, trying to eavesdrop on my parents' conversation behind the closed door of the drawing room, and thought I'd heard my mother mention a sister. Recently, I'd dared to ask her whether she'd had a sister.

'Why do you want to know?' she'd said.

Silence.

'She died young,' she finally continued.

'What of?' I'd enquired.

'The liver,' my mother had said, looking far away.

I fear for M. These letters suggest something more than physical problems.

Chapter 20

I look out of the aircraft window as Aphro and I fly into Berlin. After a lifetime of silences and my inability to peer into the quagmire of the past, I have decided to see if I can find where my mother lived in Berlin. I found the address on one of the letters from her parents and rushed out and bought a guide to Berlin. I checked it on the Tube. Amazingly, the street is still there: in Charlottenburg, on the western inner edge of Berlin. Finally I shall be able to see for myself where my mother lived and where the letters were written.

Germany was a forbidden land. My father had made that clear. The Nazis did not get their just deserts, he had often reminded me. They were everywhere, staffing the State, the railway stations, the buses, the passport offices. Impossible to go to Germany without running into them. They look just like you or me, he had said. And you had to be careful of their children as well. Anybody young enough was enrolled in the Hitler Youth. They will still be alive and kicking. Even their children will carry some mutation. When it came to Nazi beliefs, my parents appeared to succumb to a geneticist explanation. I must never go to Germany.

Yet I want to see where my mother lived, as I explained to Aphro. Aphro had invited me to Sunday lunch, which we ate off her luxurious round dining table in her large, light-blue kitchen. She was full of disbelief when I explained about my resistance to visiting Germany.

'It's well over fifty years since the Nazis!'

'Don't you think I know that.'

'It's a democratic country now. Just like it is here. The German State was completely reconstituted.'

I stared at her. How dare she? I dipped my bread into the last of my soup and chewed it slowly.

'My parents wouldn't have wanted me to go.'

'That's it, isn't it? You've really got to take your own decisions.'

'I'm scared.'

'What of?'

'What I might find. What I might feel.'

'OK. I'll come with you. Does that help?'

I was apprehensive. I did not tell her this. We had difficulty finding a mutually free time. Our journey had to wait till winter.

As we circle to land, I reflect that my father also made this journey, but the other way round, fleeing for his life. He went into hiding on the night of the Reichstag fire. He had been active in a left-wing theatre group and had earned the hostility of the Nazis as a result. The local milkman had knocked at their door at 4am to warn him. He got out a few hours before the SS came for him and had walked across Germany.

The ground below us looks surprisingly flat. We land with a bump. It has taken us two hours from London to Berlin, not the twelve months it took my father.

I have booked us into a hotel for two nights. That will give me as much time as I can cope with.

German words come crawling out of my mouth like insects, the words tickling my tongue as they emerge, making my jaw ache with the surprise and difficulty of it all.

'Wo kann man den Zug? Where do we . . er . . er . . the train?' I ask our hotel receptionist. We have dumped our bags in an over-snug room.

The receptionist looks at me with curiosity as he points out where we should go.

'You never told me you could speak German,' protests Aphro.

'But I can't.'

'Did your parents speak German to you when you were a child?'

'Oh no! They loathed everything German. They wanted me to be a proper little English girl and speak Queen's English in my nice Church of England primary school.'

Aphro, I must remember, really does not have a clue. She had grown up in the protective bosom of a proper English family. She could have no idea how horrible I found the idea of learning to speak my parents' language. I wanted nothing at all to do with it. German belonged to another time and

71

another place that I wanted no part of.

'Yes, I suppose speaking German just after the end of the Second World War could draw attention,' I hear her tell me.

'Anyway, they preferred speaking English. And did so better than many English speakers!' I admonish her. 'They felt no affection for their first language.'

'Did they never speak German?'

'When they didn't want me to understand. That's when I would listen carefully.'

I hope this satisfies her. It is not the whole truth. I do not tell her that some of my first books were in German and that, till I was about five, I could read German as well as I could English. Nor do I tell her that my mother had, for reasons unknown, started to speak to me on odd occasions in German when I was a teenager. Perhaps she suddenly understood that, if she did not teach me her mother tongue now, it would be too late. It *was* too late. I hated her for torturing me in words that carried with them meanings that were closed to me, and codes I could not break.

'You sound like a German,' Aphro informs me.

We clamber down the stairs from the overground tube station called the S Bahn into the street, and walk round the corner to visit my mother's old home. I have tried to send a letter ahead of us, addressed to the landlord, but have heard nothing back.

I am arriving unannounced.

When I was a child, my mother described where she had grown up. It was a window into her past, rarely opened. I was intrigued by the intimacy. Before the First World War she had felt safe, though she had been only five when the war started. The War destroyed all that. She had told me this as if she were still grieving for a lost paradise.

I remember my mother unexpectedly confiding a secret as we were walking down the road which passed endlessly under the railway line in Durham. 'We lived opposite a train track. I would stand on our balcony and watch as the carriages sped by. That's how I learnt my geography. I wanted to know where those trains were going. I discovered wonderful names like Paris and Prague. I knew one day I would be on that train.'

She pulled a face and added: 'Not the way it happened.' I had looked at her quizzically but she said no more about it.

'Was it noisy?'

'Not during the day. There was a row of lime trees which lay in a straight line between our road and the railway line, and they blocked the sound. But in the quiet of the night, I would lie awake in bed and listen to the engines hooting and spitting, and the clippety clop of the wheels charging along, to east and west. That's how I became an internationalist.' She grinned at me.

Here I am, walking slowly along the side of the railway line, along a row of old lime trees. The trees must have survived the Allied bombing. Not so the houses. I stare at the line of hideous post-war blocks of flats, presumably thrown up as fast as possible to provide accommodation for the millions of homeless, bombed-out Berliners.

'It's gone!' I shout, sweating and pointing to a space between the blocks, which must once have been a house. My heart is beating so fast I feel I'm going to die on the spot.

'No. We're not there yet.'

We cross the road so as to be able to count the houses. My mother's house is standing there, in all its nineteenth-century grandeur and beauty, the only house which had not taken a hit in the whole length of the street. It is four storeys high, with beautiful carved balconies on every level.

'I have to get in.' I hadn't known how much I would want this.

I ring all eight door bells. There are four flats on each side of the entrance. Aphro has taken a few steps away from the door. She looks unusually embarrassed. Nobody answers.

Then a youthful-looking man in his mid-thirties, with a little boy and a pushchair, appears out of a car which he has parked under a lime tree on the other side of the street. He crosses the road and goes up to the front door nearest to where I'm waiting. He is placing his key into the lock as I approach. I try to explain in German what I want. He answers in fluent English and invites us in. His name is Paul, he tells us.

We climb a panelled curving stairwell up to the second

floor. Paul opens the heavy wooden door to his flat. The ceilings are high, the walls thick, the rooms light.

He explains to us that he has just picked up his child from the playgroup.

'You look after the child?' I ask politely.

'Yes. My wife, Irma, she is a teacher. I am a house-husband. Is that not what you say?' He laughs.

We go in through the heavy panelled door, straight into the front room. Everywhere there are children's clothes and toys.

'The three of you live here?' I ask Paul.

'We have two other children. It can be . . er. . crowded.' He smiles again at me.

He shows us the children's bedroom, the largest of the rooms, he explains. It has three bunk beds, one tucked in on stilts under the ceiling and two on top of each other against a wall. The room is jam-packed. It must have been a squash for my mother and her sisters.

I imagine my mother waking in the cold hours of the night and hearing her sister's voice.

'Louise. Are you awake?'

'Shush. It's early.'

'Why don't we go down to the swings in the Tiergarten?'

'We're too young. You know that.'

'The zoo, then, I love the zoo.'

'Mamma and Papa don't allow you to go down to the Zoo.' Louise is trying hard to see where her sister is hiding. But she can't find her anywhere.

I imagine Louise's father standing next to her.

'Time to get up, Louise. Time for school.' She can see he is holding a book by Goethe in his left hand. He is so good-looking, so upright in his bearing. 'You don't want to be stupid like your sister.'

I remember one of the few things my mother had told me about herself was that she had left home when she was fifteen. She had got a job developing films, just as this industry was starting out.

'You were ever so young.' I had said. 'Where did you live?'

'I lived above the shop. I paid the rent out of my weekly wages. I was very proud. I had my own pay cheque. Couldn't afford to eat, though. The inflation didn't help.'

'Where was the shop?'

'As far from my parents as possible.'

'Was there something wrong?'

'I can't remember.'

I imagine my mother's parents writing their letters to Louise at a desk facing the French windows, where they looked out onto the trains and thought of their distant children. As they watched the tall, elegant trees sway and shudder, they dug deep for the right words, momentarily sheltered from their grief.

The walls are covered in twentieth-century art reproductions. The sofa has a bright, modernist throw covering it. There is the smell of food and families. I feel at home. But this *is* my home. I might have been born here, under other circumstances. How odd that some other happy family lives here, perhaps just like my mother's, when it should be me.

I cross the front room and open the old French windows onto the balcony. I breathe in the sweet smell of lime blossom. We are too high to hear the hubbub of the street. A train whooshes by on cue, travelling from east to west, no billowing smoke or squealing wheels, but I understand how my mother felt, standing at the hub of Europe.

Paul tells me I must see the hall. As we walk out of his flat I ask him how he got this flat. It is not an easy question for me.

'Ah, there is a very long list. This is a special house, you understand. It's a national, historical monument. It is one of the very few houses of its type which survived the bombing of the Second World War.'

Just for a moment he looks embarrassed. I nod to encourage him.

'Yes. It is now run by an agency on behalf of the State. We were on the list for a long time. We only moved here a year ago.'

'Who was here before you?'

'I really don't know. But before the war, there were many Jews living here.'

'Jews?'

'Yes, I must show you the plaque.'

We descend the stairs slowly. Paul points out the beautiful fresco of painted peacocks strutting across dark green lawns against a deep blue sky on the domed ceiling and walls.

'You must understand that this is not the original. The renovations were very hard to do, I believe. Most of the original plaster had disintegrated, but some old photographs were miraculously discovered. It was very lucky this house survived at all. You understand?'

We understood.

We turn round the bend at the bottom of the stairs and there is a brass plaque high on the wall. It has been inscribed with many names.

'What is this?' I ask. My mouth is suddenly dry.

'The names of all the people who were taken from here to the camps and never came back are listed here. The landlord paid for it to be put up. It is so high because of possible vandalism.'

About forty people's names are listed. Forty people from eight flats. I look to see whether *Zweig* is there. There are so many names. I am unable to see anything at all.

'There he is.' Aphro is pointing to the name: *Zweig*.

I start to weep.

'What were the first names of your grandparents?' Aphro asks me.

I shake my head. Paul tactfully draws away.

'There are only two *Zweigs* here - Johann and Rosa,' Aphro tells me. 'Are those the names of your grandparents?'

'I don't know. Probably.'

I have never imagined that I had grandparents. No grandparents inhabited my childhood. I do not even know their names. I find it hard to associate with what Aphro is trying to tell me.

Aphro has known the names of all her grandparents and great-grandparents since she was knee high. She cannot easily understand my ignorance and incomprehension.

'How about the letters to your mother?'

'The letters referred at best to 'Mutti' and 'Vater'. They didn't sign their first names.'

I don't dare say it out loud: these are my grandparents, these are their names.

I sink down onto the cold tiled floor, my back held up by the wall. From here, I try to read what is in front of me. The inscription on the plaque states that it is dedicated to those who lived here, never to return. There is a clear Star of David carved behind the names. *Zweig* is in the second column of five.

I finally get up and turn back into the hall. Paul puts two strong arms around me, and holds me tight.

'Do you know what exactly happened to the people listed here?' I ask him.

He shakes his head.

'No. I do not know. I suggest you visit the synagogue. They will tell you.'

'The synagogue?'

'Yes. They will tell you about the Jews.'

But I am not a Jew.

The three of us stand by the back door that leads into the small green courtyard. In its centre is a stone statue spouting water.

'Do you know which flat your family lived in?' Paul asks.

'No, but I think it was the second floor.'

'So it could have been our flat.'

'I do hope it was. But I would like to knock at the other door on the second floor.'

'Yes. But the old lady who lives there never comes out these days.'

'How long has she lived there?'

'She and her husband have been there a very long time, certainly since the end of the war. He died many years ago.'

'What did he do?'

'The gossip is that he was military. But they kept themselves to themselves.'

'He was the right age to have fought?'

'Probably, yes.'

'They were Nazis who took over 'unoccupied' flats?'

At this, Aphro nudges me towards the front door. Paul suddenly announces: 'I must have a photo of you.'

'I'd love that. Thank you.'

'I want to show it to my children, and tell them, 'This is the granddaughter of the people who once lived here.''

Paul runs upstairs for his camera and then places me before the fountain in the courtyard.

I imagine my mother and her sister sitting on the edge of the encircling wall on bright, even days like today, legs swinging, their arms entwined around each other's shoulders, gossiping, enjoying the splash of water.

Chapter 21

Sam and I are sitting opposite each other at the cluttered wooden table in the kitchen, over bowls of under-cooked spaghetti bolognaise.

'I visited where my mother's parents lived in Berlin,' I say to Sam. Like my parents before me, I'd hesitated to tell him, fearing that a story about the horrors of the past could infect him. But, unlike my parents, I gambled that a knowledge of his past would protect him.

Sam looks up from his bowl with a hardness of gaze which turns my stomach. What has happened to my baby, to the eyes which were pools of trust?

'They were your relatives too.' I sound petulant, but I'm afraid.

'They've nothing to do with me. When did they die? A hundred years ago. You weren't even born then.' Sam is maintaining that look of his.

'They were your family.'

'I don't have a family.' He is leaning right back on the kitchen chair, as only the tall can, balancing himself somehow on the tips of his heels. This is hard. I want Sam to be glad that I am reclaiming the dead.

'We are a family, just a rather small one.' I don't sound convincing.

'We don't count. You can't have a family made up of two people.' Sam is truculent. 'My friends have brothers and sisters and aunts, uncles and cousins. I don't. We don't even have anybody to spend Christmas with, except ourselves. I don't understand why you expect me to be interested in this. I don't actually understand why *you* are interested. Looking for dead relatives isn't going to give me - or you - a family.' He is close to shouting.

'You'll be more interested in your family when you are older.' I find it hard to use the word 'family'.

'Don't count on it. If you want to do all this, don't do it for me.'

I gulp down the rest of my spaghetti. Sam leaves his uneaten and disappears into his bedroom. I hear his door being closed firmly. I hide myself in the washing up. I cannot make him want to know. Sam is indifferent to my gift to him of a past.

Chapter 22

As the translations arrive, I file the sheets away into a purple plastic folder, a colour I like. But when the next envelope plops through the letter box, I find I cannot read the papers in it. It is as if what is before me is written in an impenetrable language. This voyage to meet my grandparents is rough indeed.

John phones me a few days later to enquire what I've learnt from the next batch of translations. It's only early evening, but I'm curled up watching the news on TV.

'I can't read them,' I tell him. 'It hurts me.'

'Because they're dead?'

'Because to me, they were non-people, as if they had never lived.'

'I never cared that I'd grandparents,' he informs me, meaning to comfort.

'What's your grandfather's name?' I ask.

'You know that! My maternal father was Harold. And on my father's side, William. You never met him. He was a Liberal councillor before the Second World War. He was my favourite.'

'I wish I could talk of favourites. I don't even know their names.'

I hear John hesitate: 'You are getting to know your grandparents now,' he says very slowly.

At the end of the conversation I get up, go to my desk and pull out the sheet with the new translations. Only two letters. I will cope.

3.March.1937

Business times are difficult. Mother is also concerned about how to send you linen tablecloths.

For the first time in about thirty years, Aunt H. won't any more be able to come on Saturdays for our little circle. S, K, Uncle W and R are all leaving for London. But Uncle H is complaining that he has to give up his trip abroad. You will understand the reasons.

81

There is no signature, no way of being sure who the letter is from. I want to say to myself, 'This has nothing to do with me.' Instead, I phone John back.

'Do you remember how you used to tell me I must have a Jewish background?'

'Of course.'

'These letters keep referring to customs that must be Jewish.' I can hear John's rich laugh. 'Listen! The family coming round to celebrate Saturdays. Isn't that the Jewish Sabbath? And in an earlier letter, there was something about celebrating Seder. Aphro had to explain that referred to Friday evening meals.'

'Don't say I didn't tell you.'

'My parents didn't tell me the truth.'

'But your parents may not have seen themselves as Jewish.'

24.May.1937

Dear Children,

Did you receive the little tablecloth and the briefcase? It is for Friedl from his father-in-law, with particular love. The gabardine was given us by Uncle W's chauffeur. I wish you health to wear it.

K can't keep her job from April 1. She lives with us and cries a lot. She is now only allowed to teach in a Jewish school.

Glad fate is being so kind to you. Always thinking of you.

From Mother

An advance - I see Friedl has definitely become a man - my father, I presume. A woman did seem less likely, given what I now know about my mother. She always condemned any form of non-heterosexual encounter as 'immaturity', if she spoke of it at all. Always coy on the fundamentals of life. 'Friedl' wasn't spelt wrong, and I hadn't misread it. The parents-in-law were using a misleading name deliberately, I guess to keep him and them safe. What fear lies hidden here!

K. All knowledge of who she was, is now lost. What must it have been like to be a teacher and to live under the Nazis as a Jew?

These dear people send letters worrying about gabardines and linen tablecloths, while their family and friends are leaving them behind, escaping the Nazis.

Chapter 23

I go to visit my mother in the Psychiatric Unit of the hospital. The Unit is one of those 1960s single-storey buildings with a lot of glass, nothing like the Victorian 'mad-houses'. But, as I crunch up to the building, I am fearful of what I shall find within. I buzz to be let in, the front door slides open after a few moments, and I find myself in a 'locked' glass cubicle. A voice asks me questions over the tannoy: 'What's your name?' 'Who are you visiting?' 'What's your relationship to her?'

'I'm trying to get in, not to get out,' I find myself saying into the tannoy. Then the second door is released and I'm through.

There's a woman waiting for me on the other side. She wants me to stick a coloured paper badge onto my coat so as to establish I've been through the vetting process. (I am later to discover the colour of the badge changes every day. I presume this is so that no visitor should succeed in turning themselves into a resident.) I peel the badge off the moment I turn away.

I spot my mother in the 'lounge' and walk over to her. She is slumped back in a sofa, her legs, badly swollen since the hospital mis-medicated her, sticking out in front. Her knees are just about parallel with her head. She is wearing stripy pink socks which are so tight that they cut into her leg, causing her flesh to bulge over the tops of the socks, which makes it impossible to pull them up above her ankles. I try to sit down next to her, but the cushions are so lacking in resilience that I have to perch on the rim of the sofa so as not to roll back onto her. This I want to avoid at all costs.

I peck her quickly on the cheek nearer me, but she does not respond. Then I make myself touch her lower leg, the bit protruding above the pink sock. Her leg feels cold. She does not turn to look at me, nor do I turn towards her. I fear what she is thinking: 'You refused to get me out of the hospital. You have reduced me to this.'

But the lounge is bright and smells clean. There are

about ten residents altogether, mostly old, but there is one woman, sitting in a corner, who, despite concealing herself behind sunglasses, does not look more than about thirty. They are otherwise all seated on either side of the room. They look harmless. There appears to be a policy that the staff do not wear medical outfits, but t-shirts with jogging bottoms. It's difficult to tell who are the staff, whom the patients.

I heave myself up from the sofa and try a youngish-looking man.

'Excuse me,' I start.

He interrupts me pleasantly. 'I'm a health visitor here. Try the office.' He points me to where it is.

I knock at the door and, though nobody responds, go in. Through wide windows I note that the office staff have a full view of who goes in or out of the front door.

'Excuse me,' I start again, talking to nobody in particular. A woman sitting opposite me looks up.

'Yes?'

'I think my mother needs to be in a chair where she can sit upright.'

'I'm the wrong person for that,' she informs me.

'And the right person?' I enquire, looking hopefully around.

'They're not in today.'

Still ignorant of the ways of such institutions, I say: 'But all that has to happen is that she's moved into one of the empty, more upright chairs.'

'The person you want is here tomorrow,' the woman answers. Later, I was to learn that the seating plan was part of a careful strategy, not to be disturbed by the mere needs of the patients.

'OK. Could my mother have a blanket for now to cover her legs?'

'You need to talk to the staff nurse on duty for that,' she tells me. 'Has your mother said she's cold?' she adds, with a look that says she knows a trouble-maker when she meets one.

But my mother is no longer talking. She no longer screams and shouts. My mother is behaving too well, sedated out of existence.

She is also unable to stand or walk. I stay till supper time and watch as the staff lift her into a wheelchair and push her to a table. Her legs are still uncovered. Then the nurse hands her a spoon with the food already on it. When she wants to drink, a nurse holds up a mug with a lip for her to suck on.

The person who was my mother is no longer with us. I want my mother back.

I arrange my next visit so that I can get to talk to a doctor. I start by telling him my mother needs to be moved out of the sofa. He nods. I ask him whether she is still being drugged. He assures me she is not, but I do not believe him. I ask to see her medical card but am informed this would break patient confidentiality.

'I was consulted at the main hospital,' I protest. After all, this was technically what had happened. 'Are you the doctor here who is responsible for my mother?'

I finally get an appointment with the main psychiatrist. We talk in the corridor. What catches the eye is that this is a man who is attempting to defy baldness and age by wiping thin strands of hair across a broad gleaming forehead.

'I want to see her medical records,' I start.

He backs his junior doctor: there is a policy not to give drugs unless totally necessary. Louise is quiescent, he assures me, because of the drugs she was previously given (another untruth, as I was later to discover). And, no, I can't see her records.

'I have power of attorney,' I insist. 'I represent my mother's interests.'

But, as the man knowingly points out, my 'power of attorney' does not apply to stays in psychiatric units.

I continue to insist that my mother doesn't have a clue what's going on. But I know when I'm beaten.

'She is getting the best possible care,' the doctor answers me. He has gone a nasty red colour.

She has, the staff joked, a boyfriend. An old man, about twenty years younger than my mother, took to sitting next to her on the sofa. They held hands. My mother appeared much calmer. And proud. She was the oldest woman there and the only one with a boyfriend. But the staff decided to separate them because the man is married, though his wife visits rarely. Every time he comes to sit down next to her, they take his hand and lead him to the opposite side of the room. I ask why they can't sit together. 'It can cause trouble,' is all I get.

Conversations with my mother are unpredictable. But at least she is speaking.
'How is Sam?'
'He's fine.'
'Does he enjoy school?' She always shakes her head at me, when asking this. It is my cue to ask her whether she enjoyed school. It is also an expression of solidarity against the repressive education system.
'Did you enjoy school?' I ask her.
'No, I did not. I left early.'
'Why did you leave early?'
'How is Sam?'
'Why did you leave school early?'
'Does Sam enjoy school?'

I want to ask her about the letters but I do not dare. I have no right to this information. I want to ask her why she never told me about my grandparents, why she never told me that they wrote to her all through the years of separation, why she never told me of their affection for Emil. She always gave me the impression that her parents did not really care for her or Emil. Now I know that is just not true.

At my next visit, she sits in silence. She clutches my hand so hard that it hurts. I try to pull away.
'Don't leave me! Don't leave me!' She is almost sobbing.
'You are hurting me,' I explain.
A light smile touches her face. 'Aren't I strong!'
Then, hunching up, she starts to moan. I hold her hand as if she were a forlorn child. Finally, comforted by my presence, she falls asleep. I am the only one left to love her.

My mother never really took to mothering. She did not find in herself the desire to provide that sense of emotional availability and solidity that most children crave. Perhaps her emotions were too carefully folded away in the bottom drawer of her life and being. Yet now, in her dying days, sitting blankly in her psychiatric ward, she hangs onto my hand and tells me in a faraway voice, 'I love you.'

After many months of my demanding that my mother is assessed, an appointment is fixed. I insist on being present. The three of us sit in the main corridor of the Unit, my mother in her wheel chair. The psychiatrist certainly stands out. He is wearing a snug, pale linen suit, with a purple tie.

'Isn't there a room we can use?' I ask.

'We are very busy here.'

I am too exhausted and worried to fight. Instead I begin: 'I don't think my mother is receiving appropriate care here.'

'Let's leave her to talk, shall we?' Turning to her, the psychiatrist asks in a neutral voice, 'Do you know your name?'

My mother rolls her eyes at me. '*Why* do you want to know my name?'

'Your name?'

'I refuse to answer such an idiotic question.'

'What month is it?'

'Look outside if you want to know about the weather.' She gestures to him to look outside.

'Who is the prime minister?'

My mother recites, eyes shining,

'*'Take physic pomp!*
Expose thyself to feel what wretches feel
That thou mayst shake the superflux to them
And show the Heavens more just.'

Who wrote this passage?' she asks her tormentor.

Neither of us responds.

'Shakespeare. It's *King Lear*,' my mother proclaims, triumphantly.

'What did you eat for lunch today?' continues the psychiatrist, unabashed.

'Rome was built on the blood of slaves.'

'My mother has been scarred by her past experiences,' I start to explain.

'I would greatly appreciate it if you didn't speak,' the psychiatrist insists.

My mother smirks at me as I roll her back into the lounge, shaking and pointing to her head with one finger, to indicate that she thinks the man is crazy.

The psychiatrist's final diagnosis, he informs me over the phone late one evening, is that my mother is of sound mind and therefore must leave the Unit as soon as it is resolved where she will go.

Stunned, I ask him what she is supposed to do, as she can no longer walk and is only just able to feed herself.

'Your mother no longer fits our requirements,' the psychiatrist explains.

'Did your assessment not include dementia?'

'Dementia' is a word that no daughter ever wants to use about a parent. It damns them for the rest of their lives. But I need not have worried.

'There is no conclusive evidence,' the psychiatrist assures me. 'Conclusive'. Such a slippery word. What, I want to know, would constitute 'conclusive' proof. But I would not get a useful response.

'Can she come to live with you?' the psychiatrist is asking.

'Cheaper for you that way,' bursts out of me.

'I suggest you look at this from your mother's point of view,' he interjects. 'Have you asked her whether she would like to live with you?'

'I can't have her living with me.'

Not a good daughter. Not good at all.

'You live by yourself with your son?'

'Yes.'

'It could be useful for you to have your mother with you. And your son would benefit from having her close by.'

This man does not have a clue. But I feel as if I'm being pulled apart.

I do not tell him how difficult my mother is when Sam is around; how my mother and Sam compete with each other for my attention; how my mother frets if I speak to Sam rather than to her, or how she cuts in whenever he tries to speak to me. I do not tell him about how much I know she disapproves of my child-centred method of child rearing, so very different from hers. I do not tell him how she accuses me of spoiling him if I serve him food first, and how she takes the food from his plate when we are trying to have a meal together.

Nor do I tell him that I've never forgiven my mother. Not since I was a child. I had not recovered from my childhood self's hatred of my mother's unavailability, her frigidity, her irrationality when all I had wanted was her love. Make her suffer! Is this not what I truly, deeply wanted? To get her off my hands. I do not tell him that I do not want, indeed cannot be my mother's mother.

I do not confess that having Sam and my mother together in my home would drive me mad.

'It isn't possible. My mother needs to be sent to a Home,' is all I say.

'How about her returning to her own home?'

It is not easy to play with your mother's life.

When I later put in an official complaint against the Unit's treatment of my mother, the psychiatrist was to accuse me of trying to slow up my mother's release.

It had started one day when my mother was still in the hospital. Lying in the hospital bed, she had raised her arm and pointed emphatically out of the window.

'Look,' she had proclaimed: 'There's a synagogue.'

I had peered intently out of the second-floor window onto the jumble of roofs beneath.

'No, there isn't,' I say, shaking my head vigorously to give emphasis.

She had given me that 'my daughter is an idiot' look of hers. 'Look! Look!' And, arm still outstretched, she turns back to me, beaming. Every time I visited, she pointed out the synagogue to me.

I had by then started to piece together that Louise's parents had seen themselves as Jewish. But I hadn't thought of my mother as Jewish. On the one occasion I'd asked her, filling out a school survey, she had said 'No' to being Jewish. Another time, when John and she had been intently discussing whether it was of relevance that Marx was Jewish, she'd provided as the clinching argument: 'He never went to a synagogue.'

But I suspect, as the present recedes from her consciousness, this deeply buried part of her past is being resurrected and becoming more important to her. I had to trust my instincts on this one. I decided to make her Jewish.

This did not go down well at the Unit.

'You didn't tell us she was Jewish.'

'I said she's an atheist, not that she wasn't Jewish.'

'An atheist can't be Jewish.'

'My mother's cultural background is Jewish, not her religion. I want her to go to a Jewish care home. She will feel more at home there.'

I had this conversation repeatedly over the months, and as her social workers and carers constantly revolved, so I went through this explanation again and again. Hackney had a limited budget, even then, and the custodians of its funds used all possible techniques to block this upstart of a Jew from siphoning off extra money by going into Jewish care. Initially unaware of how the system really worked, I'd at first accepted the social workers' refrain that, try though they might, there just wasn't a place for her in any Jewish care home anywhere within the boundaries of the M25.

So I found it ironic to be told that it was I who had delayed her move from the Unit. But, unknown to me, the psychiatrist, who won the case, had grown confident. Though their interest in her welfare did not extend to them visiting Louise, a young couple who had much admired her, had protested to the psychiatrist that it was I who was the problem, not Louise. There was nothing wrong with Louise, they had assured him, which would stop her managing by herself at home.

I did know my mother didn't want to go into a 'Home.' But I didn't want her to go back to her own home. That much was true. How would she cope? She could hardly stand, could not walk, and would not be able to maintain her personal hygiene or feed herself. And I could not cope with becoming her carer.

I knew I was preventing her going home, where she had lain her head next to the ashes of her husband, where every chair told a story, where the smell told her she was at home, where she could look out of the window and watch a world she knew.

Never be the daughter who decides that her mother cannot return to the one place she wants to be. My mother wants to lie on her lumpy, pee-soaked sofa, where the sun catches her face in the morning hours, where the draft whips round the old window panes when the wind blows east, where she knows the place and purpose of everything, and can sleep and rise as she likes. She does not want to sit in a comfortable room, filled with old people, dozing and moaning, on the way to the grave.

Chapter 24

I glance over the two sheets of translations from 1937, wishing there were fewer letters to digest. Most of the letters are addressed to Friedl and are from Vater, I note. The letters confirm that Louise was again away for much of the year. She certainly used to get around

Indeed, the letters are quite critical of their 'agitated' daughter and her failure, as usual, to keep in touch. But they show that Louise's parents adored Emil, which is not at all what my mother had told me. My mother had said that her parents did not want her to marry Emil, because he wasn't suitable. I'd readily assumed that her parents, a nice bourgeois couple, found her husband too much of a firebrand. But it wasn't so.

How normal their letters tried to keep everything. Just a light passing reference to 'unpleasant experiences' and money problems, wanting to persuade Louise and Emil that there was no cause for concern. Yet in Germany, nobody could now visit a Jewish doctor and all forms of Jewish organisation had been banned.

5.7.37

It is a long time since I wrote. L's letters appear to exude agitation. So she is going to the Sorbonne? I'm sorry for you, Friedl, that you will be alone now, but I feel confident that you will be able to look after yourself.

We are sending L 10 marks monthly. When we can get to the post office.

From Vater

4.8.37

Dear Friedl,

We write just as gladly to you and will also be glad of your news.

Despite unpleasant experiences which you can imagine, we are much rested. Today, K has still worked. I cannot go into details. You will understand. We long to hear from our daughter.

From parents

29.8.37

Dear children,

We are so grateful for the two separate letters from you and Louise.

Did you, Friedl, get the cake? We are so sorry nobody is looking after you in your loneliness. Soon Louise will return and then you won't need anyone else.

G did not contact me on my birthday. The first time in thirty-six years.

Is it worth celebrating birthdays, especially as you get old and the gap between reality and illusion gets greater? Nobody fulfils one hundred percent. One has done one's best and that has to satisfy. The applause of a few loved ones suffices.

I wish you success for your plans.

Let us know if Louise's exam will affect your circumstances.

I am so very tired.

From Vater

People's lifelong routines were being disrupted at the most profoundly personal level. Vater had to comfort himself with the regularities of the past, because his daughter had not sent a birthday greeting.

22.10.37

Dear children,

Mother wishes to thank you, dear Friedl, for your birthday card, from 'wherever'. Send us your poem, dear Friedl. We know you are hiding a poet in you.

Conditions here vary. But we are running out of money, though I am still working with exporters. I want to travel to where the lemons grow.

From Vater

This is the first time that the letters alluded to getting out of Germany. Vater's note about wanting to go where the lemon trees grow, shakes me.

10.11.37

Dear children.

Yesterday, we sent 10 marks, plus 10 marks from mother's earnings. Please acknowledge.

Any wishes, L, for your birthday? How I remember you, my daughter, when you were nine years old! You told me how wonderful it is that God made it that when you get dressed in the morning, you can start with the things you last take off!

You've both had joy and sorrow, which will bind you together. Hope you will forever move forwards.

From Vater

When Vater penned these letters to Louise and Emil, he wrote in the moment, about the moment. Now it is I, more than seventy years later, who pour the meaning of eternity into his every word.

Chapter 25

One evening, exhausted, I suggest to Sam that I order pizzas. Beats cooking any day. And Sam is home on a Friday. Reason enough for a celebration.

'Not 'pizza', Mum, 'peeza'.'

'Would you or would you not like a *peeza?*'

'Not the posh ones.'

'Fine by me.'

An hour later, we are both seated at the kitchen table, the dancing flame of a candle throwing shadows, and embracing us in its light as we tear at the Quattre Staggione (mine) and Vegetarian Special (Sam's). The dog, underneath the table, gets his share too.

'Why don't you eat your crusts?' Sam accuses me.

'I don't need my hair to curl,' I tell him, but Sam shakes his head at me, full of reproach that I am feeding the dog with my food.

'You're wasting it.'

'Grandma's going into a Home.'

Sam has been the one witness to how frequently my mother's crises have disrupted his and my life. How often he'd had to take second place to my interminable phone calls to social workers, doctors and carers. How often, unwilling to leave a young child by himself, I'd insisted he drive over with me, for him to stand on the doorstep as I'd hammered on my mother's locked front door because, yet again, she wasn't answering the phone. How often it was Sam who had comforted me when I'd moaned that she could again be lying unconscious in her home. 'It'll be all right, Mum. You'll see.'

But Sam, older now, is right out of comfort. 'About time too,' he declares, confronting me with his gaze.

'Do you remember when you used to fence with her, she would hold a broom handle and you'd have a stick? That was such good fun,' I say, hoping to remind him of better times.

'She did that *once*,' replied Sam, who knew this as one of the few instances I always gave in favour of my mother.

'Remember how she came on that demo against pit closures with us? The one in London. Amazing. She was over eighty and it was pouring with rain. And there she was, with her red umbrella and her grandchild. Didn't work,' I add. 'The mines were all closed down. Thatcher's great achievement.'

'Don't be silly, Mum.'

'How's school?' I ask.

'What's it to you?'

'Sam, why are you being like this?'

I have excavated Sam from many holes into which he was pushed, or had fallen, in his long school life in North London. He didn't have a good time of it at primary school. When I recently asked him how much he remembered being bullied, he told me he remembered every minute. Do you think it was because of your hair, I'd asked him. But Sam had replied: 'It was OK. It hardened me up for life. Nobody'll ever get away with bullying me again.'

I'd gone to the Head at the time, though I hadn't told Sam this, to complain that he was getting sticks and abuse thrown at him in the playground.

'If you got his hair cut, it'd be easier for him,' she'd told me. 'His long fair hair makes him look like a girl.'

'The length of his hair is up to him,' I'd insisted. 'It doesn't justify his getting 'gay' hurled at him.'

She'd replied: 'What do you expect me to do?'

''Gay' should not be used as abuse,' I'd persisted, flabbergasted.

'You want me to draw them pictures of gay sex so as to show them how it's done?'

'I don't want Sam bullied.'

'Not my job,' she replied, getting up from behind her desk, dismissing me.

Sam changed to a school where at least the bullying was confined to the simpler form of physical attack.

Even when I was pregnant, I already resolved that I was not going to allow my child to stand as I had done, fighting my corner, alone. But I could not protect Sam from the bullies and worried that I had transferred to Sam my sense of being 'other'.

He has grown to resent my desire to know what's going on in his life.

'I ran into my old English teacher at school,' Sam unexpectedly announces, as we munch.

'Did she speak to you?'

'What a rat. She asked me what I was doing in the sixth form.'

I remember how persistently the English teacher, who did not find Sam easy to teach, had tried to throw him out of her GCSE English class, predicting he would get a Fail.

'Did you say anything to her?' I ask.

'What's the point? 'Hey, Miss, remember me? Guess what, I got an A!''

What political or ideological tragedy, I wonder to myself, overwhelmed the comprehensive ideals of nurturing each individual child? I had strongly supported the comprehensive movement in the 1960s, and the belief that the education system should break down, not reconstruct class differences, and that each and every child mattered as much as the next, irrespective of birth. Yet many of the teachers at Sam's comprehensive school appeared more concerned with League tables and results than with the needs of the students. Sam had not fitted into the English teacher's model of 'the good student'.

'I think I'll write to her, reminding her she would only put you into the exam if I took financial responsibility for your entry when you failed. Now I'll take responsibility for your A grade,' I tell Sam.

'Don't do it, Mum! Please. If you must, wait till I've left the school.'

'I never really understood what she had against you.'

Sam grins. 'I once told her that her teaching was boring. That we could all read, so why didn't she save us all a lot of time and give us the details of the crib she was teaching us from.'

'And did you say that to the maths teacher, too? The one who threw you out of the top GCSE stream and then had to let you back in again after I'd complained?'

'He didn't like the way I used to tilt my chair onto its back legs during his class,' Sam smirks. 'I didn't learn anything in my new class. All I did was help all the other students.'

'He must have missed you when you were put back up.' I smile at Sam.

Sam's eyes brighten. Then he says: 'Made no difference, Mum, whether I was in the top or middle stream. So I got an A. Why do you always have to make such a fuss?'

'You'll be fine at university. What the school interprets as insolence, they will understand as inquisitiveness. The lecturers will love you.'

Sam nods. He looks pleased at this.

The trouble with pizza is how quickly it gets eaten. 'Pudding?' I ask, but Sam rolls his hand round his stomach with pretend grunts of satisfaction.

'Thanks, Mum. I'm off!'

'Out?'

'What do you expect? It's Friday night.'

Chapter 26

'Hello?' A woman's voice answers the phone.

'Is Ruben there?' I fear my voice gives me away. It was difficult enough ringing him, without this.

'He's in the bedroom. I'll get him for you.' I can hear a question mark hanging in her voice.

'Hi.' Ruben sounds displeased.

'It's such a lovely afternoon. I thought I'd walk the dog.' This is a lie.

'You have my permission.'

'With you. Well, not with you. With you if you wanted to come, of course.'

I'm sure he did.

'I'm somewhat pre-occupied just now.'

'Yes, yes, I quite understand.'

To my surprise, Ruben is laughing. 'Don't sound so gloomy. I'll phone you soon.'

Why don't you leave well alone, I tell myself, as I head for the warmth of a hot bath halfway through the day. I throw my clothes into a heap on the floor and get in. As I relax into the water, Ruben keeps dancing around in my head, though I tell him to go away.

I want to belong to the world through Ruben, I muse. The last years had not been easy. Between working, my mother, and Sam, I'd slipped beneath my own radar. Once, I'd been attractive - at least if the number of men who had once wanted to bed me was a measure. Indeed, soon after my relationship with John had finally given its last gasp, I'd had a lovely time. But promiscuity had rapidly got tedious. Even with Simon - great fun at first, but my boredom threshold had been rapidly reached. 'Youth is wasted on the young.'

I'd managed to conjure up one last entanglement after Sam had been born and my mother had started to disintegrate. I'd escaped to see a film early one afternoon, and a long lean man with a ponytail of lank curls, had ostentatiously held open the door to the cinema for me. We were early, and he'd offered to buy me a coffee. Flattered, I'd agreed. After the film, he'd caught up with me and suggested we meet up, which we did, once in a cafe, once for a brisk walk on Hampstead Heath. He'd explained he was a social worker, a team leader indeed, on sick leave. Stress. I was sympathetic instead of suspicious. But when he came to my house, I realised there was no way he was walking through my bedroom door.

Now I'm just about invisible. Lying in the bath, I refuse to look down at the skin, which used to wrap my arms so smoothly, now hanging loose and accusing. I want to be desired and to desire. And to be told everything will be all right.

I glance around the bathroom. I'd decided to paint it a glorious magenta-red to conceal the awful pinkness of the bath, which came with the house. But the paint looks worn and needs a fresh coat. Through the bathroom door I spot piles of books leaning up in the corner between the bathroom and a bedroom. I must get round to putting up more bookshelves. And I need to do something about the large hole in the hall carpet which the dog had dug to bury his bones. I try to block the thoughts which whisper that, if only things went well with Ruben, I'd sort everything in no time.

Ruben phones me a couple of days later. 'Let's meet,' he suggests in a matter of fact sort of way. I am relieved, but say nothing. We arrange to get together at the Kandinsky exhibition at the Tate Modern. We have, it turns out, both visited it before, but are grateful to find something easy that we both enjoy. After admiring Kandinsky at some length, we gravitate to the balcony with its wonderful view of St Paul's, and pull out chairs where we sit up against the balustrade, near but not too near each other, peering out over the river.

'I like the middle period the best.' Ruben glances at me.

'Before he succumbed to painting under the direction of the Party.' I turn towards him and grin.

'You know, he was originally inspired by mysticism.'

This is all very interesting but it isn't what I want to talk about. Still, I say: 'One of his early pictures of Murnau hangs over my desk at home.'

'I've got his *Yellow, Red and Blue* in the front room. It's later. Less nostalgic.'

'But I had that up in my room in Oxford!'

I'd discovered Kandinsky very early and loved the enormous abstract reproduction which I'd stuck with multiple strips of illicit sellotape onto the wall over my bed in my room at college.

Ruben is looking amused and nodding: 'I know.'

So he did care.

Then he adds quietly, 'I'm not really on the left any more. Not like at Oxford.'

'What happened?'

'Got a good job.'

'As what?'

'University lecturer. California. Didn't make it to Prof.'

'I had to become part-time. Too much else going on with son and mother to stay as a full-time lecturer.' I look enquiringly at him.

'Married. Had two children,' he replies.

'And?'

'I don't want to talk about it. I'm just pleased to be sitting here with you.'

For a long time we stare out over the river and the boats. A fine drizzle has started.

Glad to have a good reason to leave, I break into the silence. 'My son is home this evening. I should go.'

Chapter 27

I have decided to open the MI5 papers which I'd hidden in my son's old toy cupboard ever since receiving them. The box reveals at least five hundred sheets, some in German, many in illegible handwriting. My parents did everything they could so that I should not be sitting here, opening up their pasts without their knowledge or agreement.

'You know I'm doing research on the construction of national identity,' Aphro reminds me when I tell her, over a cup of tea, about the papers later that afternoon.

'I suspect this will be more deconstruction,' I warn her.

'The insider's definition of the outsider is always the key to how the insiders' view themselves And you couldn't get much more of an insider's view than MI5,' Aphro says.

'And there's no clearer definition of the insider than that of the outsider,' I add.

With some foreboding, I accept Aphro's insistent offer of help.

Aphro checks the ordering of the papers. 'Do you want these in date-order or do you want like kept with like?' she asks.

I sit immobile and stare at her.

'What?'

'We could put the letters from your family together, or we could order everything chronologically.'

'What's everything?' I manage.

'That's what we're going to work out. There seem to be a lot of papers relating to your mother's arrest and a transcript of her interrogation in Holloway Prison.'

'She was arrested?'

'Hold on. We must get organised.'

'I didn't know my mother was in Holloway.'

Aphro continues: 'The file doesn't finish until after 1950.'

'But I was alive by then!'

'I don't think that was MI5's chief concern.'

Aphro starts to number the pages in sequential order. But I cannot stop shaking.

Over further cups of tea, Aphro announces: 'These papers would make good teaching materials. Raises all those crucial questions about how far one can generalise from such historical sources, but at the same time learn about the individuals involved.'

'Aphro, this is my family.'

'I must find out whom the signatures in the margin belong to. Could give a unique insight into how the Home Office was vetting refugees at the beginning of the war. I couldn't borrow these papers, could I?'

'Write an illustrious research paper about it?' I snap. Aphro is emotionally tone-deaf.

'You know I'd credit you. None of that patriarchal rubbish where men take the research women have done and claim it as their own.'

'I'm getting tired,' I tell her truthfully.

'I'll take that as a 'no',' Aphro says.

Suddenly she is picking up her possessions, ready to go. I thank her. But, though initially relieved that Aphro has gone, I am then seized with foreboding. Do I really want to know what I shall soon discover?

Chapter 28

Unusually, I find myself wanting to find out about the letters from Mutti and Vater and, the day after Aphro's abrupt departure, when Sam is not yet up, and rather than visiting my mother, I sit down at the kitchen table to read the later letters from 1937.

The first letter I look at is not addressed to anybody specific.

21.11.37

Thank you for your list of wishes. We will try to obtain the necessary material. We fear the dress you requested is too risky, but other wishes may be possible. But I have sent you 10 marks, plus some food and clothes.

There is a deep shadow hanging over us. Father is losing his market. His buyers are going elsewhere. We can guess where it will lead.

The doctor intends to let M come to us for a holiday. We wonder whether they think this will help her. Do they want to discharge her permanently? The task of the Institute should be to keep inmates while they are a danger. This problem and the other one are millstones around our necks. We need to pour our hearts out to you. We are not ones to hush things up. We'll get through it.

L now in Brighton. T sent detailed and shocking news in her letter from Palestine. What terrible birth pains of the new country.

I hope your plans for your new goal come to fruition. Honour your reasons without knowing them.

May each change bring its blessings.
From Mutti

6.12.37

Dear children,

I have been looking at Louise's picture that you kindly sent us.

I miss you.

I hope you are blessed.

Ideas of happiness change as you get older.

From Vater

22.12.37

Your letter made us laugh. That is so necessary, given what is going on.

Aunt K's flat is about to be taken. We fear K will not be able to keep her teaching job. But we cannot go into details – you will understand. S. is now in England, and another friend of ours, a teacher, is leaving soon. What is to happen to us? We will soon be almost the only ones left.

The price of a turkey for Christmas has gone up and is now beyond our reach.

From Vater and Mutti

At what cost are these marooned parents still sending help to their absent children? The parents sound desperate. I suspect they are no longer able to feed themselves properly.

German Jews are no longer allowed to have passports to travel abroad. Impossible now to know whether their friends made it out to safety. The parents must have been so worried they would also lose their home, like K. 'Informal' activity by members of the SS, I guess.

Another reference to M. As an 'inmate' this time. I phone Chris, the translator, but she is adamant it is this particular word in the letter.

The drums of the future are drawing closer, blocking out other sounds. I watch as their world contracts.

Chapter 29

I am rung up one blue evening by the Director of the Assessment Unit and told that my mother is to be moved to a Home of their choice in twenty-four hours' time. The decision has been made.

'It's Jewish?' I ask. But no. There is nothing Jewish about her Home-to-be.

'Haven't you made enough of a nuisance of yourself already?' the Director replies to my objections. 'We know what you've been up to. We've talked to the staff. We know your mother wanted to go home and that you've been trying to stop her. Now all we can do is send her to the Five Leaves Home. That's what happens when you don't collaborate with us.'

'I was told there haven't been places in any Jewish care homes.'

'We don't usually send our residents to Jewish Homes. If you had wanted her to go there so much, then it was up to you to find out about it.'

Stunned, I suggest her move be postponed till I do just that. 'Nobody told me I could get involved before,' I tell him, lamely but accurately.

Every social worker had insisted the task of finding my mother a Home had to be done by them alone.

'I realise it's only one day's notice but Louise has been with us far too long already,' is his reply.

I attempt legal action to stop the move. The specialist lawyer who advises me is appalled at the abrogation of Louise's civil rights, and explains how to take a case to the High Court on her behalf. But it has to be done by 4pm that day and I am timed out.

I ring work to explain I shall be taking another day off. The woman in the office is remarkably forbearing, almost sympathetic. Everybody, it seems, has had the problem of what to do with an ancient parent.

Early the next morning, the ambulance takes Louise to a Home far from where I live, outside London. Though I leave plenty of time to drive there, I get lost and arrive late. My mother, still wearing her coat, has been placed on a hard chair next to the door, her feet dangling above the ground like a little girl. She glares at me as I finally appear, panic-stricken, in the lounge.

'I'm sorry I wasn't here when you arrived,' I tell her.

She turns her face from mine.

'I'll get you out of here,' I promise her.

The manager is hovering next to me.

'*We* are looking after her now,' he pronounces.

The Home reminds me of a nineteenth century workhouse. The residents' chairs are cramped up against each other so tightly round the room that one person's elbow pushes into the space of the person sitting next to them. I go to ascertain the state of the loos, to find they are filthy inside and outside the pan. One poor woman has been planted in the corridor leading between the lounge and the bedrooms where she sits, screaming, unseen but not unheard. Further down the same corridor, in a corner, sits a man, also ignored, who is trying, with some success, to pull down his trousers with one hand, the other already tucked inside. It's late morning, yet the residents are all slopping about in their dressing gowns and slippers, stinking of urine. This place is surely the end of the world.

So many years after Labour had taken power, I was horrified that anybody could get away with caring for old people like this, needy people whose only sins were that they had grown old and didn't have enough money to buy in their own care.

I start a campaign to get my mother out. I begin by writing letters, starting with the Director of Social Services, which gets me nowhere, then rise up to the relevant MPs and Government departments. To my amazement, an Inspector phones me up almost immediately. Could he meet me at Five Leaves? There's already an investigation into the Home. He would like to hear what I can tell him about what has happened to my mother. 'It's not just my mother,' I emphasise. 'Most of the residents from the Psychiatric Unit my mother was in are sent there.' But to this he does not respond.

Three weeks after being admitted, my mother is

suddenly released from her workhouse. She has not uttered a word throughout.

My teenage son, on the other hand, has started to complain of neglect. Where has his cook, cleaner and private tutor gone?

'*I'm* still alive,' he protests to me one evening, after I'd once again stuck a chilled dish, lasagne this time, into the microwave for him.

'So is Grandma.'

'Aren't I more important? Sam replies, giving me accusatory looks.

'Is there something I'm missing here?' I ask. 'Do you need help with your homework?' Would that it were so easy.

'Oh no.' Sam is emphatic. 'I'm just making a point.'

I stare up at the ceiling. Sam is knocking around in his bedroom next door. Then he turns his music up so high that the beat thuds through the adjoining wall.

I no longer understand him. Being a single mum when Sam was little was hard work, but patrolling the emotional parameters now that he is an adolescent is far more tricky.

I found it easy to provide for Sam's need to be loved. I wasn't going to repeat my parents' mistakes. I knew I had to be there for him, whatever the cost.

Now, Sam, like all teenagers, has pulled away, while still wanting me to be there. Perhaps other parents are able to maintain a better balance while negotiating these psychological rapids, but I feel unsteady in these choppy waters.

It is my physical self which crashes. I fall ill, as soon as I am informed that my mother is to be released, and is to move to a new Home.

Chapter 30

There is a welcoming committee to greet my mother and me when we arrive at the Jewish Home. I look around. Opposite the door, the first thing I see is a picture of a menorah.

They surely assume I am a Jew. I feel uncomfortable. I do not belong here.

My mother is shown her room. It is small but light, overlooking the garden: I had insisted on a room with a view.

'Is this it?'

First words in three weeks. So she can still speak. But her words cut me down to size. She wanted more. Good for her. I haven't done right by her again. I unpack her two suitcases; that is all she has left of her life. Just like a refugee. All over again.

When I arrive the next day, my mother greets me with enthusiasm.

'We all sat round a long table last night, with candles, and there was wine. Isn't it wonderful? We celebrated Trotsky's birthday. This is how we should always have lived.'

The celebration was Honaecker. Nothing to do with Trotsky or my mother's socialist past. 'I'm proud you're still a revolutionary,' I whisper to her.

My mother now seems to have acquired 'her' chair, which, I note, is placed at the end of the tightly-packed row nearest the door. As I pull out a footstool so that I can sit down by her, she announces: 'My mother hit me, you know.'

'Where did she hit you?'

'On the face. Hard.' She looks at me as if the blows were still fresh.

'Why would she do that?'

'She did not like me.'

'Had you been naughty?'

'I was a very well-behaved child.'

'What did you feel when she hit you?'

'I did not like her. She was ugly. I liked my father. He was a wonderful man.' She beams.

She has never before talked of her parents.

'What was your father like?'

'So attractive. He wept when I was born. He wanted a son. I won him over because I was so clever. I was the apple of his eye.'

'Who did you look like?'

'Him, of course. Except I'm not bald.' Laughs.

Then her voice grows thick: 'He was taken away.'

'I know.'

'Do you know what they did to him?'

'No.'

'They killed him,' she mumbles, head fallen forwards.

This is the terrible secret that had choked her, preventing her from speaking about so much else. This is the secret that has lain between us. Now it is I who find my grandfather's death too unbearable to speak of.

I am overwhelmed by my grandparents' sudden entry and exit into our discourse. The past is popping out unbidden. I dread the truth. I have not been positioned against a past and so have no future. That is my tragedy, as much as the loss of my grandparents. Now grown up, the child has no means of sucking in the confidence given by having a family past. I belong to no country. And there is nowhere I can call my own.

Death peeps round every corner. Every time I get into a car I am aware I may be killed. Every time I care about somebody, I fear the friendship will fail. My son - what an act of faith in the future! - could be carried away by the next puff of fate.

All my childhood I lived with ghosts. Now I am unable to touch what is real. I am afraid of the pain. I will not reach the next moment of my existence intact.

As anticipated, my mother, sitting in her chair in a line of chairs, insists she is not Jewish. I am asked to visit the office.

'Your mother is upsetting the other residents,' says the Manager, who is kind but rarely available. Trouble can be so time-consuming and all she wants is an easy life. 'The other residents don't understand why she keeps shouting that she isn't Jewish. And she is German you know. She sings German songs. She tries to teach them to us. We are really pleased that she's talking again but some of the other residents still think it's the Second World War.'

'I visited your home in Berlin,' I inform my mother on my next visit. I am frightened of telling her. It's dangerous to step over the invisible line between her life and mine.

'This is where you and your parents used to live.' I show her the photos I have taken of her home. I am anxious. I have no right to invade her past. Easier not to tell. I am terrified that she will start to cry with sadness, or with fury, terrified that I'll become the comforter, terrified that I will be swept away in a torrent of tears.

She stares at the photos of her home, the door to the house, the gloriously decorated hallway, the carved front door to the flat, the view from the balcony still overlooking a line of trees. She does not respond.

Chapter 31

I work out from the MI5 transcript of Louise's interrogation in Holloway Prison that Louise had first met Dennis at the Linguists Club. She was teaching German there; Dennis was studying it, after leaving Dublin for London.

My parents start to live in different addresses. I tremble, as if my life were under attack, at the realisation that my parents had split up, even though it is before I was born. I do not want to know this.

The next we hear of them - and now the 'them' is Louise and Dennis - is when they are travelling to Amsterdam and to Paris. It is hard following the MI5 clues. I pick apart the long log, written in different hands, as the 'watchers' present the minutiae of the departures and arrivals. The notes from Louise's interrogation, though more fluent and informative, are almost as frustrating for me as they proved to be for her interrogators. She gives MI5 nothing, protesting forcefully that she knows not why she is in prison or what she is being accused of. Nobody had told her. Was she being held as an agent for the USSR or the Nazis? Didn't they realise she had fled the Nazis? Why would she spy for them? Indeed, she no longer held any political sympathies. The interrogator describes her as hysterical. It is 1940.

Nor is it clear what Dennis was up to. Louise claims that she had supposed Dennis was nothing more than a courier between Britain and the USSR. But then she observed Dennis passing parcels and other materials through train windows and in sleazy hotel corridors to suspicious-looking men. She presents herself as fearful, and disapproving of such behaviour.

But why my mother wanted to leave England, without any papers or a passport, after she had made such a life-shattering effort to get here in 1933, or what she wanted in Moscow in 1936, or how she got there without papers, is unclear. MI5's long arm cannot have reached quite that far.

A letter written by my father to MI5 pierces me with arrows of pain. In the letter he accepts it was his fault, that he was to blame for Louise leaving him and taking up with Dennis.

After my escape from Germany, even when I became reunited with my dear wife,' my father wrote in expressive, if flawed, English, I was not emotionally available to anybody, even to her. I had myself been through a very hard time and had nothing left to give. It does not surprise or shock me that, after she had left behind all her family in Berlin on my behalf, that when I was not available for her for such a long time, she sought comfort with somebody else.

He was making excuses for her, trying to get her out of Holloway.

Other letters from my father are equally unexpected. He promises to send Louise money in Moscow. What was going on? Why would he be sending her money when she is with another man? A letter from him to Dennis's mother, who also lives in Oxford, offering his help, suggests steps she could take to trace her missing son. There is even a note. Goodness knows how MI5 ever obtained it. How ironic, my father writes, that a stateless German refugee is helping a born and bred English lady to find out what has happened to her son in Communist Russia. Maybe the relationship between Louise and Dennis was some sort of political front, rather than a reality.

A letter from Louise to Emil asks him, in a roundabout sort of way, whether he might be having another relationship. MI5 readers must have had fun with that one. But there is no recorded response. I find I want to defend my father against any suggestion of his infidelity.

Suddenly, my mother is back in London. No clue as to how she returned. No mention of Dennis. She seems to have moved back into my father's flat, but he then moves out, though he lives nearby. It is still only 1936.

Chapter 32

'Would you like to see a film?' Ruben calls one day after a long interval.

'Maybe. It's raining.'

I hear him laugh. 'Do you have any other suggestions?' he teases me.

The geography of our body positions in the cinema seats proves tricky. First, I lean up against the arm on the opposite side of my seat to where Ruben is sitting, to avoid all temptation, but, as the film starts, I find myself resting up against Ruben's still firm body. Ruben puts his arm round me. I never want to move again, as wave upon wave of nostalgia and desire pulse through me. I am not concentrating on the film.

Afterwards, we run to a nearby cheap Chinese restaurant in the maze of streets off the Tottenham Court Road. It's surprisingly crowded and we end up by ourselves at a table, squashed into an alcove in the airless basement. At least nobody is near us. I am sipping my way though some very ordinary won ton soup.

'What happened between us?' he suddenly asks.

I glance over at him. 'We were young.' I sound forced.

'I've often wondered what it was that drew us to each other. We never did talk much about that. But I loved you.'

I can hardly bear him to say that. It's as if a sadness that has lain damned inside me for all these years is just about to be released.

'I couldn't do it, Ruben.' I'm fumbling for words, my throat tightening.

'You just threw me away.'

'I knew you would leave me. I never expect anything to last.'

'I decided you were some arrogant, stuck-up bitch who wasn't interested in me.'

My stomach does a somersault. Was this how he'd thought at the time? Yet, it's not his language which upsets me, but that Ruben is saying he had been there for my taking.

'It was you who didn't turn up that time,' I remind him. How irrelevant it sounds now.

'I tried to phone you but you never answered,' Ruben replies.

So Ruben hasn't forgotten either.

'You had so many admirers, I couldn't believe that you would choose me,' I break into the silence.

Ruben, I remember, was adored by his fellow students. Even a few of the tutors, appearing in their black flowing gowns, and sweeping down the corridor between the rows of seats to give their lectures from the raised lectern, would stop briefly to ask Ruben how his work was going. Once, when a don who had leaned over me, oblivious, to address Ruben, had been given the usual 'I'm OK, thanks' brush off, I'd queried Ruben's manner. Ruben had looked amused and said: 'I'd hate to be like them.'

'But it was you I wanted,' Ruben is now insisting.

I don't know where to start. I don't know really what happened between us. Even now, I find it hard to confess to myself how much I'd desired him. 'We were only together for a couple of months,' is all I come up with. My voice is thin.

'Don't you think that's long enough to know?'

'I thought I was stupid and ugly. Why would anybody love me?'

Ruben regards me silently.

'You shouldn't put yourself down.' After a pause, he continues. 'My daughter was killed in a car accident, and soon after, my wife died. Cancer, or broken heart. Take your pick. That's why I had to come back.'

'I'm so sorry, Ruben.'

His eyes are dry, even stony.

'When did this happen?'

'About four years ago. I've been back here now for almost two years. I can almost talk again.'

'You have a second child?'

'One son, Peter. He's still there. A computer nerd. I don't see him coming to Britain. He's an all-American kid. Even supports the death penalty.'

'You miss him?'

'Not really.'

'What was your daughter called?'

'Crystalline. I don't want to talk about it.'

Silence.

'Where are you living now?' I'm trying to steady my voice.

'Just round the corner from you. Didn't you realise? I moved back in with my mother. I nursed her through the last bit of her life. One reason I wanted to come back. It's not a moral judgement.' He looks at me closely. 'My mother died about a year ago.'

'Another death.'

'But *she* was old, almost ninety. Not twenty, like Crystalline - hardly older than your son.'

'Did you find it difficult to nurse her?'

'It was the most natural thing in the world. It's only piss and shit. We all do it.' He almost cackles. 'It gave me the chance to get to know her. I had been away a long time.'

'Did she ever meet your family?'

'She met my wife but never my children.'

'How come?'

'Something always got in the way.'

'How sad.'

'We all die.'

I don't know what to say. That we both have been marked by past tragedies, tragedies which cannot be put right? We struggle past the other diners' tables and out into the night. Ruben grasps my arm. 'Losing a daughter was like losing my soul. I would lie awake in my bed at night and not want to be alive in the morning.'

As we kiss each other on the cheek, sheltering from the rain at the mouth of the tube, he whispers: 'Don't pity me.'

Chapter 33

Aphro and I are sitting in the pub. 'What do you want now?' was how she had greeted me when I'd rung her earlier that week.

'I was going to suggest we meet for an evening out,' I told her, furious at her apparent dismissal. Have I been offloading too much misery onto her?

It's a warm enough winter evening for us to sit outside under the trees, as we are both well wrapped up. The fairy lights are twinkling and my dog is curled between us under the table. Everybody admires the dog, who takes the stroking and petting as his due. 'Oh I wish we had a dog like yours,' they say to me, as I pray he never dies.

Aphro, too, it quickly transpires, needs to talk. 'I'm having problems with my father,' she tells me as soon as we are settled with our glasses of warming punch.

'You remember he had that op for cancer a few years back,' Aphro tells me. 'We were so worried about him, but he bounced back. But since Mum died, he isn't coping. When I phone him, he's never in. As far as I can see, he can't bear being in the house any more. Goes out for the sake of it. Seems to spend his days just wandering about. He had a fall last week. Wasn't going to tell me, but then it slipped out that he'd just been in the same hospital where Mum died.'

I carefully hear her out. Her voice is steady. What, I ask, is she planning to do? 'Nothing to be done,' she explains. 'He'll never leave his home.' And she won't move nearer to him. She checks up on him most days by phone. There's a brother who lives nearer than her. He drops by sometimes but he isn't up to much. Then there's her father's older sister who's still alive, and comes to see him at least once a week. The father also has a bit of savings. She knows he'd hate it, but she may have to look into getting him a carer. She's tried the local authority, but they're useless; her father doesn't have enough points. Aphro sounds remarkably matter of fact, but then she sighs and says: 'He was such a lovely dad when I was young.'

'I adored my father when I was little,' I tell her, picking up on the theme. 'But by the time I was eighteen, I wanted to

119

get as far away from him as I could. He scared me. All men - apart from him, of course - were evil and dangerous.' I glance at Aphro who doesn't appear to be listening. 'Did I ever tell you that he insisted I walk more than a door's length away from the kerb so that white slave traders in their cars couldn't reach out and grab me?'

I shiver.

'You didn't believe that stuff?'

'Why wouldn't I? I didn't know what white slave traders were, but they didn't sound nice.'

'Your parents were only trying to protect you.'

'Aphro, I know there were positive sides to my parents. I've got photos of us when I was little. We look like a happy normal nuclear family. We even had a dog and a garden. My mother read me Shakespeare. They took me to the seaside, once to Brittany, twice Italy. My father taught me to swim in the Mediterranean. They can't have done everything wrong.'

'You got on better with your father than your mother?'

'I once told my father that I hated my mother. She hadn't spoken to me for days. Maybe weeks.'

'And?'

'He wrote me a letter saying that if I ever spoke to him like that again, I would kill him.'

'You would kill him?' Aphro is incredulous.

'It worked. I never spoke like that again and he stayed alive.'

It's dark and I'm cold. 'Let's go inside,' I state, rising without regard to Aphro's wishes, and add, 'I'm aware my father wanted to protect me. But he also wanted me for himself.'

'Daddy's girl?'

'No other man was good enough for me. There had to be something wrong with all of them. Sad thing is that I don't think I've ever got over my fear of men.'

'Not what I've heard!' Aphro tells me.

'Aphro!'

'Come on! How many lovers have you had? Time to confess!'

We search unsuccessfully for a table in the crowded internal recesses of the pub. We perch in a corner on a couple of bar stools.

'I hear you're seeing Ruben again,' Aphro says as soon as we're settled.

'How d'you know that?' What I want to say is: 'Mind your own business.'

Why do I see this woman? We'd become friends at Oxford, two of the few women who'd been activists on the left, both of us opinionated, neither of us ever easy with the other. At different colleges and studying different subjects, we'd met up regularly at small, serious meetings in forlorn rooms, though her enthusiasm had been the Humanists, whom I'd considered too concerned with issues of Human Rights rather than class oppression. Always more ambitious than me, straight from Oxford she'd got a job as an organiser for a leading Human Rights Charity and, soon after, became one of its best-paid National Coordinators. I'd become a lecturer, an active member of the rank and file, and leading militant against management. All contact between us, even the token Christmas card, had rapidly ceased. I'd heard that, after a whirlwind courtship, she'd had a brief marriage to a successful lawyer, whom she'd lucratively divorced.

It was Friends Reunited which had brought Aphro and me together again. Contact had initially been tentative. But when she emailed me that she'd given up her previous job - Kafkaesque was how she'd described it - was living alone, and only a short drive away from me, I suggested we meet. I just hoped she hadn't moved too far to the right. Aphro had been surprisingly keen on the idea and it had been she who'd then proposed we meet again. However, some subjects are best avoided. We don't talk children - or Ruben.

'You haven't forgotten I knew Ruben before you? Oxford. Remember,' Aphro is telling me.

'Just friends,' I mutter, not wanting to believe that Ruben has talked about me to Aphro.

'Who needs men?' Aphro tosses out.

Time to change the subject. 'You've seen some of the M15 papers. Any further thoughts?' I venture.

'There's not really that much mystery, is there? It just upsets you because you've discovered your mother was unfaithful.'

This is not something I am about to discuss with Aphro. 'I don't believe my mother was a spy. And anyway, the USSR were our allies. I guess being a German refugee who had then visited the USSR was too much for British security, so they arrested her.'

Aphro shrugs. 'It was war-time. MI5 were doing their job.'

'There's something missing, Aphro. My parents brought me up to hate Stalin. I was suckled on the milk of anti-Stalinism. You remember 1953? My parents were so disappointed when the uprising in the Russian quarter of Berlin failed against the Communist Government. It was as if for one moment in their lives there had been hope. After that, my mother used to quote Brecht's quip at me: 'The government needs to re-elect the people.' I learnt very young the difference between a people and a government.'

But Aphro's eyes have glazed over.

'Tell me a bit more about your father,' I suggest. Aphro and I carry on conferring about what to do with her dad, who, until her mother died, had not so much as made a piece of toast.

Chapter 34

Don't get me wrong, reads an email from Chris, the translator, but this translation is as difficult as it gets. So many of the letters have the tops and bottoms cut off. It's impossible half the time to tell whom they were written to or who wrote them. This makes deciphering their meaning less than simple.

Where do I begin to explain my parents' fears? I remember how my father used to pace by the window in our front room, which overlooked the street, his watch in his hand, concealing himself behind the curtains.

'You see,' he informs me, beaming, 'that man is spying on us.'

I stare out, heart beating, frightened. 'There is no one there.'

'They'll be back in two minutes.'

Should I explain to her about how he covered the phone with cushions, telling me when I questioned this odd behaviour: 'They're listening to us.'

Should I tell her how every door was locked as we left each room, or about how the front door had five locks? My parents turned or shot each one every time we went in or out. As there were two bolts, one at the bottom, one at the top of the front door, I could not get in without one of my parents pulling back the bolts on the inside of the door. When I had overcome my fear and objected to this level of fortification, my father had said, 'Don't you want us to be safe?'

How could I be sure that he was wrong and there weren't enemies waiting to get us?

Most people's parents have not lived and slept their lives with the consequences of such double horrors: the bloody fall of the Russian Revolution and the rise of Nazism.

Chris's email continues: One picture postcard of a Goya reproduction has simply no name of sender or of recipient. Everything's been scratched off - the names, the stamp and the postmark. There's a bit of writing, very hard to read - do you really want it translated? I don't get it, Anna. Why don't they either throw it away or keep it as it was? PS The next translations from 1938 are in the post.

My parents kept everything. Each letter must have been so precious, a touch of the breath of those they love, from far away. Yet they had to protect the people who'd written to them. Or, of course, themselves.

Their anxieties frightened me. My father created what he feared. I wanted nothing to do with him. He became my enemy as well.

I do not tell Chris this. Instead I write back, thanking her for doing what is proving to be such a difficult translation, talking about the weather, the dog, about anything other than asking her what I'm about to find out.

Chapter 35

There are so many letters from 1938, the year that Germany marched into Czechoslovakia, the year Bukharin was executed in the USSR, the year that the Spanish Civil War was lost to Franco and the Royalists, that the Munich, Nuremberg and Danzig synagogues were destroyed, that German Jews had to carry identity papers, that Jewish children could no longer attend schools, when Buchenwald concentration camp swallowed up tens of thousands of Jews and political oppositionists: the year of Kristallnacht.

21.1.38

Dear children,

We confirm we have received your letter.

Relations with manufacturers and clients have deteriorated. I'm not certain whether I would be allowed to journey abroad, even if I had the money.

I can't avoid being depressed given the way things are. We share our fate with many, but each one suffers alone.

From Vater

22.3.38

Dear children,

We are overjoyed at E's good news about his work at Oxford. You deserve it after so much disappointment, which never brought you to your knees.

From today, we are incapacitated.

Lots of things happening here, so we are staying. We can now only travel if permanently leaving or finding information to do so.

But we will meet again.

From Vater and Mutti

I guess the difference between the letter sent in January and March is that 'Jews' are no longer allowed to have passports or to travel.

5.4.38

We will be celebrating Passover in a few days. We think of you on Seder night. There are so few people attending these days.

Louise – it won't do you any harm to do housework for a bit. Do you intend to work?

From Mutti

Despite the harshness of the comment, I am amused by how little my mother had changed. Doing housework was – understandably - never her chosen activity.

20.4.38

You will know of our difficulties. It is not just a lack of money. Whether a letter from you inviting me would be effective is doubtful. It would be more concrete if an English manufacturer invited me over for my special technical skills. Perhaps time will help unravel these problems.

I have sent you money.

From Vater

9.5.38

We are very cold. We only heat the dining room. Money is tight. We can only eat vegetarian.

No meat, eggs, fish, salt or coffee for a few weeks now.

S has left for London, Aunt K has reached Amsterdam. G is now in Stockholm without being able to feed himself and without a job; his younger brother is in New York. Our lives are becoming narrower.

From Mutti and Vater

24.5.38

The birthday morning began badly. Father is ill with the flu. When everything gets back to normal, we will take the doctor's advice.

I would so like to see you but there is no hope of that at the moment, despite all the efforts that father and everyone else is making.

From Mutti.

7.6.38

Father still has flu.

I have lost weight partly due to an unsuitable diet.

Father has now been dismissed from Z and K.

We want to join you in Oxford, to study an English course. Maybe, if we applied for a course in England, the police would give us our passports back. Then we would stay and be free. It may be very important to come over for more than one reason. But we would also need some money.

From Mutti

What a desperate letter. Mutti is so upset, she forgets to write in code. Or, perhaps she no longer can see the point in disguising what she wants. Which is to get out. How much worry lay behind their plan. There is nothing left for them. No job, no money, no food, no friends. No future.

4.7.38

Mother is very ill. We need medical advice. Please send us an affidavit so we can come to see you.

Friedl, your poem is full of wit – do send it to the paper.

From Vater and Mutti

How wonderful that, with all their woes, Vater has it in him to praise Emil's poem.

10.7.38

We rejoice with you now that you have the opportunity of planting new hopes in the New World which may fulfil your destiny. When will Friedl follow in your tracks?

There are two possible conclusions from the present turbulence. Either people are victims of chance or a divine providence underlines everything that happens. Father believes in the divine option.

We often have bitter thoughts but get over them because we believe and hope. My real thoughts cannot be conveyed in this letter. We all embrace you.

From Mutti

21.7.38

Dear children,

Your letter filled us with infinite joy. We don't go short of anything. We have lots of leisure to read. Because of a fault of our birth, we are unlikely ever to reach England.

There is still trade between people liquidating their assets and others looking for goods, but the market has shrunk. I did not know how necessary it would be to take other measures than before.

For the time being, we will remain here and would be very happy to get good news from you. I'm very pleased that you, my dear child, are well.

From Vater

10.8.38

Beloved children,

Thank you for the long-awaited letter from London.

We tried to get ships tickets for the *Hilfsverein* but were refused today. It has now not been possible for a few months. What can we do?

From the 30 September, we no longer have the right to carry out trade. We want to write to Uncle G in the hope that he can send us abroad as the firm's representatives.

Or perhaps we think it would be better to sell everything or give it away as we can't sell because everyone is leaving. Then we could go into an old people's home.

Go to Uncle W in London, dear Louisechen, and tell him how we are fixed. I'm sure he will want to help.

I did not anticipate how black things would get. But we don't want to let it bring us down and if we are telling you at all, it is so that you can get advice from other members of the family. Our fate hangs on what the latest decree declares.

We want to sell our piano. We are very depressed.

Love from Vater

For Vater to say he was depressed, he who pulled chestnuts of hope from the all-consuming fire, tells me how desperate he had become. They had tried to get out and they had failed.

8.11.38

Dear siblings,

One has had uncomfortable visitors before the sister travelled. She could not see her husband, nor speak to him and we hope that he is well. There are many others in the same situation.

Theoretically, our existence is clearly negative now. One is afraid of losing everything. Your queries about food cannot be answered with a yes.

The man's silence, R, should be explained. He was under great stress and risk, even though everything he'd done had been above-board. He got away but they have not heard from him.

But our souls are not broken and speaking economically, we have done everything.

Greetings from the heart.

Your siblings

How did my parents end up with this poignant letter which was not sent to them?

The letter is so coded that any interpretation could be wrong, but it appears that the husband of a sister has been sent to a camp. So the camps were already known about.

Kristallnacht took place on November 9-10th when the State finally released its dogs of hate against the Jews, one day after the previous letter to siblings was dated, one month before the letter below.

27.12.38

Dear children

We hope we can wish you a hearty farewell on the day before you travel to the New World. We feel especially close to you in these lines and we hope for you both that the separation will not be long and that you and E will be able to pursue your goal together.

We can't pay the rent. It's difficult for Jews these days. We will take up your hint of asking for Jewish Charity.

Love from both your parents

Chapter 36

At least I know what you were called, Rosa and Johann, since I saw the plaque bearing your names in the house in Berlin. I still find it difficult to use your names. Names make you real. I find this painful. Even writing 'grandparents' hurts.

Your letters shine with warmth, in the midst of despair. I watch as your lives collapse, little by little. By the end of 1938, being 'Jewish' is to be *untermensch* - without a job, without rights to send children to school, without money, without rent, without anything. Afraid the little you have will be confiscated. You bestowed charity, never believed you would need it.

You have lost the right to leave. You try, where others succeed. But you fail. I want to know why you didn't get out. What happened to Uncle W's hoped-for sponsorship for you to go to Britain? I know about Uncle W now. He sponsored other members of the family in preference to you.

I watch you. You ask for affidavits and enquire after posting abroad. You bid your tearful farewells to that long list of your friends and relatives who were allowed out, assuring them that they were doing right and you would be just fine. Why did you not try to get out earlier, like the others were doing? Maybe you didn't understand what was at stake. Perhaps you said to each other, let the young ones go. What can happen to us?

You care about being Jewish. You mourn for the disappearance of your little gathering for Seder. Impossible now to know how far your 'Jewishness' was a response to the rabid State and popular anti-Semitism. I can hear you saying to each other: 'If we're going to be persecuted for being Jewish, then being Jewish is what we are. What else have we got? Who else is there to stand by us?' Maybe I've got this wrong. Maybe, the celebration of Seder and the other Jewish ceremonies were always important to you.

I must tell you that I follow in my mother's footsteps. I do not see myself as Jewish. I hope this does not upset you too much.

What happened to you, Rosa? Were you taken to the camps, as the plaque states? My mother had told me you died of a heart attack, but I no longer trust what she tells me. You died when I could not be there for you, could not hold your hand, or whisper comforting words. I wish you could hear me now.

But I know there is a different story. My past lay behind unassailable fortifications. I am not meeting the people, but reading their words, words that were constructed to assure their distant daughter and son-in-law that they should not worry.

Maybe they succeeded too well. They wish that Louise wrote more frequently. But I'm starting to understand why she did not.

Because I now know, that just as I, later, fled my parents' home, my mother had fled hers. 'I didn't like my mother,' my mother had told me. 'I hated her.' My mother, brilliant scholar though she was, left her prestigious secondary school and her parents' home the moment she was old enough to get a job. She went to live and work as far as possible from her parents, on the East side of Berlin.

I'd asked her why. She'd told me that her mother's voice was harsh. She was 'so censorious'. Nothing was good enough for her. She expected too much of her daughters. Louise, always so good, such a bookworm, who only went out to go to the bookshop, not a gadfly, or a seeker after pleasure - she didn't deserve it when her mother hit her.

But now I suspect there is more. I'd again asked my mother about her sister. We'd negotiated her usual 'Why do you want to know?' Then she'd gone quiet. I was sitting on a footstool, facing her, in the lounge of her Jewish Home.

'My mother did not do right by Marthe,' my mother whispered, head almost bowed to her chest.

'M.' My mother's sister. So, now I know her name.

'Your mother put Marthe into a psychiatric hospital?'

'Psychiatric clinic,' my mother corrected me.

She did not say 'asylum'.

'Why?' I dared to ask.

My mother was starting to press her lips hard together, in the way she does when she doesn't want any words to spill out.

'She wasn't very clever, you know, but there was nothing wrong with her. Not really. People said she was flirtatious.'

133

'People?' I interrupt.

'My mother. She said Marthe was always making eyes at boys. What nonsense. They married her off. Do you know that? Aren't I telling you a lot. They married her off to an unsuitable man. Much older than her. A gambler. And more. She didn't deserve that. She just wasn't clever like I was.' Adding with a typical gleam: 'I was very clever, but you know that.'

I cry when Chris rings. 'Would I have liked them?' I ask her. 'Were they too judgemental, too repressive, too Jewish? I wish I'd got to meet them,' I continue, sobbing.

I want to say, 'Hello, Grandma,' and perhaps to kiss her dry, crumpled cheek.

The words rush off the old pages, sheets of paper so fragile that the slightest tension would tear them apart. But the writers are dead and gone. Whatever I do, nothing will bring them back.

Chapter 37

'I think MI5 become really suspicious of your mother after she made her trip to the USA in 1938,' Aphro suggests, sitting on the floor, studying the MI5 documents. I hand her the papers, sweating. The dog, banished from his usual position lying at my feet, looks crestfallen.

Arrived New York. All well.

'I assume that telegram is from her?' Aphro asks.

'I wonder if my father ever got it.'

'The next document is a letter from your mother's parents, hoping she can help get them out of Germany.'

'MI5 must have been opening their mail.'

'Quite useful for us in these circumstances!' Aphro lets out a hoarse laugh.

'My mother got her parents' names onto the emigration lists for the USA.'

Maybe this is why she went to the US. She wanted to get her parents out of Germany. To America: the land of opportunity. Give us your huddled masses. How hopeful had my mother been? She would have had to work hard to have any chance of success, and I don't see that happening. America was not alone in failing to open its doors to those wishing to escape death in Germany. But it was one of the worst. Even after Kristallnacht, only a tiny fraction were allowed in. My mother will probably have known, at the very time she was hoping to save her parents, that the United States turned back the boat *St Louis*, carrying over 900 German-Jewish refugees.

'Then she's back in Britain,' Aphro continues. 'Almost a year later, MI5 decided she was such a high security risk that the police should pick her up. They took her in the street outside her house. She asked to go into her flat to pick up a few things, but they refused. Just like they treat asylum seekers today. I was right - your mother was then imprisoned in Holloway and interrogated. Your father campaigned to get her out. It's all in the handwritten memos in the margins. You should be proud.' Aphro is looking pleased with herself.

But what concerns me is what my mother was imprisoned for: my mother who rarely left the house, who wore gloves if she ventured out of the front door, who tied her hair into a tight bun, and who read Shakespeare to me as a fun thing to do. She must have come to the attention of MI5 for something. Most German refugees did not get sent to prison. Maybe the frequency of her trips abroad - France, Holland, Russia, Vienna, the USA, sometimes more than once - made the security services suspicious. Or was it one trip in particular which drew their attention?

What I say is: 'How did my mother afford all those trips abroad? She didn't have a job or money. She didn't even have a passport.'

'Curious, isn't it? Maybe she was a spy. That's what MI5 seem to have thought. Their notes state that she didn't appear to know what country she was being accused of spying for.'

'That's my mother,' I tell Aphro. 'You never know whether she is creating a smoke screen or telling the truth. Indeed, she may often not have known herself.'

Chapter 38

I visit my mother in her Home, bearing a large bunch of freesias. I go out of duty rather than love. Too often, she sees me and turns her head away, as if I am her jailer, demonstrating to me that she is not happy where I've incarcerated her. Impossible to explain to her the cascade of events which finally deposited her here, far from home. She is sitting in her usual place, next to the door.

I show her the flowers, holding them up to her nose, so she can enjoy the scent. She nods.

'Lovely.'

I am delighted that she has spoken - the first time in a few visits.

'How are you feeling?' I ask. What a stupid question. I seat myself on a stool, near enough to be able to shout into her better ear.

She half nods, half shakes her head. Today's visit will not be so bad after all.

A carer arrives and asks me whether I would like a cup of tea. I thank her. She takes the flowers, explaining she will find a vase.

I seize the moment to ask her about her visit to the USA.

'Did you ever go to America?' I shout so that she can hear me. I am starting to find it easier to ask her questions.

But there is no chance for discreet conversation. The Home discourages their residents from leaving the sitting area to go to their rooms, or the small pleasant garden, as it makes greater demands on the staff. The entire room can listen to what I'm saying. Indeed, one of the other residents at this point turns to her neighbour, who appears asleep, and says: 'I remember those GI boys, don't you, Maisie?' Maisie replies: 'I wish some people wouldn't talk so loud.'

My mother shakes her head. I try again. 'Where did you go in America?'

'New York.' She looks at me as if this were obvious, but also with pride.

'Why did you go?'

'Why not?'

'Emil was living here,' I tell her, my insides feeling like

turbulent jelly. 'Was he going to follow you?'

'Comme ci, comme ça.'

'What were you doing there?'

'I was studying Economics at the University.' I pause, hoping for further comment. My stomach is cramping. But the past is insisting it be heard. I'd not known that the USA offered a faint hope for salvation for her parents till now. Why torture her with that memory?

'Did you hope to get your parents to the USA?' It is a forbidden zone.

Silence.

'You were a long way from home,' I persist.

'Home?' My mother's tone is sharp.

'Where do you see as home?'

'Yes.'

I'm all too familiar with this form of conversation stopper. 'Why did you come back?'

'What a lot of questions. Why are you asking me all these questions?'

My lips go dry, my tongue glued to the palate of my mouth. I reach for her hand but she pulls it back.

I remember the time my mother had found me in the drawing room, staring at the short row of books whose covers my father had carefully wrapped up in brown paper. 'What are you looking at?' she'd remonstrated. 'Nothing,' I'd said. 'That's a whole lot of nothing,' she'd replied.

'I've read some of your parents' letters,' I manage to tell her. I am stepping over the lintel of her existence into the forbidden contents of her soul. I'm not yet ready to mention the MI5 documents.

'My letters?'

'Yes.'

'What are you doing with my letters?'

'I'm keeping them safe for you.'

She smiles. Relief.

'What about the letters?'

'They show that in 1938 you went away to the USA.'

'Yes.'

'Why did you go there?'

She turns her head away at this question.

'Why did you not stay there?'

'The war was about to break out. I caught the last boat

138

home. I was lucky.' As if she sees herself performing on a stage before a rapt audience, she smiles at me, squeezing her eyes together, moving her head sideways, her lips slightly parted.

'I couldn't start all over again in the USA. I wanted to be with your father.' She looks sly when she tells me this.

'Didn't you want to stay and finish your degree in New York?' I know from the MI5 papers that she was one term short of finishing her degree.

'I told you. I had to leave.'

This is like drawing teeth, but I have finally developed enough courage for the extraction.

'You weren't lucky with your degrees,' I persist, feeling so sorry for my brilliant mother, thwarted three times in her pursuit of academic qualifications.

She looks vacant.

'You used to tell me that you were thrown out of Berlin University because you were a woman. Wasn't it rather that the University defined you as Jewish?' I pose this as a question and wait.

'No.'

'No, you weren't Jewish, or no, you weren't thrown out for being Jewish?'

'No.'

The carer arrives with the tea. She is staring at me. If your mother is not Jewish, says her look, what is she doing here? I know when I'm beaten.

I try a new topic. I'm in a hurry. I always fear that any conversation with my mother could be the last. She's had too many near escapes from death already and I've only just started to uncover her secrets.

'Did you like Oxford?'

'No.'

'But you had a baby there.'

At this, she reaches for my hand. 'Yes. You.' Again, that smile.

It is my turn to pull my had away. Then, instantly regretting my rejection of this rare revelation of maternal affection, I try to replace my hand in hers, but in vain.

'Tell me about it,' I say.

'We decided to have a baby after the Battle of Stalingrad.'

She has told me this before, but I am still overawed by it. If it had not been for the millions of Russians who gave their lives in 1942, pushing back the Nazi invaders, my parents would not have felt safe enough to have had a child, and I would not have been born.

'I was only allowed to pick you up every four hours. I am sorry,' my mother suddenly announces. She appears genuinely upset, as if this is something she has regretted ever since. This time, she is not acting.

'Even if I cried?'

'Your father said we mustn't spoil you.'

'Did you want to pick me up?'

'Of course.'

'Ahh.' My tears refuse to stop and start to trickle down the side of my nose. I keep wiping my face with my sleeve, stricken.

'He told me to stop fussing you.'

'Ahh.'

'He told me, if I spoilt you, I would get you into bad habits.'

'He was right.'

At that, we both laugh, though for the life of me I'm not sure what's so funny.

I am shaken and confused by her confessions. Time to leave. I kiss her lightly on the cheek and tell her I will come to see her again in a few days. She pouts and tells me: 'Don't go.' As I look back from the door, her eyes have closed.

Chapter 39

I decide to visit my childhood home, my childhood of silences.

I ring up my old school friend, Val. After chiding me for not phoning her in weeks, she is keen to make a date. I do not tell her about the letters.

This is the first time since university that I have returned to my home town. My parents had sold up without telling me. I'd just settled in London when my mother had rung me.

'We're moving down to London,' she had stated.

This was a surprise, not entirely one to be welcomed. I'd enquired when. 'Tomorrow,' she'd informed me. They were moving into a house quite near to me.

'What about the house in Durham?' I asked. She handed me over to my father at this point.

'We've been diddled,' he explained.

'Out of your own house?' I must have sounded incredulous for he snapped that they'd explain later. I'd enquired after my things.

'Didn't you hear me?' he said. 'We've had to throw all your things away because we'd no time to pack.'

To this day, I wish I'd had the chance to say goodbye to my childhood home. But perhaps they did me a favour, throwing out the few possessions of my childhood: my paints and pencils, the wooden meccano set I'd loved so much, and my books, though this is not how it felt at the time.

Durham station's fancy wrought-ironwork still holds up its sloping roof, no different from when I had last stood here, on my way to Oxford and freedom. I get off the train, remembering how the ice-cold wind used to whip in from the Siberian plains, burning the insides of my nose if I didn't wrap a scarf round and round my face. But, although it's winter, the wind appears to be taking a holiday. I didn't need to dress so warmly after all. Val is waiting for me in her car as I emerge, fearful, from the station.

Val will wait for me at the bottom of our road. She sees the visit to my home as a private journey. I start up the hill to the house. I have written to the present owners. They are expecting me.

Our road was as steep as I recollected, but the houses

opposite are so much closer than I remembered. My three-storey house has retained its mid-nineteenth century hauteur. I hesitate before I knock, staring around me, searching for the person I was the last time I stood here, sniffing out any last scent of my parents. A man far too young to be my father opens the front door and ushers me inside.

'Thank you for letting me have a look around,' I tell him.

He nods politely. 'Please. Take your time. Should we begin on the top floor?'

We start up the stairs, now revealed in their original oak, the chipped white paintwork long gone.

I remember how I used to sit on the top row of the stairs after being sent off to bed at 7pm on the dot, and, not even close to feeling sleepy, eavesdrop on my parents. They were sitting in the upstairs drawing room, and I could rarely catch what they were talking about. I guessed they were whispering in German, the language of secrets, behind the firmly-closed door. Perhaps I have this wrong. Perhaps they whispered in English.

German was the language of death and deceit; it was their language and not mine and I never wanted to learn it. Yet still, sometimes, German sounds come rat-tat-tatting on my mind's door. I try to catch the words. Sometimes I think it's just about to happen. Just one last try and I will hear what is being said.

How did my parents feel, speaking in their own tongue, the despised language of the enemy? Did it touch some essential part of themselves, which English could not reach? In the crevasses of my mother's being, she never ceased to see herself as German. Yet she spoke to me in English. A foreign tongue. Their language was not mine. My language was not theirs. Another distance, another loss.

My tiny bedroom is, strangely, larger than I recollected. The family who lives here now have squeezed their two children into luxurious bunk beds, both bunks reached by climbing up a sturdy ladder. I am envious of these children's intimacy, their squabbles and petty jealousies, the knowledge that somebody dear is near.

I remember how I drew up the bottom sash window,

and, if I pressed my knees up hard against the bedroom wall, could peer so far out that I could see the cathedral. On a Sunday morning, I would listen to the ringing of the distant church bells and be calmed. At night, as I lay awake, I would hear the clanking and grinding of the steam trains passing by over the railway bridge, which cut across at the bottom of our street. I had felt connected to the rest of the world, just like my mother had, listening to the trains in their Berlin flat. Did she agree to this house and godforsaken city because the sounds and sights reminded her of a lost and safer existence?

I stare around the forbidden zone of my parents' bedroom. Still a bedroom, it is now carpeted and richly decorated, with a large, comfortable-looking bed.

I imagine my mother, waking early in the cold hours of the night and, touching flesh, expects it to be her sister.

'I couldn't help what happened to her,' she reminds herself. 'I was too young.' Louise turns her back to the world, and shivers in the night air.

I remember my mother and father emerging at the end of the night, the light still grey, always swathed in dressing gowns and slippers, so cold I can see their breath. Louise has been woken by the alarm. Yet again, it's time for her to get up to make me a cooked breakfast, which I take as my due. It is the one meal my mother always produces, and always in time for me to go to school well-fed. But I am being tardy. The egg is getting cold. 'What is the point of my making it for you if you don't hurry up?' she chides. I swallow down my food, snatch up my satchel and hurry out.

That bedroom door remained shut, not just during the dark hours of the night, but during the hours of light. I was forbidden entry, and could not imagine what my mother could be doing in the bedroom for all that time. As with any forbidden fruit, I was tempted to discover what was going on and had once plucked up the courage to knock at the door. It must have been a weekend or the holidays, as I was not at school. It was mid-afternoon and, as so often was the case, my mother had not appeared since breakfast time to provide us with lunch. I was prohibited from going into the kitchen and was starting to feel seriously faint. There was no reply to my knock. But my father had come up the stairs. 'What are you doing here?' he'd asked. Terrified, I'd told him I was really hungry. Maybe he also needed food, not that he'd have considered preparing it himself, for he said: 'I'm sure we can find you a biscuit somewhere.' I never knocked on that door again. Today is the first time I'd entered this forbidden zone since early childhood.

My host invites me into their kitchen, where he offers me a drink. But this is not the tiny kitchen galley where my mother turned out her meals and created her unique filter coffee. That has become a utility room. The long thin formica table which I used to squeeze behind, sitting on a high stool if I wanted to try to hold a conversation with my mother, is no more.

Their kitchen is where our front room had been. One side is taken up by a magnificent hob, where the anthracite stove once stood. My father had fed it twice daily with the coal he carried up the steep stone stairs from the dark basement. Here had stood the table where I did my homework and the three of us ate our meals. The ghosts that hung around over the doorway have gone. We must have taken them with us when we left.

I look over to the corner of the front room where, every year, we placed a freshly-cut, sweet-smelling tree at Christmas. But in the corner of the room now stands their gleaming hob.

My father would proudly carry the tree up the long steep hill from the local market, balance it in a large bucket packed in with coal, and lovingly dress it with tinsel and baubles. On Christmas Eve, the branches were lit up by burning white candles, casting swirling shadows round the darkened room. We three stood round the tree and sang *O Tannenbaum* and *Stille Nacht*, in German. It was the nearest I ever got to seeing my parents in tears. The ghosts danced around us in the candlelight and I, unable to understand what was going on, wanted to run away.

My father had furnished our house from auctions and the local market, returning, beaming, with another bit of carpet to cover the bare floorboards, another coal scuttle, another nineteenth-century vase to feather the nest. We lived in a run-down part of England and beautiful things were easy to come by.

'What are we going to do with that?' My mother refused to accept his presents with grace, refusing to accept that where she had ended up, stranded by the storms and eddies of world politics, could be her home, and rejected my father's offerings of love. She never felt, I suspect, that she was more than camping. Nor did I ever feel this was my home. I too was just passing through.

Finally, carrying my mug of tea, I go out to look at my beloved walled garden, where I could stare out over the hill opposite. I escaped to here whenever I could. The garden is gone, covered over by the luxurious kitchen. The hill is an estate. Even the tall swaying poplars, which I loved and which told me the way the wind was blowing, have vanished. This is not my home. Nor was it my parents' home. Germany was their home. I thank my host, who shakes my hand quickly, and I am gone.

We spend the afternoon visiting the secondary school where we had met as children and grown into young adults together. Val had liked the school, though neither of us had fitted in. Val was one of a rare species: a bookworm. But as boys had become an increasing source of wonder, she'd made a circle of school friends, of which I'd not been a part.

The tree is still standing in the tiny courtyard, on whose surrounding wall Val and I had once sat and chatted in those impossibly long-ago days. Now we perch next to each other on the wall. The youthful Deputy Head photographs us, a moment resounding into eternity.

We chat about the girls we'd once known: Doris, Ann, Dorothy, Veronica, Kathleen and Eileen. Whatever happened to them?

'What's your life been like? Have you achieved what you wanted when you were eighteen?' I ask Val.

'Not really. But I have so many riches that I wouldn't complain,' she replies. 'I have two wonderful children and six grandchildren. I couldn't have wanted better. And you?'

'I haven't finished yet. I still have lots to do.'

'Better hurry up, then.'

Chapter 40

'Mum, there's somebody at the door for you,' Sam yells.

'Who is it?' I'd just got home and pulled on my sloppy skirt and red top, jettisoning the well-fitted, almost flattering matching trousers and top I wore to work.

'A man.'

Damn. I run down the stairs in my slippers.

Ruben is standing there, sort of smiling.

'Hi.'

'I was just passing.'

'Come in.'

'No, thank you.'

That's a relief.

Pause.

'Is your mum OK?' Ruben enquires.

'As well as ever.'

Pause.

'I had a premonition that she was very ill.'

'She's not well.'

'But nothing more than that?'

'No.' But it feels good to have somebody other than me care how she is. 'Why don't you come in?'

Ruben looks down at the ground and steps inside the door. 'It isn't easy when one's parents get very old. You know, if there's anything I can do. . . '

'Thank you.'

'I do mean it. How is your research into your family going?'

Why is he asking me this? 'It's hard. Nobody much cares about that either.' The 'either' slips out before I can stop it.

'It's not surprising your friends don't understand. Most people know about their pasts - their grandmothers smacked their bottoms and tucked them up in bed.'

'I don't think most of my friends can cope with what I'm discovering. What do you say to somebody who finds out their family may have been wiped out? 'Oh dear, how awful'? Doesn't quite fit the bill.' I look down at my fluffy slippers. 'I'm so scared of what I'm finding, I can hardly breathe.'

Ruben appears to nod, though in my haste I hadn't switched on the hall light and I can't see him clearly in the descending twilight.

'It's hard losing people, especially if you never knew them,' he tells me softly.

I try hard to bite back my tears, though whether they are for him or for me, I do not know.

'Mum!' shouts my son. 'Mum!'

'Yes?'

'What's happening?'

Ruben seems to bow. 'A good call,' he tells me. 'Time to take my leave. Glad your mum is OK. You look after yourself.' And Ruben is gone.

'Have you forgotten again that you're taking me to football practice?' My son is shouting at me from the top of the stairs, ignoring my streaky face.

Chapter 41

I open the Yale and Chubb locks of my mother's house. She has passed the Home's three-month probation and will not be coming home again. This was not how she had planned her exit. 'I'll only leave my home in a wooden box,' she had told me.

I had only understood how much their new home in Hackney was not to be my home when I'd realised there was just the one bedroom. Yet I look at it now with nostalgia.

The grandfather clock meets me in the hall, still standing tall. It has ceased to tick. Every day, my father proudly opened the catch on the glass door and pulled gently on the loops of chain. It chimed insistently every fifteen minutes. I remember how to open it and wind it up, but the clock refuses my touch.

I go into the sitting room, first door on the left. The long broad Georgian windows look out over the park and the trees, the room lit up by the afternoon sun. For the first time, I realise that this house has the same proportions as the house where I grew up. My parents must have demanded well-proportioned, spacious rooms with large windows and high ceilings.

Every inch of wall is covered with my father's German Expressionist paintings. What am I to do with them? The paintings show miners crouching in far-too-low tunnels of coal, a woman lying in blood, entitled *Ode to a Fallen Soldier*, and even the occasional hopeful portrait of my mother. I love these pictures.

What is to be done with the light walnut table, with its wobbly legs?

'Could you lay the table,' my mother would instruct me, when I still lived with them in Durham.

These were moments of great excitement. We ate in the front room only on those rare and special occasions that we had a guest.

I would go to the varnished mahogany sideboard and pull out a crisp, newly-laundered and ironed damask tablecloth. With luck, it had initials embroidered in the corner. I knew better than to ask whose initials they were. I gave each person their own linen napkin. My mother placed a hand-embroidered runner down the middle of the table, with a delicate bunch of flowers at its centre. Then she would ask me to get out the green Wedgwood tableware and the silver. This is what we called it. Not cutlery, or knives and forks. The 'silver' had personalised embossed lettering at its palm end. I did not know to whom it had once belonged. These were happy occasions.

The walnut table is invisible under years of unsorted bills and letters. They will have to wait. I pull optimistically at the leaves, and the table shudders, finally quaking open, its legs splayed. It too has died.

I lift the lid of the walnut piano. Its tone is still soft, for all the years it has been ignored. I had loved that piano. I have a sweet memory of my mother sitting there, one calm, dark evening, playing Mozart so effortlessly I thought I would swoon with pleasure. I had insisted on music lessons in a painful and unsuccessful attempt to discover the sublime.

Here is my polished desk, with its impractical, sloping top. It has a secret drawer, with a tiny carved key which turned the lock, which opened the drawer, which nobody but me knew about. Here I had sat, with my school homework, my friend. Here I found solace and a life apart from my parents. Books were my companions.

I phone up John.
'God speaking.'
'My life is being taken over by ghosts.'
'I'll be right over.'
Some time later John arrives. 'I have two hours,' he announces.

John had never made friends with time. I remember how, already late, he used to rush round our flat looking for a book, or his notes that he had to take with him to a meeting or to work, then tear out of the door, waving his goodbyes as he ran.

We take down the once beautiful moth-eaten Kalim rug from the wall over the fireplace and throw it into the skip. My parents had acquired it in the 1930s from a street vendor, long before such artefacts were fashionable.

'Remember,' I begin, 'that beautiful Turkish carpet we bought together?'

'The one that's mine!' John retorts.

We'd been on holiday to Istanbul, soon after we'd got back together. The trip had promised us a future. We'd climbed down from our three-day journey by train into a horizon of minarets, the smell of warm earth and a firework of light. John, guidebook in hand, had directed us on our first day to the Blue Mosque. There, I'd fallen in love. I sat down on the floor, mesmerised by the soaring blue geometrical tiles. 'Food,' John had to remind me. 'You'll get hungry and then you'll be bad-tempered.'

Later, we'd collapsed into the sagging bed, me with a decorous band of gold around my marriage finger. It had been John who'd suggested we should try to conform to local expectations. 'I don't want to marry you,' I'd protested. All he'd said was: 'You can wear a wedding ring without being married.' We'd bought it in a pawn shop and, though I refused to wear any ring when we did wed - I didn't want to be turned into anybody's possession - I have it to this day. The heat no longer bit the skin when, later that afternoon, we ventured out.

The carpet had been one of thousands displayed amongst a maze of tightly-packed stalls in the souk. We'd already passed through the spice quarter, filled with every colour and smell of powder, and the ironmongers' quarter, where young boys and men were hammering out old metal into exquisitely-decorated 'objects d'art'.

The carpet was hanging over a wall, glowing. John and I had both stopped and stared. 'I wonder how much it is?' I'd muttered. 'Where would we put it?' John had replied. The stall-holder had come over and offered us cups of thick Turkish coffee, which we'd drunk squatting on small stools. 'It's silk,' he'd explained and had given us a history of carpets which I still remember. After we'd paid, he'd rolled the carpet up and tied it tightly in string. John had carried it over his shoulder, first back to our hostel, then to London. We'd nailed it to the wall of our bedroom where it caught the sun and reminded us of Istanbul.

'It's mine,' I'd informed John when we were carving up

our home and our possessions some years later.

'I carried it everywhere,' he'd replied.

'It was my idea.'

'But I paid more towards it.'

'Only because you were earning more than me.'

I didn't say that I wanted it because I wanted to remember my time with him.

'This is getting us nowhere,' John had stated. 'You can have it if I've first choice on all the books and records.'

'Not the record of songs of the Spanish Civil War,' I'd stated.

'Especially that record!'

'Where've you put it?' John is enquiring.

'It's on the floor in the hall.'

'But it'll get worn there.'

'Exactly.'

John sits on my floor, sorting out the books and papers with painful slowness, amazing accuracy and a scholar's relish.

'Couldn't you go a little faster?' I suggest.

'Might miss something.'

'Don't think I don't remember how our flat got taken over by stacks of unsorted newspaper,' I chide. I want to say: 'I wish we'd had a lifetime of memories.'

As John searches, he discovers a collection of well-thumbed classics from the Greeks to the modern day. Then John spots the books wrapped in brown paper which, when unfolded, reveal texts by Marx, Luxembourg and by Gramsci in Italian, published in the early 1950s. He's thrilled.

'At last I know what books your parents were hiding in that brown paper. It's amazing to have such an early edition of Gramsci. I wonder how they got hold of it. I must take a look.' He leans up against the bookshelf, studying the text.

I find a stack of left-wing magazines, including *Partisan Review* from over fifty years ago. My mother had a few articles published there that I'd known nothing of. We find boxes of Louise's and Emil's published poetry. A whole closet is filled with my mother's unpublished plays, many properly typed and bound. They fall out of drawers packed so full that they have to be forced open. This is a lifetime's work that I knew nothing of. Now I have some clue what she was up to in that bedroom. If you are mid-scene, a hungry daughter does not compete.

I had known of one play of hers. It had been put on in the West End of London. I'd refused to attend. The play was about life in Moscow in the 1930s. My mother had returned from the previews, frantic. The front row, she had explained, had booed the play. They were Communist Party agents who disapproved of the play's anti-Stalinist message and had come to stop the play from running. She is quite mad, I'd mercilessly assumed; but I now know better. I wish I had been there for her.

There is one last large unsorted cardboard box left on the floor. John picks it up and places it on the table, the papers piled so high they spill out. I retrieve them and check to see what they are. They appear to be a stapled collection of handwritten and near illegible notes.

'Give me,' says John. 'Did you know your mother ran creative writing classes in the local Hackney Community Centre?' he asks. I shake my head. He burrows further into the box, appearing with an assortment of yellowing news-sheets, run off on old Banda machines, and A4 stapled magazines. I look at them gingerly to find that in almost every magazine and pamphlet there are poems and stories by either my mother or father.

'I knew they were going to a local writers' workshop, but they never told me that they were being published.' I suddenly feel terribly sad.

But John says: 'It's wonderful. Have a read of this. It's a lament on the death of Blair Peach. And there's another poem on how the Tories freeze the old to death. They were finally doing what they wanted to do and they were doing it together.' He turns towards me, smiling. 'It's probably the only time they were happy together after they fled Berlin. These writings are precious.'

What am I to do with this mountain of words and inspiration? There is no one I want to give the plays to, except back to her. This is a new mother I have discovered.

But this understanding does nothing to change my experience of childhood.

Chapter 42

'There are some letters from 1939 I just can't translate,' Chris phones me to explain. 'They're in an archaic handwriting. And what doesn't help is that the writing paper is so thin it's almost translucent. But I know somebody who should be able to help.' She gives me his name, Ernst, and phone details.

I go to see Ernst. He had fled Nazi Germany as a young man and now lectures about his experience of anti-Semitism and the Holocaust. I've already spoken to him a couple of times on the phone and explained.

I feel at home in his flat. There is even the same painting by Cocteau that had hung on my parents' walls. He reminds me of my father – the high-domed head, curious eyes, and his guttural way of speaking English.

Ernst takes the fragile sheets and starts to read, then begins to shake, and his eyes go moist and pink.

'You have to go now,' he says, and standing up, shoves the sheets back into my hand and firmly shows me the door.

I stand outside the house, horrified. I had forced this man to attempt to revisit a place within him to which he was unable to return. But, even more, I'm afraid of what the letters will reveal.

Later, a friend introduces me to a specialist in old German, Veronika, who had originally fled Nazi Germany owing to her marrying 'the wrong sort of man', rather than herself being Jewish. I explain to Veronika how difficult translating these letters is turning out to be, and ask whether she'd seen letters like this before. 'Rarely,' she replies. 'Many German Jews got out. Those left behind mostly perished. The letters to their loved ones from 1939 and 1940 were often their last. Many of these letters were then either left mouldering in an attic or thrown away. Their children couldn't bear to look at them and their grandchildren either didn't want to be weighed down by the tragedies of the past or didn't want to know.' Then she said: 'I'm glad you're giving voice to those who could no longer speak for themselves. I wish more were like you. These people's stories are being thrown into the dustbin of history. There should be a law against it.' And she'd laughed sardonically down the phone.

I arrive at Veronika's house with flowers and trepidation. She opens the door, a beautiful woman, dressed in a subdued flowing dress, which suits her well-cut grey hair. We sit down at her large desk, overlooking a peaceful verdant garden. Her excitement at the unusualness of the task ahead appears to overcome the impact of the words she is translating. I'm not sure, however, if I finally want to find out what they say.

1.1.39

Dear Boy,

For people with our fate, hope is the most important ingredient in the sea of life. The New Year begins with good portents for us and we all want to believe that its contents will be as good as its overture. Mother thinks we should write a bit more delicately, rather than factually. May your work, Louise, be blessed. Joy in work is a particular gift of God. Since we do not know the future, we can only hope for the best.

We see greater loneliness for us approaching. We are following your advice, dear child, and not burdening our thoughts with fantasy. And at this moment we are grasping the difference between fantasy and illusion, which one must not be without.

Love from Vater

14.2.39

I lie awake at night and worry. Are you healthy and earning enough to feed yourself? Are you planning for your husband to follow you? He is a wonderful human being. How many men would be happy to stay on their own? I don't think father would.

Father is throwing himself into learning English with real fanaticism and I'm convinced he will learn it, We are inclined to think that we will need knowledge of the English language.

Apart from us, only the HGs are still here, but they already have an affidavit to the USA. Even our sisters have left. Our house is so very quiet.

From Mutti

12.3.39

Dear Louise,

Today we had a questionnaire from the American consulate. We asked for a particular form (575), which is based on an application through one's child. How should we answer these questions, of course truthfully? It is clear that our hopes have a very weak base.

You are the young ones and, taking a bird's eye view, more important for us than we could be for ourselves.

From Vater

I do not have Louise's side of the correspondence. I can only imagine how she wrote to her parents. Did she write:

Dear Vater and Mutti, Don't worry about me. Everything went fine in New York. You are on the emigration list. I will see you soon again. All my love, L.

Or did she write:

You are now on the list for a USA visa, but there are thousands and thousands before you. I can only offer a little hope.

20.3. 39.

My beloved daughter,

Tante K's flat has to be evacuated by the 4th April, where she's lived for 26 years. Everything is so difficult and causes so much bother, so that every person who has to face this says 'I can go no further'. She has absolutely no idea where to go. I would wish that we were spared

155

all this. I have trained myself to live for the moment and not to worry. I embrace you, liebes kind, and call out to you: Be strong, be strong, and be strong. I think of you every moment.

From Mutti and Vater

25.5.39

Louischen,

If fate decrees that we could live with our children, then such a meeting would be the crowning of our lives. Today, write to your mama.

With love from Mutti

5.7.39

Beloved children,

We are delighted that you are together again. Lots of love to you both. May this new phase of your living together be the start of happiness in every respect. With fondest love and greetings from Father and Your faithful mother.

From Vater and your faithful Mutti

My parents are back together. After about five years apart. This is cause for me to celebrate as well!

It is their last letter before the outbreak of the war. Germany invaded Poland on 1ˢᵗ September 1939, the formal beginning of WW2. Perhaps that was enough insecurity to be going on with.

1.10.39

We are in an uplifted state because we heard the G Major Concerto of Beethoven Opus 58 on the radio from Vienna. This music is like a bath in which everything bad and wicked is exchanged for everything good.

From Vater

5.11 39

We have not heard from any of you now for so long. We sit by the stove every afternoon sharing our worries and think about you and all those we love but can't change anything. Your replies are so important to us so do write more often.

Many kisses.

From Mutti

12.12.39

Your letter was like a speck of light in a long dark tunnel. We will try to stay healthy and not crumple morally. Hope these lines reach you soon and that we will be able to exchange letters more frequently. Blessings from afar.

    The envelopes I found on my mother's desk are finally empty. Their letters are now translated. There are no more. I hear the silence.

    I can never know the lived meaning of these letters. I grope for some sort of understanding, some recognition of who Rosa and Johann were. I want the letters to transport me to them, but this they cannot do. What I want is for them to become mine, these two old people, who watch as all that is true and good is taken from them and who can yet tell their child always to choose hope.

    I condemn myself for feasting on their pain, a pig at the trough of their misery. I fear that I am gaining some sense of self from my acquisition of their past, as if their tragedies are a source of life for me.

I sit at my father's old desk, in my safe warm house, and watch as the iron fist moves ever closer. I can do nothing for them.

Chapter 43

Another winter. I enter my father's dark study. This room had also been out of bounds. Once, I'd peeped in through the open door, to hear my father say: 'It's only polite to ask before you go into somebody else's room.'

Paper covers every surface. I start with his desk and go through the drawers. I find an old ink stand, a green glass weight, an assortment of chipped wooden rulers, many useless biros, a variety of pots and tubes of oil paint, brushes irregular with use, a broken painter's easel, a large quantity of feathers, fragments of shell, piles of unused yellowing paper, inelastic bands, every size of paper clip, unrevealing old passports, (his and my mother's pictures have been cut out, along with all the official stamps inside), old, partially-used coupon books from the period of rationing after the end of the Second World War, and many bags of string. I find cheque books from 1936, all the stubs meticulously completed, bank statements in perfect order till the month of his death, a bill from Paris in 1936 for a typewriter, and a receipt for the nursing home in which I was born.

In another drawer I find the bills and brochures of past holidays from their visit to France in 1962, and to Portugal in 1974, whose hope and revolutionary spirit they loved so much. Here are the guest houses they stayed in, including copies of typed notes of gratitude to the surprised owners. My father has even kept the tickets to the films they attended. I find boxes of maps, largely deteriorated, showing most of the capital cities of Europe, and bunch upon bunch of old keys.

On the desk's top, there is a photo of my mother in a wooden frame. The frame has disintegrated, the tacks which held the sides together sticking out like small bayonets. I take the photo out from behind the smudged glass and place it in a plastic bag with the things I want to keep.

In one drawer are a lifetime of university union cards, one of the last manifestations of my father's militant past, held together carefully in an elastic band. I stare hard at them, gulping for air.

Another drawer is jammed full with old diaries, plus an old, battered black address book. I decide to keep this. I rifle

159

furtively through it, with its dark crumbling cardboard cover. My father had been careful in his recordings of family and friends. It had almost every name crossed through, with a diagonal line. Were my parents attempting to keep the past alive by keeping this paper record of old friends and family? Two names are familiar and I copy them down: Leon, who lives in San Francisco, and Susanne, in New York. I also copy down the name of a woman, Elizabeth, who lived in Cambridge. How come I'd never heard of her?

I tell my conscience to be quiet at this underhand behaviour. My father surely kept this record so as to be able to touch a fragment of his past. I now in turn preserve it.

Stuffed down the side of one book case, I find a blue, battered metal box crammed with little containers of every length and thickness of nails, tacks, screws, and an ancient collection of strong metal pliers, screwdrivers, hammers and wire. I take this home.

One ancient, dark wooden bookcase, with glass doors, has opened up to shelves two deep in German classics, mostly bound in leather, from Goethe to Schiller. On the walls of his study hang more of his Expressionist paintings. I discover a passionate man who poured himself into painting and poetry. He also had a fine line in rhetoric; I find many rumbustious letters to the editors of newspapers, ranging from complaints about the state of the public lavatories or the inadequacy of a packet of biscuits he had bought, to the horrors of monopolisation.

Finally, I succeed in pulling out the bottom drawer of the massive bookcase to reveal hundreds of old Christmas cards. Here lie clues to their pasts, a guide to my parents' social web. I flick through them all, panicking. There is too much. Who can these people be? I fill many black bags with this history of their lives. I both want to keep this record so that I can trace their pasts, and to throw it all away, so I can free my life from theirs.

But a big part of me wants to keep everything, to sit on the floor and trace where my parents travelled, check out the guest houses they stopped at, look up the films whose leaflets they stored away. It is as if I want to slip into their skins. I shall follow in their footsteps. This way I shall keep my parents alive forever.

As I rifle through an old battered trunk in my father's

study, pulling out the now familiar plastic bags filled with decomposing string and shells and moth-eaten blankets, I find something wrapped in a faded flannelette sheet. I unfold it carefully. It is a cheap exercise book, written in German in my mother's tiny, scrawly handwriting. Intrigued, I put it to one side.

I tackle the second shelf in my father's study, which has yet to disgorge its secrets. It is heavy with paper and I am pulling stuff out and swinging it into the black sacks in one swift movement. At the very bottom of one cascading pile lies a small, weathered black leather wallet. I open it with care and look inside. There lies, hidden, the stub of a train ticket.

My father had told me when I was still little how he had escaped from Germany. He'd been wanted by the Gestapo and had gone into hiding the night of the Reichstag fire; it was February 1933. Other little girls are told fairy stories. The story my father told me became the prism through which I saw him, and indeed myself: a story of courage and triumph against the Nazis. It gave my life a significance, and me a strength, that nothing else my father did ever robbed me of.

He'd walked across Germany from north-east to south-west, dodging the SS and police patrols. He'd been lucky, or so he repeated to himself. He'd had the sense to flee when the man from the corner shop had woken them up, knocking softly at the door of their flat, before the sun had risen, to tell him: 'Beware. The Reichstag is burning.' He'd thought he was going to fall, climbing out of the first-floor window.

The cobbler whom he'd turned to for help had not given him away. He'd walked so far, the soles of his shoes had worn out, but he had walked on to Basel. Then, realising he was unable to swim the River Rhine to France, had walked back north. The closer he'd got to the frontier, the more he chose to walk at night. The terrain was hilly. Even when the moon was out, it was easy to lose your foothold.

Then he'd discovered a local train to France. One train was checked by the German police, the next by the French. He had no way of knowing which was which.

He couldn't wait on the station platform or in the foyer. Far too obvious. He looked around for a nearby field of corn where he could lie and try to work out the pattern of inspection. His life depended on it. But all there was, was a dusty road, ditches on either side, and beyond that, flat ploughed-up earth. He saw there was nowhere to hide. He'd made himself too obvious already. He joined the queue for a ticket, glancing surreptitious around him. Though he hadn't eaten for days, he'd kept enough money for a return ticket. A single would never do. Arouse suspicion immediately. The man selling him the ticket hardly looked up. It was early in the morning, when the sun is only just tasting the grey sky. He'd hoped that at this early hour the locals would be more likely to be travelling into France for work and that he wouldn't stand out, as he might on an emptier train. He knew his clothes were so worn after his long march across Germany, that he looked more like a tramp than a working man.

Emil stepped onto the next train into the 3rd class compartment, and squeezed into a crowded carriage, seating himself on the wooden bench. One of the men turned to him, politely said: 'Guten Morgen'. If he spoke, he could give himself away. His southern German accent would mark him out in this gathering of men from the West. He nodded his head at the man, smiled. He was sweating too much. This is what is meant by smelling of fear. The journey would be over soon. He had a fifty percent chance of life.

The carriage door was pushed open and before his stomach finally gave way, he saw that the Ticket Inspector was wearing the uniform of the French railway police. He walked out of the train into France a free man.

The ticket is from Saarbrucken to Forbach, to France, dated 11.11.1933. The train had run as a shuttle, taking men to and from their work in France. Saarland was held at the time under a League of Nations protectorate, though it was claimed by Germany.

Suddenly, I've proof. This is no longer a heroic story whose reality is uncertain. There is a ticket. My father got into France nine months after going into hiding. This is what happened. This is how my father escaped. I had grown up amongst shadows where nothing was ever clear. Now I have touched the truth.

A couple of days later, I'm walking my beloved dog across the frosty Heath under a pale wintry sun and decide that I can again face clearing the past. I return next day to my father's study.

From deep behind the drunken stacks of statistical journals, there emerges a big battered brown envelope. I want to throw it away but first peer inside. It contains dozens of letters, beautifully-written in an ancient German script. I cannot decipher to whom they are written, or sent. A few have an embossed letterhead which I fail to recognise. Trembling, I place them into a cardboard box.

Next to emerge from beneath the stacks are leather-bound photo albums, every page separated by a thin sheet of galvanised tissue. Out falls the past, not dead at all, looking up at me, some beaming, others serious.

There are no names besides the photos. I want to ask them, 'Who are you?'

'Don't you know?' They glance at each other, concerned.

I turn the pages, terrified that I am looking unknowing at pictures of my family.

'When were you alive?'

An attractive woman, frills round her neck, holding a lacy umbrella which casts a poetic shadow over the side of her face, her hair knotted back, eyes looking gently into the future, turns to peep out at me. *'You'd be better to find out,'* she tells me.

A lean man, still young but almost bald, regards me through his spectacles.

I can hardly catch his words: *'I wouldn't stay here.'*

'Here?' I ask.

But his voice is dissolving.

On fire, I snap the book shut.

Finally, the room is all but bare. The rest of my parents' past lives I throw into a big black plastic sack. Shivering as the winter darkness descends, I deliver four van-loads of paper to the dump. I have robbed my father of his room and of his life. I am weighed down with guilt.

A crumpled faded foolscap envelope has emerged from beneath all the other papers. It had been completely hidden. Inside, amongst other letters, is the letterhead of the Red Cross on small, faded sheets of paper. I tremble, fearing the cascade of further secrets.

Chapter 44

Without even the decency of a knock, I enter my parents' bedroom.

'*What are you doing here?*' I imagine my mother demanding of me.

'*I'm here to clear up.*'

'*This is my room. What do you want?*'

'*You've left it in such a mess. I'm here to sort it out.*'

'*How dare you! Get out.*'

The bedroom was the seat of my parents' power. I am about to depose them from their throne. It makes it harder that my mother is still alive. She has lain here alone ever since my father died. The room stinks of urine and the sorrow of an infirm body.

I first tear away at the myriad of boxes and bags which loiter on top of the cupboards and in every crevice. From a battered hat box emerge old floppy straw hats, carefully preserved in tissue paper. One is made of shiny black woven hessian, with a large brim, smelling of mould. When did she wear this? From the top of the wardrobe I pull down suitcases, which, opened, release an ancient and extended family of moths.

Out of the wardrobes emerge a variety of elegant leather handbags; three exquisite fur coats, one with a Berlin wholesaler's name sewed inside, in its pocket a Paris Metro ticket dated 1937; an exquisite black dress with tiny black and white sequins sewed in a sparkling swathe from shoulder to waist; revealing, delicate lace blouses, and a sexy, tight-fitting little black dress. As I parcel them up for charity, I wonder when my mother would have worn such outfits.

Out go my father's laced leather shoes, polished as if he had brushed them yesterday, the shoes in which he walked to the rose garden in the park; to the theatre; to the local workers' poetry group to read his poetry; to the pub on the corner for an occasional Sunday treat, and along the canal. Out go his tailored suits; his cloth caps, which he used pull down over one side of his head, worn as an act of solidarity with the Durham miners; a galaxy of socks, many darned by my mother's hand, and his many shirts, in a rainbow of colours from white through to purple. I had never noticed before how well turned-out my father had been.

I am shocked as he comes alive before me, so many years dead. I did not know him. I want to carry his clothes home with me and hang them in my cupboard, glad that he will put them on the next day and greet me in the morning with an enthusiastic, 'Good morning, Anna.'

Next to my mother's pillow by her bed, sits a compact square parcel. I see it and realise what lies within will be the urn which contains my father's ashes. I turn the box over carefully, looking for an indication of sender. COOPERATIVE FUNERAL PARLOUR, HACKNEY, reads the greying label. She had lain with my father's ashes besides her every night since his death.

She'd hidden him here, where I could not mourn him. I'd mused, in the years since his death, about where my mother had secreted his ashes.

Now I have to decide what to do with them. I could return the ashes to her - they could bring her comfort. But I can imagine the Home' manager's horror at this suggestion. Moreover, so many of my mother's few possessions have already gone missing from there, I do not want to trust the Home with my father's ashes. Nor has my mother mentioned them to me. She hasn't nodded, in the way she can, to where the box would have been on the small table next to her bed and raised her eyebrows questioningly at me, as if to say: 'Where is he?'

I carry the box to my car, place it upright into the boot, and tuck it in carefully with the dog's blanket. Then I walk down to the local cafe and, shaking, order a cup of tea and two slices of toast. I don't have to decide straight away what I want to do with my father's ashes.

I return to confront the chest of drawers, with its ornate brass handles and carved wooden corners. When I was a child, I'd told myself that the reason I wasn't allowed into the bedroom was because this was where my parents hid their drugs and secret potions. Here I would enter the heart of my parents' kingdom, the kingdom of life and death. I look in where no child should. Nothing. I am disappointed.

The chest of drawers contains underwear; torn, soft, silk black knickers and petticoats, armpits stained, hems uncurling, exhausted by long and loving use, which my mother so much prefers to the new, modern cotton knickers and vests I give her. Did the silky slips remind her of an almost forgotten erotic past, as they slithered over her old roughened skin? So much more comfortable than cotton. Were my gifts to her of cheap cotton knickers an expression of my refusal to accept that my mother had enjoyed pleasure?

But in a drying machine, unlike anything seen for fifty years, stowed behind the bedroom door, I find old jewellery, wrapped up in rags, buried under a small mountain of discarded shoes. When had my mother worn the sparkling sapphire and golden necklace, interspersed with pearls? I imagine her glittering, throwing back her dark bob of hair, blue eyes trained on the nearest man, charming and remote.

I am starting to possess what I have never possessed. This is all mine now; yet it can never belong to me.

Chapter 45

Ruben has invited me out for a meal. 'You always liked French. Let's go to *La Cuisine* in Covent Garden. My treat.'

'Great. How come?'

'It was my birthday last week. Bit of a celebration. A surge of the super-ego.'

I decide to dress up in my matching, multi-coloured top and trousers, but make the mistake of glancing at myself in the hall mirror, hoping for reassurance. Who is that old woman? Not old exactly, but with saggy dewlaps round her mouth and sad shadows carving the flesh beneath her eyes. I reach for a lipstick, but all it does is increase the paleness of my skin. Or should that be my soul?

He picks me up at six o'clock, insisting on waiting for me at the front door. The dog is trying to block my way out.

Ruben has reserved a table upstairs, by the window, where we can look down on the hustle and bustle of the world outside.

'You always liked sitting next to the window.'

He has ordered a bottle of expensive Chablis. Bread and olives are brought and the waiter lights the candle decoration. We are enjoying ourselves.

'Are you sure you can afford this?' I ask him.

'Oh, don't worry about me. I have no mortgage and nothing much to spend my money on. I live a careful life. My work paid me off with a professorial lump sum on compassionate grounds. I live off the interest. I've become a stock market gazer. *FT* every morning before breakfast.' He grimaces at me, both of us remembering how we used to condemn the way the capitalist system worked. 'Beats working any day,' he adds. 'Let's order and this time I want to hear about you. How's your mother?'

'Not changed.'

'Do you remember I met her that time?'

'Of course I do. She flirted with you.'

'You told me she always did that.'

'Yes. Unbearable.'

'No change, then.'

'I've been finding out a lot about her I never knew. The

167

letters now reveal I have more of a Jewish heritage than I had supposed.'

'You aren't surprised?' Ruben sounds amused.

'Are you still partly Jewish?' I retort.

'It's not something you lose along the way. Ah, where did I mislay that Jewish bit of me? America is different, anyhow. Being 'ethnic' is like a badge of honour.'

'Only your father was Jewish, right?'

'Identity is a construction. But I always assumed your family were Jewish. There was no other explanation.'

'Explanation for what?'

'Their silences. Your ignorance. You bore the imprint. Why did you call your son 'Sam'?'

'Is it short for Samuel, you mean? No, it's simple Sam. I wanted to give him a short name that went easily with Weilheimer.'

'Why didn't you give Sam his father's surname?'

'Wasn't my thing, Ruben. You know that. Why shouldn't the mother give the child her surname, rather than the father's? I didn't even take my husband's name!'

The waiter brings the food. It looks wonderful. I'm having Duck à l'Orange, my favourite.

'So, you've been around? Had fun?' Ruben asks me.

'That's not how it feels. It's been hard. It feels as if I have been working my way slowly through a long dark dank tunnel towards a distant point of light. Sometimes, I couldn't even see that. Sometimes I thought I would drown in the puddles along the way.'

Ruben is regarding me closely and says nothing.

The words start to tumble out of me: 'It's been one crisis after another. I don't know how single parents manage. When the child-minder didn't turn up before Sam went to school, I had to take him to work. When the primary school Head phoned up to say Sam had fallen over and needed to come home, I had to walk out from work. When I had to attend yet another meeting to calm down one of Sam's secondary school teachers, I had to miss my union meeting. When my mother's social worker phoned to say my mother had yet again not opened the front door, I often had to drop both work and child to rush over there. When the hospital phoned me on my mobile to tell me Sam had broken his arm, falling off his bike on some youth rally, I had to desert my mother when she was really ill. And that's not to mention that the guy at work, who is my immediate superior and younger than me, is one of those men who make it very clear that women can't do their job properly if they have children. Sometimes it feels as if I'm drowning, not waving.' I finally come up for air.

Silence. Ruben looks peaky.

'I'm sorry, but I need to go.' Ruben is throwing back the rest of his glass. 'I'll pay on the way out. Why don't you sit and finish the wine. Pity to waste it. Such a good year.'

What have I done?

He leaves his pigeon breast with grapes almost uneaten on the table. Shaking, I gulp down the rest of my wine and leave the restaurant as soon as I can be sure Ruben has had time to disappear.

Chapter 46

It is time to leave. I have pulled out the guts of my parents' home. Their furniture, collected over a lifetime of exile, had been sold by the auctioneers. £1000 for the fruits of a second life.

I hand the key back to the estate agents. They make a cursory inspection of the insides, now naked to the view, shaking their heads at the dilapidation and decay. Only the sun-drenched wallpaper with its orange and yellow stripes still shines its stuff.

I take a last long look around the empty body of the room. The curtains are all that is left, hanging, lopsided as ever, on either side of the tall Georgian window, so worn and dirty not even a charity shop would give them a temporary home.

From the beginning, the purchase of curtains had been a source of discord.

'We're not going to sleep in here,' my father had argued.

'But we don't want the world staring in on us,' my mother had insisted.

They had compromised on ready-made curtains.

Red had been my idea. 'Goes with the sofa.'

'Bit dangerous,' replied my mother.

'Just because you have red curtains, doesn't mean you must be socialists.'

My father had given me his sad, 'You are too young to understand' gaze.

The curtains they brought home were a deep maroon, not a socialist red at all. Nor did they close in the middle. My father had measured the window to the fraction of an inch, but failed to take account how much ruffle a curtain needs to do its job properly.

I had arrived one winter evening to find my father trying to balance an ancient battered screen in front of the offending gap. We stabilise the screen by finally jamming it behind the table.

My mother, curled up on the red sofa, observed us. 'If you move that table again, it's going to fall apart.'

'This way, nobody can look in,' he says. 'You never know

170

when there might be intruders. You know that.'

My mother has started on her high-pitched laugh. 'I told you we should get fitted curtains.'

A hurt look from my father.

My mother phones me a couple of weeks later: 'I've got news.'

'What?'

'We are having bars put up across the window of the front room. Your father feels insecure.'

'You've already got three locks on every window.'

'And so should you!' My mother slams down the phone.

When I next drop by, I observe that the bars are of gleaming brass, catching the rays of the sun and the eye. I ask my father whether he's pleased with them.

'Your mother wanted them. You know how she is.'

'But it's so gloomy inside. It feels like the room's in some sort of institution.'

'We'll draw the curtains when it's dark. That way we won't see the bars. It'll be cosy.'

But the curtains remain undrawn.

About to close the door on my parents' home, I spot a paper box on the floor, so squashed and battered I almost ignore it. Exhausted, I pick it up, peek inside, and spot that name: Dennis.

As I hand in the keys, I mourn. How much I had hated being here, yet how much I regret leaving. I may never have had a room or a bed here, I've found no relics of myself, no toys, no books, but I mourn the home I never had. I want my parents back. I want us to sit around the table eating the overcooked roast chicken. I want them to love me: in this house: now.

My mother is still alive. Yet, without even telling her, I have emptied her home. This time it has been her daughter who has left her homeless on a foreign shore.

I am winnowing out the artefacts of her life, while she would want to live amongst them still, an act of power on my part, or even aggression.

The past is no more. Her home has been destroyed and I am the avenging angel. I have not saved my mother. I have killed her as surely as if I had taken a knife to her heart. Neither have I rescued the dead.

Yet I am still angry. I do not want the responsibility of clearing my parents' lives and home, which reeked of wild neglect. Was it because they lacked so much that they held on to so much? I suspect the turbulence of both my parents' pasts compelled a harmony, where neither could challenge the other's excesses, that their joint need for silence created an inability to query each other's obsessions. Maybe my mother's fury paralysed her ability to keep control of her surroundings.

But whatever its origins, what did they think would happen to this crazy chaos? Did my mother think that she would, one day, miraculously sort out her past? I suspect she never believed herself to be old, never saw the inevitability of death, the slow rise of decay. It is as if Emil and Louise believed themselves immortal. There would always be time to tackle the relics of their life. Yet it is I who have to face this decomposition.

Did they suspect, or even hope, that one day I would come along and delve deep for their secrets? Yet they never spoke to me of what they must have guessed I would one day disinter.

Chapter 47

5am. I find myself sitting at my computer table in my room downstairs; I stare through the French doors onto the white painted wall in the garden, a triangle of the outside world.

The geranium, in its small red pot, planted to welcome the spring, is not thriving; I water it too irregularly. I had tried to grow a honeysuckle in the corner, between the wall and the house, to climb up the pole. All that's left is the pot and a stick. On the ground is a trough with flowers, a mixture of newly-planted pansies and a pretty but enthusiastic weed, with many sprays of tiny purple flowers, which I refuse to pull out, though it is spreading fast.

I cannot sleep. The last batch of letters, found in my father's office, is before me, translated.

8.2.40

We are very worried about Uncle N. and we fear the worst. The truth must out. Not knowing is torture. Do not keep news from us. May you be protected from all evil.

Beloved Louischen, our sweet baby of the family. Thank you for DM 150 which we got from your friend Frau R. Lovely for young to feed old.

Your letters made us very happy.

Love from your loyal ones

19.3.40

Dear all, Dear L,

We ask you again urgently to free us from our nightmares and please let us know what you know or found out through E.

We want to stress our intense wish to emigrate as soon as technically possible. No reason needed. We are so jealous of those who are not here with us. May all our hopes come true.

Love, Vater

Why were the letters from 1940 in my father's possession? What distinguishes them from the letters from 1939 is that my mother's father is now calling out to her, telling her of their need to escape.

Was it that my mother could not bear to see the guillotine's slow drop onto her parents' necks?

'If only I'd tried harder to get you out,' my mother may have thought. *'If only I'd realised I was on a one-way ticket out of Berlin. I should not have left you to die. I should have stayed with you, to break bread with you, to care for you, to step outside into the fear of the streets, to buy you a loaf of bread or a packet of coffee, to be there as the world contracted to the view from the windows of the flat.'*

Did you think: *'I wish I could have loved you better, Mutti. You were so strict with me, so unforgiving. And you panicked so over every little thing.'*

Did you think of your father and wish: *'I hope I did not hurt you when I left home so young. I loved you so much, Vater. I want to sit with you again on the balcony. We would pause our talk as the rumble of the train passes. You would quote me from Goethe, hoping to entice me away from Marx. I will remember you always.'*

Did you curse your husband? *'It was you who got us into trouble, you with all your left-wing political activities. Emil, you may have become a good shot when you took on the SS, but that was going to change nothing, except our fate. Do you remember, Emil, it was I who forced you to leave. I wanted you to live. I told you I would leave Germany with or without you. But then I had to leave my parents. I should have died with them.'*

Is that what you thought? Is that why my father buried these letters where you would never find them?

Chapter 48

'This has nothing to do with you. Leave those papers alone.'
My parents' ghosts obstruct my way to the boxes which
occupy the floor of my large front room.

'I want to find out about my history.'

'Our history. You are merely the postscript.'

I consider the photo albums. I sit cross-legged on
the floor, my family piled on my lap. Other people have
the photos of their nearest and dearest presented on
mantelpieces, sideboards, TV. Entering Val's house is like
entering a family gallery; on one side of the hall are her father
and his parents, and her mother and her parents; on the other
side, a more patchy selection of her husband's family. In her
front room are pictures of herself at the age we first met. She
looks so young. Her two children, at different stages of their
young lives, smile out, getting married, and then with their
own children, a gallery of belonging. They keep the images
near them, holding onto their souls.

I grew up without pictures. Photos, my father had
informed me when I was little, are an irrelevance. Families are
what you make them. Relations are not more important than
any other group of people, and are often less. Families, it was
intimated, are for the weak-minded.

Yet at some point, a photo did appear in my parents'
London home. It sat on the old gas fireplace in the living
room. It showed two elderly strangers. I never asked about it.
My mother once broke her usual silence and asked me:

'Have you seen the picture of my parents?'

'Don't know what you mean,' I'd replied, pretending that
it was not there.

I've adorned my house with photos of Sam. Every year of
his being is celebrated.

Most of the photo albums on my lap had belonged to
my father. I recognise his writing on the leaves. A photo
appears of an 'old' woman. She is in three-quarters profile,
sitting stern and stiff-backed in a chintz chair, her hair in a

175

tight roll at the nape of her neck, steel-rimmed glasses shielding her from our vision. His mother, he had told me, died when he was a young boy. He remembered virtually nothing of her. I look at this picture of a woman in middle-age and am afraid, afraid that my father's mother also died at the hands of the Nazis.

A locket falls out of an album on to the floor and springs open. Horrified, I look down at the two tiny photos which have fallen out. I cannot pick them up. They look at me, and I ask them who they are. But they will not tell me. *'How will you save us?'* say the faces in the photo. *'How could you leave us, forgotten? How could you let us die? You are responsible for us now.'*

I remember my terror when I had once illicitly gone up into the attic of our Durham house. My father was looking into an opened old trunk at what appeared to be a soldier's uniform. He snapped down the lid as he saw me. The uniform belonged to his brother: killed in the First World War, I'd conjectured. The boy in the sepia photo had worn it, I now add. Yet I cannot imagine how the uniform got from Germany, especially from the trenches of the First World War, to an attic in Durham.

Soon after my father's death, I'd enquired of my mother:
'Did my father have a brother?'
'Why are you asking?'
'What was his name?'
'I can't remember.'
'What happened to him?'
'I don't remember.'
'Yes, you do. Your husband's brother. Did you ever meet him?'
'He died before I knew your father. I can't remember what happened to him. It doesn't matter.'
I don't believe her, but I nod.

Now I chance on a ring, its diameter too small to be a napkin ring, too large to be jewellery, buried at the back of the drawer of the walnut chest where my father kept his cheque book and other financial papers. My father will have touched the ring each time he reached in.

Behind the tarnished silver was inscribed the name Alphonso. It was a birth ring. Every day my father will have remembered.

With the ring, I find a cup, shaped like a tulip. I rub the dull metal and again the name Alphonso appears.

I stare down at the photo in the album I had glimpsed as a little girl, before my father had dragged the album away. Now I have a name for the little boy standing in his sailor suit, so proud beside his brother. Now I know who he is. I stare hard at the boy's thin lips and his averted gaze. Alphonso: what an unlikely name for a German youth born at the beginning of the twentieth century. Alphonso, my father's brother. Never to know me. I clench his birth ring in my hand.

I find photos of a grave. Not so much a grave as an unmade pile of earth with a small ordinary stone lying upon it. My father had written next to the photo a date of birth and death. What a short life.

Alphonso is writing a letter, the letter I am to read eighty years later. It reads,

How can I live without you, my love? You are the only person whom I have ever cherished and who gave my life a meaning.

Alphonso's lips are twitching. He keeps removing his glasses to rub his eyes, dry from weeping. He stands at the window and sees the reflection of a weak and unattractive man. His life no longer has any intrinsic value. He sits back down onto his narrow bed and signs the letter, though the signature is faint.

I check the date on the letter. It is a few days before Alphonso's death.

I am looking at the photos my father took of his brother's grave.

My father's grief at his brother's death condemned him to a collusion of silence with my mother. Never able to tell me he had a brother, yet every day he remembered him.

I've had enough of silences which shout louder than words.

I go to visit my mother: 'Alphonso committed suicide,' I tell her.

'How do you know that?'

'But he did, didn't he?'

'He died of a broken heart.'

I reclaim my uncle. The cup is placed on the bookcase next to where I am sitting.

I unearth my father's family tree from out of a dusty, unlabelled file. The ancient yellowing foolscap has been folded into a small square, inscribed with tiny Gothic handwriting. But I now know what I am looking for. It is the last birth on the tree, at the bottom of the page. I find Alphonso's full name: Alphonso Martin.

'I have a son,' I inform Alphonso. 'His second name is also Martin. I gave him your name, never knowing.'

Chapter 49

───

7th January 1941

Dear Mrs Louise Weilheimer,

Today I received a letter from your friend Mrs R, dated 9 December, with the sad news that your sister died, far away from her parents and from you. Your parents are very upset about it. At least, she is now delivered from all suffering. Please accept my heartfelt sympathy.

From EP, New York

I know you lived, Marthe, though your parents' letters rarely speak of you and by initial only. I have tried to find you. But I find it hard to hear your voice over the waves of time.

I have to break down the walls of resistance which have held back my mother's memories. I may not have long. She has shrunk since she was so ill. Her breathing is difficult. But to ask, to approach the truth, is to feel dread.

I sit down on the chair next to my mother.

'Tell me about your sister.'

My mother hangs her head.

I persist. 'What happened to Marthe?'

'I don't know.'

'What did she die of?'

'Liver failure.'

'You know that isn't true.'

'If you know so much, why are you asking me?'

'Who sent her to the mental hospital?'

'I don't know. I was so young, you see. I couldn't do anything.'

My mother is still not able to talk, either because grief has dammed her voice, or because what had happened was too awful to put into words.

A few days later, hunting through my father's thick files,

a photo slips out onto the floor. I bend over to pick it up and take a look. It is a black and white photo, corners curling with age, of two girls. The younger girl, who looks about five years old, is beaming straight into the camera, and I know this to be my mother. She is wearing a plain dress with a large lacy white collar, and long socks in tightly-laced shoes. Her hair is parted and pulled back. The other person, behind Louise, wearing the identical dress and with a similar hairstyle, but significantly older, is resting her hands on Louise's shoulders. She has her head slightly turned, and though smiling, does not meet the viewer's gaze.

I turn it over and in my father's hand, I read: 'Louise and sister'. I have found Marthe.

There are so many questions I would like to ask.

'Tell me, Marthe . . ,' I want to begin. I want her to come and sit down next to me and put her arm around my shoulders. I stare out of the bedroom window, imagining who Marthe had been.

It is 1930. Berlin. Marthe has not done well at school and her parents have decided the best thing for her is to get married. Now that she is almost twenty, they are getting concerned. No problem about her looks. She is a beauty, doe-eyes, a moist, well-formed mouth, clear skin. Young men whistle at her. She looks down, but smiles softly, glancing at them out of the corner of her eye. Sometimes, when her mother sends her out to do shopping for the family, Marthe goes and sits on the swings opposite their block of flats and chats with the boys, who cluster round her as if they were bees at a flower. Her mother watches her from the large window overlooking the street, and frets. She calls her husband.

'Look,' she says to him, 'no daughter of ours should be behaving like that.'

'She should cover up more,' says the father, though the only thing naked about their daughter is her face. Even her hands are gloved, and all that can be seen between the hem of her skirt and her boots is a short flash of white stocking.

'I'm going to talk to the Liepmanns,' the father says. 'Their son has never married.'

'But he's twenty years older than her!'

'It's a respectable family,' her husband continues. 'Nothing ventured, nothing gained.'

The mother finally says, 'I've heard he's a bit of a wastrel. Gambles.' She does not say what she wants to say, that he consorts with prostitutes.

'The final decision will of course be hers,' her husband reassures his wife.

Marthe remembers when they introduced Fred to her: his greasy clothes, the middle-aged spread, his shining scalp. She didn't say no. How could she? She knows she is a problem for her parents. Her mother often says to her: 'You idiot'.

Her mother also frequently tells her that at Marthe's age she was already holding down a respectable job as a book-keeper, not mooning around at home. 'I want to look after children,' Marthe says.

'You're not bright enough to get the necessary qualifications,' her father informs her.

'You'll have lots of your own children soon enough,' her mother says, with forced encouragement.

Marthe has moved into Fred's family's house after their marriage six months previously. Her parents congratulate themselves on solving the problem. Marthe knows that. She tries to be a good wife but does not understand at first why it is so difficult. Then she overhears her normally quietly-spoken mother–in-law damning her son for his folly.

'But marriage won't change his ways,' her mother-in-law advises Marthe gently when she realises Marthe now knows about her husband's errant behaviour. 'You will get used to it.'

Whereupon, Marthe packs up her case and walks halfway across Berlin to get back to her old home.

'What are you doing here?' is how her mother greets her.

'Marthe,' her mother chides her, when she comes back in, 'how come you've been so long?' The mother glances over at her elder daughter, annoyed at that innocent gaze of hers. Marthe perches herself on the edge of the armchair. 'I've done the shopping, as you asked.'

Her mother sighs. 'That takes you an hour? To go to the

181

shop at the end of the street and back?'

'I went to the park for a few minutes,' Marthe confesses.

The swings in the park provide Marthe with a brief refuge. And Matt is sometimes there. 'Not good enough for you,' her parents had told her when they had observed her chatting to Matt one time when she was still at school. 'We don't want you seeing him again,' they had instructed her. Matt lived a few houses down and they often used to walk to school together. Matt would talk to her about his local youth group, and he always asked her how she was.

Marthe closes her eyes. She wants to go back down to the swings, to lean another time into Matt's firm body. The last time he pushed her on the swings he'd grasped her around her shoulders, his hands slipping down to places which left her giddy. 'Stop,' she'd pleaded, and he had. But she wants him to touch her. Not anywhere too personal, though. That wouldn't be right. Her skin feels tight and hot as she imagines running her hand over the strange fairness of his short scrub of hair and remembers the sweet scent of his sweat.

Her mother is speaking in that hard voice of hers: 'Your father and I have been talking. We know what is going on. You must make some effort towards your husband. Nobody's marriage is perfect. You've got to stop gallivanting around after everybody and anybody who wears trousers.' She does not tell Marthe what her husband has also said: that Marthe is leading men on, that she is putting her parents to shame.

Marthe could have told her mother that the closest she has been to Matt is in her dreams.

'It will be easier when you and Fred have your own home together,' her mother is advising, her tone softer. But Marthe observes her mother eyeing her stomach and folds her arms over her body to conceal the bulge.

Post-natal depression is not an accepted illness at that time.

Martha's mother is frantic. The birth of a child should have sorted Marthe out, given her a purpose in life, stopped her silliness. Instead, Marthe cannot stop crying. Even when she holds the baby, she hides her head in its warm snugly body and weeps.

It is Marthe's father who bites the bullet.

182

'There can be bad blood in any family,' he tells his wife. 'It isn't as if we haven't been understanding. She needs the sort of help that we can't offer her.'

'Our responsibility has now to be to the child,' says the grandmother.

A doctor is called to see Marthe and give his professional opinion. The good doctor's opinion is that she is a nymphomaniac. 'Don't be alarmed,' he reassures them after Marthe is told to leave the room. 'It's not an inherited disease,' his Jewishness no protection against his faith in eugenics. 'And,' he continues, 'it's only a mild case. A short stretch in a suitable clinic and she'll be as right as rain.'

Marthe is taken by her father to a clinic on the edge of Berlin. 'Only for a short while,' he tells her, as he hands her over, sweet as ever, to the waiting staff.

But Marthe never came out. The Nazis came to power. A person in a psychiatric clinic became *untermensch*. Marthe's parents had not planned for that. The Nazi programme of euthanasia did for Marthe.

Her death presses down on my mother, who, I suspect, never forgave her parents for what they did to her sister. But my mother also fears that she too betrayed Marthe when she fled the parental home. She cannot tell me about her sister and so she cannot tell me about herself. But she looks at me and sees Marthe.

Marthe, you are lost in history. Yet someone must carry the candle of your memory.

Chapter 50

I write to the Red Cross. I'd discovered that they still trace people who 'died' under the Nazis. Could they try to find Marthe? I have almost no information, I tell them, but I cannot bear the idea of this person disappearing into dust.

A Holocaust specialist rings me from the Red Cross. She assures me she will do everything she can to find out what happened. I have to fill out a galaxy of forms. I explain that I also want to find out about the deaths of Rosa and Johann.

Eventually, her reply arrives. Rosa Weilheimer had been buried, it informs me. I ring up to ask what this information means. Does Rosa have a named grave after all? Was hers a natural death? Could she have died and been buried in a camp? Is she buried in Germany?

Apologetically, the woman from the Red Cross explains that they know nothing more than that Rosa is named in a document of people who died and were buried during the war. 'It is difficult getting detailed information,' she warns me, but they are continuing to try.

I write to the Berlin Synagogue Research Centre and ask them if they can help find my grandmother's grave, and explain I want to find out what happened to her and Johann. The past crawls into every crevice of my life.

Chapter 51

I almost missed the cardboard box that I'd found on the floor of my parents' home. My mother must have kept the box hidden under the sofa where she used to lie. It was one of those old-fashioned cardboard things which come with small sheets of blue writing paper and matching envelopes. I now gingerly take off the lid.

My mother, who could not distinguish a shopping list from a council bill, who denied all knowledge of ever having known Dennis, had kept cuttings and letters about Dennis, organised in date order - from an article from 1948 about Russian political prisoners up to a recent letter from Seamus Arbouth.

My mother hadn't forgotten Dennis.

A few days later, I get home to find a long awaited email from Seamus Arbouth about Louise and Dennis. My stomach starts to cramp as I read:

Date: 12.4.06

From: Seamus Arbouth

To: Anna Weilheimer

It's such a pity your mother refused to talk to me when I came to London. That makes any paper records all the more important. I have now had a chance to study the photocopies of Louise's diary which you kindly sent me after you unearthed it from the bottom of your parents' trunk. You told me it was wrapped up in rags - at least that preserved it. But I do wonder how she got it safely out of the USSR!

While it is possible that she was a spy for the Russians, I incline to think she was not, but could be persuaded to the contrary.

I cannot be sure why she went to Moscow or how she and Dennis supported themselves. In spite of what she told you, she was certainly not a translator in Moscow.

She and Dennis got into trouble with the Secret Police, who thought the two of them had Trotskyite sympathies. Of course this was 1936, so anybody who ran up against the State was accused of Trotskyism. Louise's 'friend', Dennis's sister-in-law, was actually a secret agent, so everything they discussed 'in private' went straight to the Secret Police.

I think your mother got out of USSR by the skin of her teeth.

Date: 12.4.06

From: Anna Weilheimer

To: Seamus Arbouth

Easier to talk about this maybe? I'd like to know what my mother was doing in Moscow with Dennis.

I'm in for the next few hours if you can afford a phone call from the USA.

My phone rings almost immediately. Seamus goes straight to the point, before I've even said 'Hello'.

'I thought you might ask me that. There's no way round this, Anna. I know your mother was already married to your father. But there is evidence of a civil marriage ceremony in the Russian records. Don't forget,' he continues into my silence, 'that there could be many meanings behind this ceremony. Her relationship with Dennis doesn't have to have been a personal thing. She might have been a spy for the British, not for the Russians, and took up with Dennis in order to penetrate the Communist Party. Or to find out more about what was going on in Moscow. Or because she was acting for one splinter group of what was a highly factionalised Communist movement. We just don't know and we may never know.'

I thank him for telling me all this personally. 'I'll get

186

back to you when I've had time to think about it,' I inform
him.

Date: 23.4.06
From: Anna Weilheimer
To: Seamus Arbouth

Surely, if she's acting on behalf of the British government, they
wouldn't arrest her in 1940? I don't see my mother as a spy for
anybody.

Date: 7.05.06
From: Seamus Arbouth
To: Anna Weilheimer

This is a looking-glass world. But whatever the explanation for
what went on in the USSR, Louise was a young, impetuous woman
who did something very silly.

Date: 1.06.06
From: Anna Weilheimer
To: Seamus Arbouth

You've grown cynical in your old age. Or have you been too long
immersed in the USA? You know my opinion of the USSR. The
'revolution' had been defeated by the end of the 1920s. By 1936,
the USSR was a state capitalist regime of a particularly nasty
Stalinist kind. But at the time, the USSR was seen by many on the
left as a bulwark against fascism and an attempt to construct a
socialist alternative to capitalism. I prefer to think Louise was an
idealist who wanted to see what USSR socialism, 1936 style, was
like.

Whatever reason Dennis was in Moscow, he provided her with a unique opportunity. If they did get married, I guess it was because it made them safer.

Did Dennis ever get out of the USSR? The MI5 documents suggest Dennis 'gave' himself to the GPU secret police in return for Louise's freedom.

I finish the email and, shaking, go and curl up on the chaise longue. It's easy to defend my mother, another thing entirely to accept what she'd done. It seems my parents' perfect marriage was anything but. My father may not have been the love of my mother's life.

Emil had taken Louise back. Damaged goods. He had stood by her when she returned from Moscow. He had even tried to find out what was happening to Dennis. Did she feel indebted to Emil and so no longer free, no longer able to stretch her wings and fly? Was that why my mother hid away in the bedroom? Did she mourn for a past love? Did she feel compromised?

My father had written to the Home Office, defending Louise. I am looking back over a spread of papers on my desk, sweating and sick. He was trying to get her out from Holloway prison. He claimed responsibility for her liaison with Dennis Casey because he, Emil, was in no emotional state to settle down after his escape from Germany. It cannot have been easy to accept his wife gallivanting about with another man, when he had just arrived in a new land, without roots, family or friends. My parents were not having an easy time of it. Living with death can be exhausting.

My mother, as I see it, may not have wanted to settle down with her husband, but now had little choice other than to accept domesticity. What a defeat! She did so with limited grace and a kind of despair. Did she choose to have a child to deafen herself to the snarl of death? To smooth down the jagged edges left by her infidelity?

'Were you an accident?' I remember a child once asking a small group of us in the Junior School playground.

'I was wanted,' I'd replied, uncomprehending.

'Well, *I* wasn't,' one small snotty child had declaimed, for all to know what terrible odds were stacked against her. The little group had nodded, then turned to glower at me. I had shown them up. Now it is I who feel exposed.

I'm not surprised that my parents found parenting difficult. The power of past desire was irrepressible. When my mother tried to stop me seeing men, real or imagined, she thought of Dennis. When my father lectured me on the sins of pleasure, he thought of his wife's infidelity. Dennis lay between Emil and Louise, and his shadow hung heavy over me. Yet even when I ask her explicitly, my mother denies any knowledge of Dennis. The more I know, the more pity I feel for her. Her need to bury her love affair formed a barrier between the two of us. She lost Dennis and I lost her.

Chapter 52

It has taken me months before I can face reading Chris's translations of the Red Cross letters.

Early one morning, a morning of transparent light and no clouds, I gather up the file and return to bed. I lean up in the corner, duvet pulled up to my neck, and open the purple folder.

The letters are from the British Red Cross, tiny slips of paper, which only allow for a strictly limited number of words, the only form of correspondence then allowed between Britain and Germany. There are so few letters. On one side of each sheet are a few words from either Louise's parents, or Louise, and on the other side, if they were really lucky, a brief reply.

I can hardly bear to look at them.

The following letters were addressed to the Berlin flat, via the Red Cross.

8.5.40 To Vater. Very concerned about momma. 1000 birthday kisses. All our love. We are always thinking of you. Be healthy. We embrace you. From Louise

6.6.40 Dear children. Your news thrilled us indescribably after a lengthy wait. We are healthy and hopeful. We bless and kiss you all.

This answer is on the back of the previous letter.

9.2.41 News about you made us happy. We are healthy and hopeful and just long to be with you. We embrace you. From Vater

15.6.41 Dear children, Mother's failing health is somewhat better. We bless and kiss you and we hope that we will be able to do this sometime in person. From Vater

5.8.41

My beloved children!

Your mother is no more among the living. She passed away peacefully in the hospital at 6:30 this morning. She had a foreboding of what was coming. I cannot believe the unbelievable. What was mortal of her will be committed to the earth on Friday 11.15 o'clock, where she will rest, instead of Aunt S, next to her parents. The death of my beloved wife has to be accepted as an Act of God.

Stick together, beloved children, and endeavour to think and act similar to mother. She was the very best of us all.

I kiss and bless you and hope that God will give us the strength to bear this hard trial.

Love,

Your Vater

22.10.41 Dear Daddy, I embrace you and try to be with you in my thoughts and share your loneliness. Stay healthy for us. We are. Love, Louise

Reply: Dear children, I am healthy and hopeful and working at home. To have you makes me happy and strong. Blessings

9.11.41 My beloved child. Congratulations and blessings to you, little Louise. Today like every Sunday I stood at the grave of your mother.

I cannot go on reading. For the first and only time, I go out and buy a Jewish memorial candle in memory of my grandmother, and place it, lit, on the piano, by the photo of Johann and Rosa, the piano which had belonged to my mother's parents and which my mother had loved. It has taken my lifetime to discover the truth. The plaque in the house in Berlin was not accurate; my grandmother was not murdered.

My poor mother! There was no way for her to reach her mother's side. No chance to know how her mother died or to mourn at her mother's funeral, to say, 'Goodbye, I love you.' All she is able to do is send her father a consoling telegram.

How hard it must have been for you! The Germans, the people whom you had gone to school with, shopped, danced and worked with, had stood by as your family were blown to the four corners of the earth. Your loved ones had been slain. They had 'disappeared' your sister, for no greater crime than for being sick. Who would have killed *you* had you returned to stand at your father's side and grieve at your mother's funeral? Your beloved father had to stand alone.

My mother had understood her mother's death as murder. She had told me: 'I should have died too.' I now know the truth about my grandmother's death and I am glad. Yet when I tell her that Rosa did not die in a camp, my mother, shaking, is unable to hear me.

I study the photo of Johann and Rosa. Johann is looking proud, a tight-fitting waistcoat under his jacket, a bullish head, no hair, a typical German: Rosa, demure, pinched, a dark austere dress covering any sign of her female figure. They both stare into the camera. They look so old as they are flashed into infinity, though probably only in their fifties, not so long before their premature deaths.

How did Louise have this photo at all? Did her parents send it to her before the outbreak of war?

'Remember us,' they told her. They glanced at each other as they wrapped it carefully in the brown paper that was so hard to find. And the father held the parcel for an extra moment before handing it to the clerk in the post office. 'It's going to England,' he informed the clerk, who looked at him in that particular way which made him afraid.

Louise hid the photo away. Remembering them was what she could not do. The granddaughter they never knew now possesses their image. They live with me now.

Chapter 53

'Elizabeth speaking. You don't know me. But I am looking for my mother's cousin, Louise Weilheimer,' the voice at the other end of the phone informs me.

'I'm Louise's daughter.'

'Call me Beth.' Elizabeth laughs nervously.

The line goes silent. 'Yes?'

'My mother started to look into her family just before she died. She remembered that Louise married a Weilheimer and they lived in London. I looked you up in the phone book.' Another nervous laugh. 'Not many Weilheimers. My mother's funeral is next week and I wanted to invite Louise. Could you give me her phone number?'

'How amazing that you traced me!' I tell Elizabeth, excited, but also apprehensive. I'm not sure I'm ready for this, but I'm not my mother's daughter for nothing. My mother had once mentioned a Sarah and her daughter, Elizabeth. It had been in one of her 'you will thank me for not introducing you' moments when I had asked her about her family.

'My mother was never very strong on family connections,' I tell her. 'I'm afraid she is now very old and infirm. I'm very sorry about your mother.'

'Her death was a relief in the end. The big C. You know the way it is. I'm not quite sure how you and I are related either. It was only towards the very end that my mother started caring about the past. Perhaps you'd like to come? The funeral's in Cambridge.'

'That's where you live?' I can't stand her use of polite abbreviations or the pretentiousness of her voice.

'My parents, yes. But I live in London.'

She gives me the details of the funeral, which is to be held at St. Michael's - Church of England, of course - in Cambridge, and more out of curiosity than any identification with Elizabeth or her mother, I agree to attend.

I spot Elizabeth outside the church. I know it's her. She's in her late forties, smartly dressed in a black silk trouser suit, with naturally greying hair which she has in a severe bob, and is surrounded by a small group of people.

I go up to her: 'Elizabeth?'

She turns towards me: 'Yes?'

'I'm Anna.'

Suddenly, she smiles, and waving her hand round the little group, announces: 'This is my long lost cousin.'

Then she shows me to the antechamber and excuses herself, saying: 'You do understand, I have to greet the guests.' I sit and regard the gathering. They are a well-heeled group, all dressed in black. I had finally chosen to wear my one smart black skirt, with my favourite, brightly-patterned flowing jacket, to counterpoise any suggestion of false respectability. Nobody speaks.

I stand towards the back of the church so as to know when to stand, when to sing, and when to bow my head, whilst others pray. Wouldn't do to get it the wrong way round. The ceremony is led by the priest and is so much more formal than the humanist funeral we gave my father. Afterwards, we all stand round the coffin and throw clods of earth onto the bier. Elizabeth invites me back to the wake but I excuse myself, suggesting we meet in London, as we appear to live close to one another.

I'm curious. Why, I wonder, did my mother warn me off this part of her family? Nothing ostensibly Jewish about the family, so that can't be it. Nothing more respectable than a decent Church of England service. Perhaps my mother just wanted the past buried, whatever form it took.

A few months later, we meet midway between my less and her more prestigious parts of Islington. I had suggested an open-air café. Despite being early summer, it was only just about warm enough to sit outside. She had hesitantly agreed. She arrives in an unsuitably thin but smart linen suit, while I snuggle into my warm cagoule. She orders a small espresso, me a hot chocolate.

'Your name is Weilheimer? You never married?' Elizabeth asks me, as, carefully carrying our cups, we settle down at a table near enough the building to offer some limited protection from the wind.

'Oh yes, I was. Married. But I didn't take my husband's name.'

'You've got your father's name!'

I can't be bothered to argue that I grew up with 'Weilheimer', so it's my name now. 'Tell me more about your parents,' I suggest. I cannot stop myself feeling intrigued. I silently tell myself off for disloyalty to my mother. She would be so disdainful if she knew I was talking to the very people she hoped to save me from.

'Er . . . my mother lived in Cambridge and met my father at the university.' She has started to grin.

'Do you have any idea how we are related?'

'I'm not sure, you know. Maybe we are second cousins. The only thing my mother told me about Louise was that she was a spy.' Elizabeth giggles, but is looking at me enquiringly.

I guess this 'knowledge' represents family prejudice against the 'reds', for how could Elizabeth's mother possibly know such a thing? But instead I ask: 'What do you know about your mother's family?'

'Well . . . not much, really.'

'When did your mother come to England?' This is always a telling question.

Elizabeth appears unsure. 'She came out of Germany in the late 1930s. She was very little. My mother never really . . . you know . . . talked about that time.'

This all sounds so familiar; I feel excited to discover such congruities. 'Who brought your mother up?'

'My mother was sent off to some ancient relatives of her father's, who ran a boarding house in Brighton. She wasn't happy there. They both died, you know, shortly before she went to college. She used to refer to them as 'Mummy' and 'Daddy'. But I didn't hear her mention them very often.'

'Did you know your father's parents?'

'Oh yes. The Gardners. They were sweeties. They lived in Cambridge, you know. My father's father was a Conservative MP. But his mother ran the family. They had four sons apparently, but the first died when little. My father was the youngest.'

'So you have relatives on your father's side?' Elizabeth appears to prefer talking about this side of her family.

'Well, no. My father died a long time ago, sadly. The oldest living brother was a bit of a womaniser. He was in politics, like his Daddy. Never settled down. Died suddenly in his fifties of a heart attack. Had just decided to marry the woman of his dreams. And Uncle Albert is still living, you know. Such a sweetie. You'd love him. His first interest is not women, though.'

'They all vote Conservative?' I couldn't stop myself.

Elizabeth looks perplexed. 'I've never asked them,' she informs me.

'Were your mother's side Jewish?'

Elizabeth's voice rises. 'Well, of course they were. But I told you. I don't know much at all.'

'Lots of people had to leave Germany for reasons other than being Jewish.'

Silence.

I risk a last question and wait: 'What happened to your mum's parents?'

'My mother only started talking a few days before she died.' Elizabeth suddenly continues in a high, upset tone: 'Her father survived, but her mother and my mother's two older brothers were taken away.' Her face is suddenly pinched. 'My mother's father was spared because he was the only doctor for miles. They lived in a small village in southern Germany somewhere - Bavaria, I think. It was a very rural area. He was too useful. That's what my mother told me. I hate the Germans,' Elizabeth bursts out. 'I hate anything to do with Germany.'

'Are you going to try to find out more? Your grandfather could still be alive.' I've done my sums quickly.

'What is the point?' Elizabeth retorts, eyes blazing. 'The past is the past. Nothing will bring those people back. I'm not going to let myself be dragged into their miseries. I'm getting on with my own life.'

I change the subject, ask her what she does. Turns out she is a successful property lawyer. Never had any children. Not interested in them. Married to Edward, the headmaster of a private but progressive school. They lead their own separate lives. There is a brother, but he lives in the USA with his wife and two daughters, and didn't even bother coming over for the funeral. She attends Church regularly. Important to her. Yes, she sees herself as English. What else would she be?

Chapter 54

'I'm hungry,' Sam announces down my mobile after a weekend away at camp.

'And how are you too!'

'Really hungry. Not pasta.'

'So you're coming back for supper?'

'I like that apple pudding you do.' Then he adds: 'I'm sure whatever you make will be nice.'

'Grandma was suspected of being a spy. That's why she was sent to Holloway Prison,' I inform Sam as we sit stuffing ourselves on my favourite creamy risotto.

Sam doesn't stop eating. 'What makes you think that?' He sounds hopeful.

'Seamus was in touch.'

Another email from Seamus had arrived that morning. I'd hesitated before opening it, made a cup of tea, washed up, stroked the dog, done anything rather than be faced with its contents.

Seamus, the email told me, had discovered the missing link - why my mother had been imprisoned in Holloway in 1940 as a potential spy.

Louise had gone to the USA in 1938. She had been accepted onto a degree course, presumably to get the degree that had eluded her in Berlin. While she was in New York, she'd visited C. She had spotted a couple of articles in the *New York Times*, written by C, about a man she took to be Dennis, though the article, typically, only referred to him by the use of a capital letter: B. C apparently made Louise welcome, agreed that B could be Dennis, but said that he knew nothing more than the articles had already stated: B had been kidnapped by the Soviet Secret Police, present whereabouts unknown.

What Louise could not have known was that C was a double-agent, working for both the USSR and Britain. He suspected Louise of being a Soviet spy and had written to MI5: 'She is a dangerous woman who must be watched.'

Louise was already being observed by MI5 and this 'information' brought about her arrest.

The double-agent didn't survive. He was murdered by the Russian secret police.

She had no idea what she was walking into. Your mother was very lucky.

I can imagine the scene. My mother would not have found it easy to track down C, indeed I do wonder how she found his address.

She decided against writing to him – her stay in Moscow had taught her a thing or two. She knew C had defected from the USSR and, from the articles, suspected he would be on her side. She would have dressed up for the occasion: a bow in her hair, red lipstick carefully applied and, if the weather warranted it, wearing a fur. She'd gone to the hotel, was initially taken aback by its opulence. How could a defector afford such luxury? But she'd pushed the thought to the back of her mind. She announced herself to the hotel receptionist in such a way that her request for the man's room number would not be challenged. At his door, she knocked firmly, smiling, as the door edged open. The man did not at first look pleased to see her. She adopted her most coquettish pose and introduced herself, explaining that she was interested in his articles on B. The man had to take a quick decision. Louise might be an attractive woman - shining hair, dark eyes and a neat figure - as his one glance had already revealed, but he knew all too well about how the Soviet Secret Service sent temptresses to lure defectors to their death. Better to entertain her, find out what she knew, and then act accordingly.

My poor mother didn't have a clue.

It was the Cuba crisis of October 1962 which revealed to me that the USSR had nothing to do with socialism. America had discovered Russian missiles on Cuban soil, their 'back yard', and was making frighteningly warlike noises. I was keen to stay alive and had turned out to demonstrate. But what was I demonstrating against? Supporting the lot from the Communist Party, with their placards supporting the USSR, was impossible. Then I heard the small but vocal International Socialist contingent shouting: 'Neither Washington nor Moscow!' So I marched with them.

At small meetings in drab rooms, I was convinced (as I still am) that the Russian Revolution of 1917 had been destroyed by the hardships caused by the subsequent Civil War, when the Allied forces invaded, joining with the Whites, and by the international blockade, and that the failure of revolution in Hungary and Germany left the USSR isolated. Socialism could not exist in the USSR alone. The USSR became a State capitalist society, its working class exploited by the State.

The possibility for socialism had been extinguished long before Dennis, and then my mother, were drawn to the USSR. But fascism was on the march, and my mother, exiled from her own land, was hoping to find a land of dreams: instead she found nightmares.

I ask Sam: 'Are you interested in hearing about Grandma?'

'It's you who want to tell me. I'm eating. Just carry on.'

'She didn't know why she'd been picked up and sent to prison, or whether she was suspected of spying for the USSR or Germany. Her interrogators don't seem to have given much away. You can imagine how she'd have hated being accused of spying for the Nazis.'

'Poor woman,' Sam says, unexpectedly.

'MI5 did pick up other German exiles whom they suspected of having Communist sympathies, but she wouldn't have known that at the time.'

'But she'd been to Russia?'

'Yes, she was seen as a trouble-maker there. Even a Trotskyite.'

'Trotsky what?'

'Leon Trotsky. The revolution's 'prophet'. Murdered in Mexico where he'd fled, by one of Stalin's henchmen. To be accused, rightly or wrongly, of Trotskyism in the USSR was a death sentence.'

'OK.'

'I suspect she was afraid that the Russian secret police were out to kill her, even when she was back in England.'

'Not the Nazis?'

'I think she was more afraid of the Russians. The Nazis didn't pursue oppositionists outside their territory, but the Russians did.'

'No wonder she's a bit strange.'

'Yes. It's not surprising my parents were so paranoid, but it made for a lousy childhood.'

'Is the pudding ready yet?'

'You haven't had any salad.'

'You know I don't like watercress.'

We sit together silently, slurping at the apple pudding.

'My mother leapt faster than she could think. Unlike now, when she thinks but cannot leap,' I finally comment.

'Do remember that the sins of the mothers are not visited on their daughters - or their sons!'

'Isn't that a bit of a grown-up thing for you to say?'

Sam grins, jumps up and waves at me from the kitchen door. 'Got to go. Lovely meal.'

Chapter 55

I go to visit my mother. My mother is now in her third Home in less than a year. The carers in her previous Home had diagnosed double pneumonia as constipation. Despite their objections, I had insisted an ambulance was called. The hospital doctors warned me that she was hours from death. But obstinacy has its advantages and she survived.

We both like the new Home. She has a large, light, en-suite bedroom with a view stretching out towards the sky and the clouds. The lounge is spacious, the chairs are spaced sufficiently apart to allow their inhabitants room to stretch, and the staff are positively cheerful. It does not smell of pee.

When I walk in, she is sitting propped up in her reclining chair, her head sunk forwards, her cheeks like withered tissue paper, her eyes closed, her mouth hanging open.

'Hi.' I lean down to speak into her ear.

She does not reply and I am afraid.

I touch her hand and she wakes. She peers at me, not yet focused, unclear who I might be. Then her eyes sharpen and she smiles. She suddenly looks alive. She nods. She is happy to see me.

I am in luck.

I am hunting for a hinterland. But the guardians of the past are dying and my mother is neither with us, nor is she dead.

I want my mother to talk to me about hidden territory.

'How are you?' I first ask.

But she says nothing. Her skin is too grey, but I can see the veins pulsing in her neck. Finally, I ask her why she isn't speaking.

'You are beautiful,' she replies.

Why have I disliked my mother most of my life? Have I forgotten the good times? For a moment, when she tells me that I am beautiful, I know that she loves me.

Then she returns to silence, putting her warm knotted hand over mine in an act of unique tenderness. I am terrified that she is about to die.

A moment later, she takes her hand away. All is normal.

I ask about Sarah and Elizabeth. Does she know them?

'No.'

'Has she ever heard of them?'

'No.'

This is familiar territory.

I lean over towards her: 'You went to the USSR?' I am about to enter a forbidden land.

'Who told you that?'

'You did go, then?'

'It's a long time ago.'

'You went to Moscow?'

She nods.

'Why did you go?' I wish I could expect a truthful answer.

'I was interested.'

'What was it like there?'

'You had to spend the whole day queuing.' She wrinkles up her nose at me, to emphasise how awful it had been.

'How long were you there?'

My mother hangs her head. Something is up.

'I can't remember.'

'What were you doing there?'

'I was a translator.'

So she is sticking to this fabrication.

'You speak Russian?' I ask.

'I can translate into four languages.'

'Did you want to stay?'

I catch an expression that I don't understand.

She frowns at me and states with much emphasis: 'I can't remember. It was a long time ago.'

The conversation has been terminated. The past beckons me to enter its pages, but its owner denies me access.

'I'm going on a 'Hands off Lebanon, End Israeli Aggression Now' demonstration this afternoon. I have to go,' I tell her in a loud voice, imagining the near-apoplexy of some of the residents when they hear my betrayal: didn't Israel provide our families with a homeland when no other country would take us in? Hezbollah is trying to drive us again into the sea, and this snake in the grass turns on her own.

But my mother nods at me; 'I don't approve of the nature of Israel either,' her expression says. I'm reassured, both by her approval and her awareness. Leaving, I raise the clenched fist salute of solidarity to her. She raises her fist high. For a moment, she appears proud. Deeply moved, I glance back at her from the hall. She is already dozing, but her face has changed.

Chapter 56

'I saw your friend in the street,' Sam informs me, as he swings his bike through the front door into the passageway, yet again scraping the paint off the hall wall.

'Do watch that bike!'

'You should move that bench.'

'Which friend?'

'That man you talked to for ages at the door.'

'Ruben? The bald one?'

'That's him. He was with a woman.'

I try to look unconcerned.

'They were holding hands.'

The world gets a whole lot darker.

'What was she like?'

'Thin. Younger than you. Long hair. Didn't see her properly.'

So that's why he hadn't been in touch for such a long time.

'What were they doing?'

'Don't know. Talking.'

'Did he see you?'

'Very unlikely. I was going very fast.'

'No helmet?'

'Of course not.'

'Mistake.'

'I've never had an accident.'

'The point about accidents is that you don't know they are going to happen. You still get hurt.'

But it's I who feel as if I've been run over.

Chapter 57

One day when I get home and compulsively check my emails, I discover Leon has contacted me.

Your letter was a lovely surprise, **he emails.** I am not sure how we are related. **He signs off with,** New beginnings.

I had plucked his address out of my father's address book. I remembered my mother had once referred to a young boy called Leon. Assuming an intimacy which did not exist, I wrote to him.

I am excited to have made contact. We try to establish how we're related. He knows more than me because his mother had talked about their family past. We work out that his mother was my mother's cousin. They had lived in the same street, and played together. My mother, Leon tells me, was always bossing his mother about.

Leon's grandmother, parents, and sister had all fled Germany and escaped to Palestine just before the outbreak of the War. Not much political insight, then, I think, proudly aware of my politically savvy parents who escaped in 1933. He'd been born in Israel, but had left home straight after school, first for New York, later for San Francisco.

Why did you leave? **I ask in my next email.**

In order to have a better life, **he replies.**

Not because you disapproved of Israel? **I query.**

I did disagree with some if its policies, **he confides,** but I still support Israel's existence.

Do you still have your dark curls?

Sadly too old for that, **comes back his reply.** I became officially bald when I reached my fifties, a couple of years back.

I tell him about clearing my parents' house and finding all the old letters. He writes back,

I know this may sound a bit dumb, but try to enjoy the excitement. We all have a curiosity about where we come from and what that might mean. We are lucky if we find stories, some of us sooner, some later, and can develop a sense of kinship.

We start to correspond regularly. It feels like coming home.

Soon, he phones me. We introduce ourselves. I like his deep voice.

'Why did my parents cut themselves off from your part of the family?' I've been waiting to ask him this.

'Louise and Emil did not want anything to do with the Jewish part of the family.'

My stomach suddenly starts to tense and contract. I don't want to hear what he is telling me.

'Didn't your mother try to stay in touch with Louise?'

'I don't think there was much response. Your mother saw my mother as inferior. And Jewish.'

I want to defend my mother. Instead, I ask, 'You count yourself as the Jewish part of the family?'

I could hear Leon laughing thousands of miles away. 'Being a Jew is the most important part of me.'

'What does that mean?'

'I'm not religious. Don't get me wrong. But it's how I was brought up. It's the food I eat, the celebrations I enjoy, whom I want to spend my time with.'

'I'm not Jewish.'

'How can you say that? Didn't you celebrate Hanukkah?' I hear Leon asking me.

'I don't even know what that is. Why should I know about these alien rituals?'

Leon is roaring with amusement.

'I'd be Jewish as far as the Nazis were concerned,' I continue. 'But I believe whether I'm Jewish or not is something I can decide to adopt or to refuse.'

'But your parents were Jewish.'

'No, they weren't. They rejected being Jewish.'

'How is that possible? You can't just say, 'I'm not Jewish'. That's to reject who you are, and the history of your family. It's like letting the Nazis win.'

'My father took to the streets against the Nazis because they were anti-democratic and anti-rationalist, as well as anti-Semitic. He did not oppose them as a Jew.'

'I'm so pleased you contacted me. It's amazing. I'm so very happy,' is Leon's response.

'I'm amazed to have found you. We're family now,' I tell him, delighted. Yet, at the same time, I feel he has emerged from a different planet.

I suddenly hear my father telling me:

'You're right, Anna.'

'Papa?'

'Being Jewish is not the point at all. If you want to stop a mass movement like Nazism, then you need to build a mass movement.'

'I'm so proud of you, Papa. You understood far earlier than most the way the wind was blowing. I'm proud that you were already organising against the Nazis back in 1929. It took courage to stand up against those street gangs and murderers. Even you didn't understand just how far anti-Semitism lay at its core.' I strain to catch his voice which is fading in and out.

'Don't tell me what I know, Anna. I watched the Nazis organising in the bierkellers of Munich to bring down the Weimar Republic. They wanted to destroy all democratic organisations, particularly of the working-class movement. The people the Nazis imprisoned in 1933 were the left and the trade-unionists, not the Jews. You forget that. The only way to have stopped the Nazis would have been for all the left and anti-Nazi groups to have agreed on a united approach, not based on sectional interests, like being Jewish.'

'You did not see yourself as Jewish, did you, Papa? You told me that you were a Catholic.'

No response.

'You remember Leon, Papa? He doesn't accept that I'm not Jewish. He believes that's anti-Semitic.'

'You've been mixing with the wrong people, Anna. Why do you think we never introduced you to the rest of the family? Some Jews were active anti-Nazis or socialists, but others colluded, or even collaborated with the Nazis. 'Better to work with them, than against them,' they said. Don't ever forget that, Anna.'

'But Papa, when I hear that Israel is bombing Lebanon, I feel culpable in a way I do not in Darfur or Iraq, though their dead are many. But how is that possible when I'm not Jewish?'

207

'Anna, Anna.' My father gives one of his exasperated sighs. *'I told you to stay out of politics.'*
'Papa. Aren't you proud of me?'

But I cannot hear the reply.

Chapter 58

I had tried to persuade Aphro to go on the 'Ceasefire Now' demonstration with me. One thousand Lebanese have been killed and many more wounded, almost all civilians.

'Demonstrations really aren't my thing. Do you think that the two million march against the invasion of Iraq made the slightest bit of difference?' she asked me.

But, in the morning she rang, and explained she was coming because this time Israel had gone a bit too far. We agreed to meet en route to Marble Arch.

She is wearing sandals, I note, not the favoured footwear of the experienced demonstrator. But it is a warm, clear summer's day and at least she's here.

I cannot bear the bombing of Lebanon. While the modern techniques of warfare which target civilians are generally barbaric, and the bombing of Dresden, an 'enemy' city, was, as I see it, a war crime, Israel's aggression against Lebanon particularly gets to me. How can the Israeli state and so many of its people, the heirs of the victims of the Holocaust, become the perpetrators of such carnage. I can deny being Jewish all I like. But many of my family were killed for being Jewish and some of my distant relatives escaped to Palestine. It could be their Israeli children who are now responsible for the attack on Lebanon.

My parents fled the Nazis to watch and weep in foreign lands. Now the Lebanese flee for their lives. I cannot watch the news. The man wails over his dead family. 'Why did you spare me?' he moans. I find I'm crying for my family as well as for him. It feels as if it is they who are being murdered. History has a long arm. Even my far-seeing parents did not expect that their defeat by the Nazis would make possible Israeli bombs raining upon the people of southern Lebanon.

Would I feel differently if my grandparents had got themselves to Palestine and survived? Maybe then my grandparents would still have been alive when I was born, and my mother could have celebrated my birth with a lighter heart.

Aphro and I are inevitably arguing. Hyde Park is packed with demonstrators and we wait endlessly for the march to set off.

'For every Israeli, six Lebanese have been killed,' I tell her.

'The death of an Israeli child is no less tragic than the death of a Lebanese child,' Aphro retorts.

'I refuse to make a moral equivalence between the aggressor State and a people trying to protect themselves.'

'That's what Israel says: that it has to protect itself,' protests Aphro.

'While Israel exists as a settler state, refusing Palestinians their rights, taking over their land and leaving them in refugee camps, it will inevitably be vulnerable to attack. It's always playing on the fear of the 'other' at their gate. No ceasefire is ever going to hold.'

'You will lose a lot of public sympathy with that position,' Aphro chides me.

'Sometimes one has to take sides. I critically supported the Vietcong against the Americans. I go on demos demanding America get out of Iraq now.'

'You can't support Hezbollah!'

'Yesterday's terrorist is today's freedom fighter. You know that, Aphro. Mandela is really popular now, right? Statue going up near Parliament. But I was marching for his release from prison when he was condemned as a terrorist, and his side were putting burning tyres round the necks of their enemies.'

'It's the USA's fault, really. They let Israel get away with murder because they want it as a military outpost.'

I nod, taken aback at our sudden concord. Yet, blaming the USA is the easy option. I wonder what Leon perceives as the USA's role in the Middle East. But it is Israel, not America, that is the main target of my visceral anger.

The phone rings the moment I get home from the demonstration.

'It's Leon. There's something I have to tell you.'

I've walked for four hours calling for a 'Ceasefire Now' and 'Israel out of Lebanon'. 'Could this wait?' I suggest. All I want is to sink onto my bed and watch whatever is on TV.

'I'm thinking of going to Israel,' Leon continues.

'You can't.'

'I'm going to visit the graves of my mother and grandmother.'

Would Leon have gone on a similar demonstration, I suddenly wonder. 'Israel is a terrorist state,' I retort.

'What would have happened to my family, Anna? Where were they supposed to go? You're suggesting that the Israelites should again have to wander the earth?'

'Of course not!' I shout down the line. 'But there will never be peace while Israel exists in its present form.'

'What was left of free Europe had all but closed its doors to refugees. You know that. If my family hadn't escaped to Palestine, they would have perished.'

'Of course I'm not arguing that your parents shouldn't have found a home in Palestine. But I'm against the establishment of an Israeli state for Jews only, when the land was already inhabited by Palestinians. Anyway, there are now more Jews in New York than Israel!'

'Did you know that the USA had such a strict quota system that most of the Jews on the immigration lists never made it to America?'

I think of my grandparents and say nothing. Though Leon's family were torn from their home and country, unlike mine they had all survived. He had even lived with his grandmother as a child. She had told him the stories of his forebears. No ghosts at his table. That divides Leon and me.

'I'm meeting up with a Palestinian-Israeli peace group,' Leon is telling me. 'I'm going to try to persuade Israelis to be more critical of their actions.'

'We have to demand one secular Israeli-Palestinian state. How can a religious state solve racism? It's a contradiction. The existence of Israel will never get rid of today's Nazis, anti-Semitism or ethnic cleansing. If anything, the opposite is happening.'

'One united state between Israelis and Palestinians is a wonderful idea, Anna. But it's not realistic. For now, we have to demand that Israel should withdraw to its 1967 borders.'

'It isn't safe, Leon. Go some other time.'

'It will be five years since my mother died. I have to visit her grave.'

211

'Have you been before?'
'No. This will be the first time since her funeral.'
'Not a good time.'
'Doesn't feel like much of a choice.'
'Stay alive for me, Leon.'

Chapter 59

'Enquiry' from Louise via British Red X
1.4.42 Dear Vater, Thanks for your answer in January. We are all healthy and long for you. Stay healthy and strong for us till we see you again.

Answer:
21.5.42 February letter gave me joy. I am healthy. Address unchanged. I am trying to cope with everything that comes and make sense of it love, Johann

20.5.42 Today, on 5 May, the first birthday of my beloved wife after her death. So many thoughts assail me once more that I have to relieve my soul and speak to you.

This letter is not signed, nor addressed, nor does it come via the Red Cross. But it surely is from Vater to his darling daughter Louise.

Reply, via Red Cross
19.6.42 Dear children, April letter gave me joy. I'm healthy and undauntedly and undeterred working. I hope to stay at the old address. All my love, Johann

This is the last letter.

Chapter 60

I try to hear you, Johann. I'm reading your last letters from 1942. Every word is weighed.

No more appeals from you to be allowed to leave. It is too late, and you know it. You are living through a novel stage of horror. When you write, 'I am still at my old address,' I know you are warning Louise that 'they' are trying to get you out. You're afraid. You weren't allowed to stay at the old address for long.

You say to yourself: at least my darling Rosa was spared this. That is something to celebrate. I could not have protected you, my liebschen. At least, we have the comfort that our children, Emil and Louise are safe. That alone is a blessing.

He is sitting in the heavy armchair, which he had asked a younger neighbour to move for him, so that he can see out of the window onto the lime trees. He regrets the absence of the lacy doily which used to hang over the back of the chair, protecting it from wear. His collar is rubbing his neck. Can't be because he's getting any fatter. He remembers how Rosa always had a supply of fresh collars.

The maid, Trude, who had been with the family since the children were babies, had helped, but she too must be getting on in years. He hears a discrete knock at the door and there she is. He tells himself that he is lucky. She isn't supposed to visit a Jew, never mind work for one. He cannot afford to pay her anything, and he hopes therefore that what she is doing does not count, in a strict sense, as working Not that the Gestapo understood sense.

She had brought some food a few days back, covered with a napkin. Arrived with her woven basket swinging off her arm, went into the kitchen, and with a proud smile extracted a little sausage and black bread. He hadn't asked her, of course, how she had come by it. She was always so upright. He had no need to worry. He had been embarrassed, explaining that he couldn't pay her, but she had said it was for old time's sake. His family had always been good to her. He runs his finger under his collar. His collar never used to chafe like this. His neck is getting sore.

214

'If only, Louise, you hadn't got involved in all that mischief,' he thinks. 'You were the baby of our family, our favourite.' He smiles at the memory of the little girl who always had her head in a book. Just like him. 'You left us so young. We hardly had time to get to know you before you were off on your own path. You were always a bit of a rebel, weren't you, Louise?' and he smiles again, seeing her standing before him. 'You fly too close to the sun,' he warns her. 'Beware. But I shall always be here for you,' he starts to tell her. Then he stops. He strokes the top of his high, bald-domed head. 'Louise, come to me', he calls out aloud, 'before it is too late. Louise, can you hear me?' And he buries his handsome head in his hands and weeps.

Chapter 61

The Red Cross correspondence is all mixed up. My father must have just crammed everything together into the large brown envelope. What was the point of sorting out letters, he must have thought. Won't bring anybody back. It is I, the granddaughter, who, too late, tries to piece together what befell my mother's father. It is I who now must not fall apart.

Mixed in with the letters between Louise and her father, are letters from Louise to the International Red Cross, trying to find out whether her father was still alive. It is difficult to put them into a logical sequence. One letter enquiring about Louise's father's welfare is dated before another letter from her father arrives. The post between Germany and the UK must have been taking months. Louise must have hoped beyond hope that her father's letters were simply delayed. Did Emil comfort her? Did he tell her: 'There's no point worrying. Another letter will arrive in due course.' But I don't think that is what he said.

From Louise to Red Cross
22.10.41 I am enquiring about the whereabouts of my father. I hope you can help me

From Louise to Red Cross
23.6.42 I am very worried that I have not heard from my father. Father wrote to a friend stating that he had been told to leave his flat. I am particularly worried given what has befallen the other members of my family. During 1940/41, my mother died, and my sister died following deportation. I am especially anxious given the recent deportations to Poland. Please could you find out more.

From Louise to Red Cross

5.2.43 I have not heard from my father, since his letter of June 42. Could you please continue with your enquiries?

Chapter 62

My mother hated Germany. That is what she told me. Would never put a foot on German soil ever again. She did not make that fine but crucial distinction, as my father had, that it was the Nazis, not the Germans, who had murdered her family, who had robbed her of her father, when they killed him for being Jewish.

Even so, this is only one part of her truth. If anywhere represented 'home' to her in old age, it was her parents' flat in Charlottenburg. When she insisted on singing German songs in the first of her Jewish care homes, despite the attempts of the staff to stop her, what was she doing if not, consciously or unconsciously, proclaiming her 'German-ness'. When she believed Sam was supporting the German football team against England, how great was her happiness. 'That's my grandson,' she had proclaimed, beaming, while Sam protested in vain that she had misheard.

'Why don't I have grandparents?' Sam had asked me once when he was a young boy. We were walking the dog across Hampstead Heath, back in the days when the dog was more Sam's than mine.

'Why, you *do*, darling. There's grandma.' I remind him. I do not refer to the absence of his father's parents. That will have to wait.

'She doesn't count.'

'It's a pity Grandpa died when you were a baby.'

'I don't remember him.'

'You were only just over a year. I'm glad for him he knew he had a grandson.'

'Was he nice to me?'

'He adored you. He came to see you in the hospital almost every day after you were born. He wrote you a poem. It said that your birth alone made his life worth living.'

'Did grandma come?'

'Well, of course, once or twice. She was pleased, too.'

Sam had found a stick and thrown it for the dog. The dog had never understood the rules of the game. He retrieved the stick but lay down with it for a chew. Sam was trying to pull the stick out of the dog's mouth. Our conversation was over.

Even when Sam was little, I had wondered at how difficult my mother found being a grandmother. I remember how I'd once asked her whether she could babysit for me for half a day as my child minder was unavailable, so I could get to work

'Oh no,' she had told me, 'I always have a bath in the mornings.'

I took Sam into work with me and knew never to ask her again. There was the time we all went for a walk together in the local park, and I left Sam in Grandma's care while I bought ice-creams, to return, a few minutes later, to discover neither child nor grandmother. Distraught, I found Sam playing, unconcerned and out of sight, down the hill. Grandmother, I was much later to establish, had set off for the bus stop to take herself home. It was one of many times that she marched off on Sam and me, but I never left Sam alone with her again.

Now I know far more. When my parents celebrated the bloody defeat of the Nazis at Stalingrad in 1942 and decided the world was safe enough to bring forth another child, did they anticipate that the Nazis, understanding they were defeated, would stop their killing of the Jews (for make no mistake, this was known about), and I would have a grandfather? Did my mother hope, as I lay, a gurgling baby in her arms, that she would introduce me to her father? That once the war was over, her father would enfold me in his arms and bless her child?

How could she be Sam's grandmother when her own father had not been there for her and her child. Or is it rather that grief and guilt had sucked dry the well of love?

It is hard without grandparents to draw on ancient wisdoms or have the security of knowing that there is a world before that of one's parents. The future starts to look uncertain when there is no past.

219

Chapter 63

'Ruben, can I meet up with you?'

'Come over.'

Whether because or despite of his own experiences, Ruben, I knew, would hear me. He lives, I discover, in a road less than five minutes' walk from me. He leads me straight into the kitchen, an immaculate space which, to my surprise, sports a surfeit of stainless-steel surfaces.

'A drink?' He had taken my coat and is hanging it up in his hallway.

'Water.'

'What's wrong?' His green eyes seek mine.

'I think I know what happened to my grandparents.'

'You haven't said 'grandparents' before.'

'I haven't had grandparents before. I want to talk to them.'

Silence.

'The dead can hear you, you know,' Ruben says softly.

'Don't be silly.'

'How do you know they can't? *You* can hear what you have to say to them. I find that's some sort of comfort.'

'I want to say, 'Come back. I wish you had got away. I wish you had been there for me'.'

Ruben keeps silent. My eyes are filling.

'Come into the garden,' he suggests, opening up the sliding patio doors. We step outside into a small, walled paradise and sit down carefully at opposite ends of the wooden bench.

'My life would have been so different if my grandparents had lived. My mother would have been happier. And I would have known more about who I was.'

'How's that?'

'I don't mean that blood is everything, but knowing your grandparents helps to know where you come from.'

'They were probably nineteenth century ogres.'

'Possibly. They certainly didn't do right by Marthe.'

'She was your mother's sister, the one who wasn't as bright as her?'

'Yes. My mother, I suspect, also felt compromised by

220

her parents' behaviour towards her sister. That could have been hindsight, of course. I know she wanted to get away from her parents as soon as she could. And actually she can't have known, any more than her parents did, that the Nazis would murder Marthe. I need to find a way to mourn them.'

'Have you found out something new?'

'Rosa, my grandmother, died a natural death after all. The plaque for people who died in the camps in my mother's house in Berlin was wrong.'

'You know, some inaccuracies are inevitable, given the numbers . . .'

'Yes. I think it was knowing her daughter had been deported that killed her.'

'I didn't know you knew that.'

'I don't know if I do. There's half a sentence in a letter from my mother to the Red Cross that refers to Marthe being deported. I don't know how my mother would have known or how reliable that is. But it's probably true, isn't it? Maybe Rosa felt implicated. She probably never knew for certain what had happened to her daughter, but she will have guessed. Then she took to her bed and didn't ever really get up again. Not much different from being killed.'

Ruben gives me a keen look. 'You could organise a ceremony of some sort. That's one way of talking to them. Then you might feel less that they have been taken away from you.' And he adds, 'Every year, on my daughter's birthday, I organise something.'

'Does it help you?'

'Well. That's one of those unanswerable questions. I continue to do it. That's as much as I can tell you.'

I try hard not to cry.

'I think my grandfather was murdered,' comes bursting out of me.

'How do you know?'

'In June 1942, my mother sends a panicky letter to the Red Cross, asking them to find out what has happened to her father. She wouldn't have known, even when she got a letter from him, whether he was still alive or not.'

'Can you imagine what that must have been like? First her sister, then her mother, and then, fearing that her father was also lost. Losing *one* member of my family, was like losing my soul,' Ruben murmurs.

221

'I can't bear that this good man was being torn apart for no other reason than his Jewishness. I can't bear that Johann was blessing his child, Louise, while his life was under threat. I hope you're right. I hope he can hear me talking to him. I hope he knows he is remembered.'

Ruben puts his arms around me softly. 'You've done so well,' he says quietly into my ear. 'But now it's time to open a bottle of wine. We will toast your grandparents.'

He goes off into the kitchen, fetches a bottle, hands me a glass and pours.

'It's 6pm. We're allowed to drink,' he tells me. And then he lifts up his glass and says: 'To your grandmother and grandfather.'

I raise my glass and stare at the rich yellowy wine: 'Prost.'

'Don't cry,' he tells me, fishing a large ironed handkerchief out of his pocket and gently wiping my eyes. Then he hands it to me: 'Keep it.'

Shaking, I lean up against his shining, stainless steel hob and take another sip, but find it has lost its taste.

'What happened to your parents?' I ask.

'Till death do us part. Except that it did. Bloody early too. My father died in his sixties. About the same age as I am now. Heart attack. My mother had a great time after that. Would never have thought it of her.'

'Did she remarry?'

'No, but not for lack of proposals.'

'Did you mind?'

'Why should I? I'd left home anyway by then.'

'Did she talk to you about your dad?'

'Not particularly, but I'd a large family. Impossible to keep secrets for long. Everybody knew everybody else's business. Quite unbearable.'

'I wish I'd had a large family.'

Ruben looks at me for an unusually long time. I feel myself getting hotter. Then he says carefully: 'Try not to live too much in the past.'

'I have to find out what happened.'

'But do you feel better as a result? Have you laid your ghosts?'

'I've learnt to hear some of what was never said.'

'Anna, there is no way of going back to the past,

222

however much we might long to. A few everyday pleasures wouldn't come amiss.'

He is smiling at me, but I can't make out what he is telling me.

'Who was that woman who answered the phone that time I rang you?' suddenly bursts out of me.

'So that's what's upsetting you.' Ruben winks at me, and says, 'A mistake.'

He comes up behind me and puts his arms around my body, the first time he has hugged me since our first re-union. Kisses me on the neck. Takes a gentle nibble. I can feel myself melting in the warmth of his body against mine.

Then he whispers: 'I can't do this now. I didn't know you were coming. You understand?' And unfolding himself from my body, he nods at me. Wanting me to nod back.

He finds my coat and helps me into it. Leads me to the front door by the hand.

'Ring me if you need me.'

I walk down the stairs and do not turn to look back at him.

Chapter 64

'Did you love my father?' Sam asks me over Sunday lunch. I hope to cover my confusion by pushing a large quantity of roast chicken with red cabbage and stuffing into my mouth.

'How old was I when I last saw him?'

'He last visited you when you were six.'

'I want to meet him.'

'Good.'

'Good'? Did you want me?'

'Darling, I wanted you more than anything in the world.'

'Did my dad want me?'

Try for the truth. 'He wasn't sure at the very beginning, when you were still in my tummy, but he wanted to be with me when you were born, and then he was so pleased he went out and got a red rose.' I hope I don't have to go into more detail at this point, but Sam does not press.

'I want his address.'

'OK.' I tell him, nodding emphatically, while I feel lightning travelling along the nerve-ways of my body. I had always hoped that one day Sam would want to find his father and yet I also fear it. What will come tumbling out of the emotional cupboard? I regard my almost-grown-up son and remember how his father had failed to turn up for his weekly Friday visit one sunny July afternoon all those years ago, without any explanation before or after, and how his son had sat on the staircase leading to the front door, despite all my attempts at comfort and distraction, every Friday afternoon after school, for years and years, waiting for his father's knock.

'I'm going over to see him this afternoon. My friend, Joel, is coming with me.'

I glance up at Sam. He is talking as if finding his father is an everyday event. He must have discussed this life-changing moment with Joel. I am shaken by the disappearance of my baby boy and the appearance of this brave young man.

'OK. Does your father know you're coming?' I ask.

'How would he?'

'Do you want a lift? I'll drop you off nearby.' My arrangements for the afternoon are no longer important.

'OK.'

'I think it's great, but why now?'

'He's my dad, that's all.'

I cancel my plans, and, heart in mouth, drop the two of them off.

'I love you, Sam,' I call after them, as he and Joel disappear into the broad doorway of the Edwardian block of flats.

When Sam gets back late that evening, I enquire how it went.

'All right,' he says, then adds, sounding indignant. 'Why did you call after me: 'I love you'?'

Chapter 65

'It's Elizabeth,' a clipped English voice at the other end of the phone informs me.

It's almost 10pm. I am watching TV, lying on my bed, and not at my tactful best. 'Oh,' is all I can manage.

'There was a child,' Elizabeth announces.

I think back quickly to our previous conversation about the deaths of her grandmother and her children, frantically trying to remember what Elizabeth had already told me.

'In Germany? Your grandparents had another child?' I query.

'Probably.'

'Why do you think that?'

'There was talk that a child survived.'

'Whose talk?'

'I think it was my mother's. Something about somebody phoning her.'

'The child phoned her?'

'Perhaps.'

'But there was a phone call?'

'He traced her, anyway.'

'Was he your mother's brother?'

'I think he was adopted.'

'How on earth did he find you?'

'My mother was only four when they put her on the Kindertransport.'

'Elizabeth, what is it you want to tell me?'

'That's it, really.'

'Imagine this boy,' I suggest. 'He is found by a kind German couple who heard crying and discover a little child with flaxen hair and blue eyes, not much more than a baby, hidden away in an abandoned flat. Their son had been killed on the Russian front and they took the boy as their own. The boy grows up and has children of his own. He starts trying to work out who he really is, and what the people who had become his parents might have been.'

'That's all make-believe.' Elizabeth sounds furious.

'Has he contacted you? Is that what's happened?'

226

'No. Yes. But it just wouldn't work. Not given who I am. I'm a happily married woman. You do understand. I can't reverse what happened because of the Nazis. Nobody can.'

Chapter 66

I run into the house to answer the ringing phone.

'Could I speak to Fraulein Weilheimer, bitte.'

'Entschuldigung?'

'Dr Brandt here. I am the person looking into what happened to Berlin's Jews. I have news for you.'

'Hello. Yes?'

'I did research after I received your letter.'

'Yes.'

'I have found out what happened to your grandmother.'

'Yes.'

'Yes. I also know exactly where she is buried. It is better if you come over and we talk. Yes?'

'Yes.'

In a letter I'd found from a Herr Messerschmidt in my father's files, I'd found what might have been a clue to where my grandmother was buried. It was to my mother in Oxford, dated 1946. Part of it read:

I can make enquiries about your mother's grave when I go to Weisensee [the Jewish cemetery on outskirts of Berlin] but I go seldom. It is questionable whether it can be found. In the office, I will only be given a field and a row but since the wooden plaques have been completely destroyed by the weather in the last few years, you can't tell one grave from another in the new fields.

Deeply upset, I imagined a field outside Berlin where the bodies of dead Jews are shovelled quickly into the earth, with no marking to tell who has been buried there. I have to find out.

I shall go to visit my grandmother's grave. I want to carry flowers. I want to throw myself down on the grave. And shout: 'I'm here! I survived!'

I want to believe that she will know that I am there. I, a disbeliever, want to believe that she knows I have found her. That it was not all in vain. That they have a granddaughter, and a great-grandson.

Should I pay for a small headstone? Is there indeed a grave? Let me be practical here. I know from Herr Messerschmidt's letter that she was buried in a dug-up field. I still need to find out what is really there. Did she, amongst so many others who died during the war, have no grave? Or is there a grave of some sort? Does it matter?

I wish to have a grandmother. I shall honour her.

'Why was I never told anything about you?' I want to shout. 'Do you know who I am? What business did you have not living long enough to say hello? How could you leave me with my parents? I did not feel loved.'

You will not know. You will not return. Your ashes will remain dust. But I shall go and weep by my grandmother's grave.

Sam, his friend Joel and I, are waiting at Stansted airport on our way to Berlin. To my delight and surprise, Sam wanted to go too, on condition he could bring a friend. 'It's a free holiday,' he had informed me when I tried asking him why he was coming. I am scheduled to see Dr Brandt.

I can see two girls wandering across the waiting area in our direction.

'Are you brothers?' one of them asks.

I hide behind *The Guardian*, pretending to read. I hear Sam and Joel guffaw.

'I'm the older one,' Sam is declaring.

'Why do you tell them that? Just because you're taller,' Joel retorts.

'And the more beautiful. Look into my eyes.'

Can this be my darling son speaking? This time, I can hear the girls giggling.

One of them is saying, 'But you have fair straight hair and green eyes, and he has dark curly hair and brown eyes.'

'I'm the handsome one,' Joel is stating.

'We have the same mother but different fathers,' Sam explains, wickedly.

On the plane, I ask Sam whether he is coming to see Dr Brandt with me that afternoon.

'How long will it last?'

'As long as it takes. Why?'

'I'll come with you if Joel can come too.'

The three of us are seated in an arc waiting for Dr Brandt in his office, which is attached to the Synagogue. Dr Brandt bustles in, his presence filling the room, and heaves himself into his chair behind his desk. I have already informed him of my questions. He addresses us in impeccable English.

'I checked the records for Rosa Zweig,' he informs us. 'She died a natural death.'

'But my mother told me that her mother, Rosa, died in a camp. And the inscription on the wall in her house also says she was taken away.' I forget about the letter which described Rosa's final resting place as an unmarked field. I find it hard to remember what I know, and even harder to make sense of it all.

'I have checked exceedingly carefully. She died in the Jewish Hospital in 1941,' Dr Brandt assures me.

'Jewish hospital?'

Do I detect a moment's hesitation? 'The hospital was allowed to continue. Her husband, Johann, visited her there and was involved in organising her funeral. She has a marked grave. Her husband was there when she was buried.' He looks at me to check whether I understand his meaning. I am wiping away the torrent of tears with my hand.

'Johann was still free then?'

'Exactly.'

'Do you know what she died of?'

Again that look. 'It was a natural death. I am sure of that. Unfortunately, the detailed records were lost when the hospital was bombed.'

Only much later did I understood what he was implying about the role of the Jewish hospital in the fatal destiny of some of its patients.

'I understand you would like her death certificate?'

'Yes. I wrote to you that the Red Cross explained how complicated that was. That I need a money order.'

'Your mother did not obtain the certificate?'

'No.'

Another look. He opens a book, makes a phone call, and disappears round the door of his office.

'Why are you bothering?' Sam asks in the lull.

'I want to honour her. I wish to have her as my grandmother.'

'I find that strange. The importance of the family can be exaggerated.'

Is Sam being intentionally obtuse? I glower at him; he replies with a noisy shrug.

Dr Brandt has reappeared. Almost bowing, he hands me the death certificate.

'A gift,' he advises me, brushing aside my proffered Euros, as I try to wipe away my tears.

'What about . . . Marthe?'

'Ah. Not much luck there, I fear. Tell me what you know again.'

'She was in a psychiatric clinic near or in Berlin. I don't really know why. I suspect her parents placed her there, probably in 1932 or 33.'

'Ah. The date matters, of course.' Another knowing look. 'How was she related to you again?'

'She was my mother's elder sister.'

'And does she have any other relatives?'

'Only my mother, but she has dementia.'

'She never wanted to find out?'

'She couldn't bear to find out.'

'And why do you want to find out?'

'I owe her. She would have been my aunt. I don't want her memory to be lost. It's as if she had never been born.'

'Shut up, Mum,' Sam growls at me.

'I understand, but there is the difficulty that you are not the next of kin. It is very difficult to gain access to records like these.' Dr Brandt sounds sympathetic. 'Also, many of the records were destroyed, either deliberately by the Nazis or as a result of Allied bombing. Records that survived are generally still unresearched.'

I stare at him.

'There has been some hesitation over looking into this area of Nazi crimes.'

'By 'this area', you mean the records relating to the euthanasia of 'mad' people?'

'Correct.'

'Suffering is graded, is it? First come the Jews, then the communists, and the 'imbeciles' come last.'

231

'Something like that. But I'm sure you understand there's more to it than that.' Another look. Then, Dr Brandt suddenly announces: 'I have an idea.'

He reaches for the phone and makes a couple of long calls, in German.

Then he informs me: 'Marthe was still alive in 1939. It isn't clear what happened next.'

'She was not alive in 1940?'

'She was still alive in 1939.'

'In the Clinic?'

'In the Clinic.'

'What happened next?'

Dr Brandt is looking at me. How many interviews like this he must have endured. 'You know as much as you need to about what happened next.'

I have to ask: 'Injection?'

'Maybe.'

'Deportation?'

'Very possible. This is a very difficult area. It was only sixty years ago.'

I stare at him. What is he telling me? What can it mean? It is so difficult to comprehend such unbearable news. It is almost as if it is not real, as in a dream.

I get up to thank Dr Brandt, aware he will not say more. So my mother was right in that brief reference to M's deportation in her letter to the Red Cross. How and what had she known?

Dr Brandt is suggesting we all go for a coffee and cake at the café next door.

The proprietor looks as if he is Turkish, or maybe Lebanese. Another refugee. They clearly know Dr Brandt well. He comes over to our round, formica-topped table and I order coffee and 'Apfelkuchen mit Sahne' for the three of us. Dr Brandt has already been presented with a cup of rich, sweet-smelling Turkish coffee. 'I'm trying to lose weight,' he informs us, but agrees to take a taste of mine.

'Is this the best of German cooking?' Sam demands. He has already consumed almost the whole cake.

'I love it,' I tell him.

'Whatever for?'

Dr Brandt laughs. 'It's better straight after they've baked

232

it,' he tells Sam. 'If you want real German cooking, go to southern Germany.'

'How come you don't speak German?' he asks me.

'My parents wanted me integrated.'

He nods.

'How come you are living in Germany?' I ask.

'My mother was hidden.'

'Here?'

'Yes. She spent the whole war in a cellar, unable to ever go out. The German family who looked after her risked their lives.'

'They got away with it?'

'Yes. She was one of a handful of Jews who survived in Berlin. She married one of their sons. But that wasn't why they hid her. She didn't know him till they took her in.'

'Do you remember that time with Grandma?' I ask Sam. 'It was the time of the European cup and Grandma was still coherent. Germany was playing England and she asked you which side you were supporting. You mocked her and said, 'I support Germany!' She misunderstood you and said, 'Oh, how wonderful! My grandson supports Germany.' And you got so cross and said, 'Of course not, I'm supporting *England*, Grandma,' but she didn't hear you.'

'Didn't want to hear me, more like,' adds Sam.

'But, so interesting. That, when the chips were down, she supported the side of the country which had killed her family and turned her into an exile.'

'She's mad,' is Sam's reply.

'It's not so simple. She never felt Britain was her home.' And I ask Sam, 'Do you think of yourself as British?'

'Of course I do. What else would I be?'

'I don't know what I think I am.' Joel speaks slowly. 'I was born in South Africa but my parents fled to London when I was very little. My sister is older than me and I think she sees herself as more South African than English. But we are Jewish as well.' He turns to Sam. 'How can you not see yourself as Jewish?

'I wasn't brought up to be Jewish. I hate all this PC rubbish about the importance of ethnicities.'

'Maybe I'm three things,' Joel replies.

'Are you OK?' Dr Brandt turns to ask me. 'I've brought you a map of where your grandmother is buried. I have it with me in my bag.' He starts opening the clips on his voluminous, creased leather attaché case, and fishes inside. 'The old Jewish cemetery is on the edge of Berlin.' He brings out two pieces of paper and hands them to me, pointing out where he has arrowed the cemetery and the exact burial site. 'It's easy to find. One tram ride.'

I stare at the sheets.

'It's a real cemetery? With marked graves?'

'But of course.'

My tears start to ooze out. Dr Brandt nods, aware, I guess, that he can never predict which bit of the information he imparts will upset. Rosa was not dumped into an unmarked grave after all

'The cemetery wasn't destroyed?'

'No. The newer cemetery in the centre of Berlin was smashed up, but Weissensee was far from the centre, and it miraculously escaped.'

'I can't cope with anything more today. I'll go tomorrow.'

'That's OK. They are open tomorrow. As you haven't made an appointment, you will have to find the grave yourself, but that should not be difficult.'

'I have a last question.' I hesitate before continuing. 'I can't decide whether to visit the camp where my grandfather died.'

'Theresienstadt?'

'Yes.'

'We don't need to do that. We carry our dead with us always. And we carry the grief. Who would it help if you went?'

I nod, comforted.

It is time to leave. We all shake hands. I thank him profusely, as he disappears to his next assignment.

'Don't get back too late,' I tell the boys, who are about to set out to explore Berlin.

'Oh, Mum, we can find our way around.'

'I'll get him back OK.' Joel nods reassuringly at me.

'Are you coming to the cemetery tomorrow? I want to make an early start.'

'Let's see how it goes,' Sam tells me.

The next day, I go alone to the cemetery. It was indeed

an easy journey. Once there, the map guides me quickly though tranquil wooded avenues, lined by old trees, still in leaf. The sun obligingly appears and slants its light through the boughs. It feels as if I am walking through a dappled misty glade in a German fairy story. I reach the stone, simple to spot because of its surprisingly large size. It is a family grave. There are four names written here, three of people I have never even heard of, all either born with or married into the Zweig's. Rosa's name was the last to be entered. The words on the tombstone are, I guess, in Hebrew. I'll have to get them translated. I take a picture.

The tombstone is set back from the avenue, at the head of the grave. Nobody has been here for a very long time. Luxuriant green weeds cradle the stone and curl in profuse knots across the earth. At the foot of the tombstone I lay a stone which I have carried from home. I had chosen it with care. Sam had decorated it, when a child, with beautiful rich colours and glittering tinsel. It glimmers at the foot of the grave. I sit down on the kerb of the grave. I have found my grandmother.

'I'm so pleased to have found you,' she tells me.

'I wish you'd been alive for me,' I say to her.

I hear her say, 'You must look after my daughter for me. I know she can be difficult, but she needs you now.'

'I've been looking for you,' I tell her, but I can't hear her reply.

In the airport lounge late the next day, waiting forever for the flight back home, I finally get a chance to ask Sam and Joel how it had gone.

'I love Berlin,' Sam informs me.

'How come?' My feelings are far more mixed than this.

'There's so much to see. We just wandered around. It's great. I'm going back some time.'

'We found the Tiergarten and walked along the river to the Theatre Island,' Joel informs me.

'Did you look at where the Berlin Wall was?'

'Yes. But we couldn't find the notice boards and signs and stuff about Nazism you told us about.'

'Did you go to the Jewish Museum?'

'It cost too much.'

'I wanted to go in.' Joel is pulling a face at Sam.

'Why? It all happened such a long time ago,' Sam retorts.

'I never got past the first bit. It's brilliantly done. But I found it too upsetting,' I confess. 'The Museum shows the different directions of the Diaspora on different corridors all diverging from one hub: from San Paolo, to the USA, through Holland, Italy, India, to China, just like our family.'

'We don't know any of them.'

'We might have known them if we'd all been able to stay in Germany.'

'But then there wouldn't have been a 'you' or a 'me', so how do we know what it would have been like? Ahha, ahha.'

'I dropped into the Synagogue museum as well.'

'How boring.'

'It shows that the leaders of the Berlin Jewish community collaborated with the Nazis right up to 1942, even on the deportations, I suspect.'

'Dr Brandt was hinting at something about the Jewish Hospital. Maybe that's it,' Joel adds. I hadn't realised he had been listening.

'What?' Sam's interest is slipping away.

'They should have been leading a fight back, not collaborating,' I argue. 'There wasn't even a mention of the Euthanasia programme in either the Jewish or Synagogue museums.'

'Why should there be?' objects Sam.

'Don't you know? Jews never have mental health problems.' Joel winks at me.

'Have you heard of the poem by Pastor Martin Niemöller?' I start to recite slowly:

'First they came for the Jews, and I did not speak out, because I was not a Jew.'

To my delight, Joel breaks in:

'Then they came for the Communists, and I did not speak out, because I was not a Communist.

Then they came for the trade unionists, and I did not speak out, because I was not a trade unionist.

Then they came for me, and there was no one left to speak out for me.'

On the way home in the car, I ask them: 'Are you hungry?'

Sam and Joel check silently with each other. 'Not really.'

'What have you eaten?'

'We had some disgusting German sausage in a roll for lunch. But we got a delicious Turkish kebab last night. Enormous. Somewhere around Friedrichstrasse. And it was so cheap. It only cost us about five euros each, it was really good. Not like German food,' Sam informs me.

'But it *is* German food now,' Joel replies.

I drive Joel home. As he is about to get out, he thanks me. 'I wouldn't have missed it for the world.'

'My pleasure,' I tell him. 'I was glad to have your company.' I glower at Sam.

'Me too.' Sam giggles.

Then Joel asks quietly, 'Will you keep going about your aunt?'

'I suspect the paths through this particular portal are still heavily guarded. But I will keep on looking for her.'

Chapter 67

I haven't told my mother that I have found her mother's grave. How would it go?

'By the way, Mother, I've found your mother's grave. I've visited it. It's in a Jewish cemetery. Your mother is lying with her parents.'

She might not respond. That would make it easy. Or perhaps she'll be upset. 'Why did you do that?' she will demand, reminding me of the mother of the past, for whom nothing I did could ever be right. She will not cry, for she never cries.

It feels as if I am poaching on her life, taking from her what is hers. Her mother, her loss. By what right do I claim it for my own?

I wonder why you never tried to find out what had happened to your mother. Maybe you thought: 'What is the point? Finding her grave will not bring her back to me.' Maybe you never wanted to set foot again on German soil, grave or no grave. The past is very noisy, is it not, Ma? You needed to stop your ears to its din.

Yet now I don't tell you either. What iniquity is this? I am protecting you. Just as you 'protected' me. Now, I deprive you of the life-blood of information, just as you did me. Kindness or cowardice?

My poor mother. All you had was Herr Messerschmidt's letter, which told you very little, except that there was probably no marked grave. And you never wanted to find out more.

Chapter 68

I invite Sam to celebrate his excellent A level grades. We walk to a nearby French restaurant, the sort where you pay to be given the impression you are sitting in a friend's dining room, eating home cooking. The waiter arrives to light the candle and gives Sam the wine menu. There's a first for everything.

After we've ordered, I ask: 'How's it going?'

'I don't want to talk about my dad.'

'OK.' Our family certainly excels at keeping secrets.

'I know what you did,' Sam confronts me.

I take a long mouthful of the deep red wine. I have not asked Sam again about his visit to his dad, not wanting him to feel I am prying into this embryonic relationship.

'You stopped him seeing me when I was little,' Sam continues.

'That isn't how I remember it.' I am shaken. How could Sam believe what he is accusing me of?

'I know what happened.'

'In that case, there's more than one version of what happened.' I'm amazed that I am able to say something so remarkably balanced.

'What's your version?' Sam retorts.

'Your father simply stopped coming to see you. He gave no warning and no explanation. I wrote him letters, pleading with him to see you. After a very long time, he wrote back that he wanted to start a new life.'

Sam is glaring at me.

'Even if I'd wished to, do you really think I could have stopped him from seeing you, if he'd actually wanted to?' I continue.

'I don't believe you. You made it impossible,' Sam shouts.

'You'll just have to make your own mind up.'

The waiter arrives with our food, but we eat without appetite. It feels like I've lost my son.

'Why are you so interested in all this old family stuff?' Sam is trying to make up. I hunt for an answer.

'I was brought up without knowing anything of my past, yet that past flows through every bit of me. I have to decipher the code. You don't know how strange it is not to know who any of your grandparents were or that there once were aunts and uncles.'

Sam is giving me one of his penetrating looks: 'You should think before you speak.'

I cannot believe that it has taken me till now to appreciate that Sam, like me, has had no links with his father's family, that a circle of absence has been recreated.

'I'm so sorry, Sam. I didn't think. I'm sure your dad will tell you about his parents, now you are back in touch.' I try a smile. But Sam's face is unforgiving.

'Why didn't your parents tell you about their parents?' Sam is asking, nodding at me, but his eyes are cold.

'What happened to their friends and relations was unbearable. And Grandma feels responsible. She feels that she shouldn't have left her parents and sister behind in Germany. She wished she had died with them, she once told me. Guilt is a potent kill-joy.'

'She couldn't have saved them by staying, could she?'

'The guilt of the survivor.'

'I suppose she did survive.'

The puddings arrive. We have both ordered chocolate tart. Comfort food. We eat it in that amicable silence which can descend when food is pleasurable.

'You've a new girl friend?' I finally say, the last spots of pudding scraped up and eaten. I'd been waiting to ask Sam for weeks.

Instead of the outburst I feared, Sam smiles.

'I hope so. Jaz.'

'Congratulations. How did you meet?'

'Friend of Joel's. Just a friend. They used to go to school together. I thought I might invite her back home tonight.' Sam glances across at me.

'OK.' He's as much informing me as asking for my consent.

'Time to go?' Sam suggests.

I nod, impressed that Sam had not tried to hurry the meal. 'I shall miss you when you go to university.' It's something I have to tell him.

We are done. Sam disappears into the night and I go home alone.

Chapter 69

I drive to Elizabeth's house, guessing correctly that this is not going to be a boozy evening. The house, in an expensive part of lower Islington, is pre-Victorian and, when I enter, discover that it is furnished in corresponding style. I wonder whether they've tidied up specially or are always fastidious. No children, of course.

Edward, her husband, shows me straight to the dining-table. A good sign. I hand him my bottle of dry New Zealand white.

I'd been walking the dog on Hampstead Heath. The dog might be Sam's, but Sam is at university and it is I who now love the dog. He takes me for walks and lies on the floor in my bedroom at night. Every morning, he pushes his old face into mine, knowing that it is time for me to wake up. I listen to him, concerned that his heavy breathing betrays his age. I fear for him and for myself.

It was the gloaming, when the light disintegrates into the dark, when the greens dissolve into grey. I like this time. Fewer people. Coming towards me in the growing gloom, I'd spotted Elizabeth with her husband. I'd not have expected to see her here.

She'd introduced us: 'Edward, Anna'.

'I recognise you from Elizabeth's mother's funeral,' I'd told Edward, bowing ever so slightly towards him. I was surprised by how much older he appeared than she did. He must be well past retirement age.

'How are you?' Elizabeth had enquired.

'I love it here. Walking the dog keeps me sane.'

'I've been thinking about you,' she'd gushed. 'It would be good fun to have more of a talk. I suspect we have a bit in common.'

Without my deciding to do so, I'd found myself thanking her and accepting an invitation for Saturday dinner, in three days' time.

'Would you like a glass of sherry or glass of wine?'

Edward asks me, politely. Is Edward here because he and Elizabeth always spend Saturday evening together, or has he come as her protector?

'Wine, please.' I try out a smile.

He goes off to the adjoining kitchen and returns with a small crystal glass of red. Definitely not alcoholics, then. Elizabeth opts for sherry. She suddenly arrives with my plate of the full English: semi-rare beef, thinly cut, and two veg. I am amused. Edward seats himself at the head of the table, one woman on either side.

We eat and chatter about our jobs, retirement, houses, holidays, and pastimes. Elizabeth talks enthusiastically about her Church charity work. Her way of giving back and especially to those most in need. Last month they'd held a fun day for the local hospice. So worthwhile.

We are eating our pudding, which turns out to be a choice of ice cream, when Elizabeth asks me, 'Have you ever wondered why your marriage failed?'

Not what I'm expecting at all. I consider whether I can ask for another glass of wine.

'That's just the start,' I reply.

'Edward's my first successful relationship.' She glances at him from the corner of her eye. I hold my tongue. 'Did your parents try to put you off boys?'

'Oh yes. They did everything imaginable. You first.' I suddenly find that I am pleased I came.

'It wasn't anything specific. Not that they locked me in the house. But it was made very clear that boys were bad and if I went near one, I would be even worse.' Elizabeth glances up at me quickly. She appears to hesitate. I nod, understanding all too well. 'And my mother was always telling me what a frump I looked. *She* was always so glamorous. Never went out without her furs. She used to tell me I should take better care of myself. When I was a teenager, she used to laugh at me and say, 'If you don't lose some of that puppy fat, no boy will ever look at you.' Elizabeth is staring hard at the table.

'What happened?'

'What you would expect. I had a couple of relationships, nothing serious of course, but I could never settle. I was always . . .'

'Afraid?'

'Yes, it's difficult to put one's finger on it. I was never relaxed. It felt as if I wasn't good enough to have a proper relationship. And I always blamed myself when things went wrong.'

It's as if she's telling me my own history.

'Till Edward?' I suggest.

'There was a long gap. I was by myself for at least ten years. I stopped caring about relationships. Or that's what I told myself.'

I look at her, questioning. Edward is hearing all this.

'Met Edward through the Church. Haven't looked back since. Been together now for - how long is it, Edward? Almost fifteen years?'

Edward says nothing.

'But you must have changed?'

'I finally understood that I was as good and as attractive as anybody else.'

'When I first saw you at your mother's funeral, you struck me as an attractive, well-turned out woman.'

'I got there in the end. How about you?'

'I went to a second generation group recently. You know, for the children of those who survived Nazism. There were about six of us and our different lives all had such similar themes. That was so reassuring. The facilitator told us that the second generation often grow up late. We are much older than most other people before we do things. Like getting married to Edward.' I smile appropriately.

'Yes.' Elizabeth is sounding stressed. 'I've always done everything later than my old school friends. It's like I only woke up to a belief in myself about twenty years later than everybody else.'

'It's typical for us to feel that we must look after our parents. As they've already suffered so much, who are we to add to their misery? So, while others cut the apron strings, we don't want the responsibility of hurting our mothers.'

To my surprise, Elizabeth appears to gasp. 'That fits me and my mum. I've spent so long feeling responsible for her, I don't want to go anywhere near her. The most I want to do is have Christmas dinner with her. And I start dreading that in November.'

She is still talking of her mother in the present tense. What has happened to the composed Elizabeth? I glance quickly at Edward but he looks no different from usual.

Elizabeth continues: 'Of course, it was different with my father. He was a super man.' I remember her enthusiasm for her father from our previous conversation.

'I'm only just beginning to feel that I'm growing up now,' I interrupt. 'I've wrecked more relationships in my time than most people have had hot dinners.'

Elizabeth is nodding. I rush on: 'I never took myself seriously. It was like I was some sort of cardboard cut-out or puppet, going through all the right motions, but lacking a heart or soul. Waiting for the puppet master, I suppose. But of course, he doesn't exist.'

'I recommend marriage.'

That pulls me up. Elizabeth is offering me coffee which I refuse.

I change the subject.

'I'm intrigued that our families, so closely related and so similar, made no effort to get in touch.' I notice the quick glance between Edward and Elizabeth and feel the atmosphere freezing up, but continue. 'There were some letters in the MI5 file . . . Louise had a rich cousin called Max, who made so many business trips from Germany to Britain and was so successful, that he was able to claim British nationality.'

Elizabeth is frowning: 'Of course. A great achievement. He's part of my family.'

I plough on. 'Being rich does help, doesn't it? He first got his Jewish wife and children out of Germany to England. It was his money that saved them. Then he got out my mother's aunts and uncles, but not my mother's parents.'

'They were never satisfied.'

I gasp. 'What?'

'That's what I heard,' she adds hastily.

Indeed, there was one appalling letter from Max which somehow ended up in my father's stack, complaining about my grandparents being so unreasonable and always wanting more money.

'What I think is that my mother could not bear to be close to any members of her family who survived when her parents didn't,' I suggest to Elizabeth, scared at how she may respond. I do not add my suspicion that the bourgeois (and Jewish) part of the family did not support my mother's parents because of their daughter's perceived Bolshevik politics.

244

'I think you're being quite one-sided here.' Elizabeth's voice has lost its warmth. 'For example, my mother's cousin, Violet, did everything for your mother. It was one of the stories my mother told me before she died. Violet . . .'

'Yes, yes,' I interrupt. 'I know. I found a letter from 1946 from Violet.'

'Well, then. You know,' Elizabeth continues icily. 'She went to try to find your mother's father, Johann, in Berlin. Her half-brother was stationed in the British sector, and despite foreigners not being allowed in, got Violet a pass. She searched for information about Johann. My mother told me all about it.'

Elizabeth seems extraordinarily well-informed. She is also glaring at me. I try a mollifying approach: 'Maybe the reason Louise had no desire to be in further touch with Violet and your side of the family was because she blamed Violet as the messenger of despair. My poor mother had waited in vain for good news about her father.'

I have said more than enough. I explain that it is past my bedtime. Edward and Elizabeth both look very relieved. I over-thank them. 'Maybe we'll meet again,' I suggest as I leave, but Elizabeth does not respond.

Chapter 70

From Red Cross to Louise

13.2.46 Thank you for your letter of the 9th February 1946. We regret that we have not received a reply to our original enquiry about your father.

From Herr Messerschmidt

15.5.46 I can't tell you much about your father. He was evacuated in July or August 1942. He took his luggage with him to the collection point in the Lewetzow Strasse. From there, I believe he went to Piaski, near Llublin. Nobody ever returned from Llublin.

From Louise to Vater

14.7.46 Today we got the most wonderful news from the World Jewish Congress and got your address in Berlin. We can hardly dare to believe it. The only news we had from you for years came 6 weeks ago from Herr Messerschmidt that you were sent away in 1942. Our dear father and grandfather, we are so eternally happy. The best news first. We have a delightful little daughter, Anna. I am enclosing a picture. Anna's first words shall be Grandpa 'Opi'.

Vater, it can't be too long now till we see you again and I kiss you and embrace you, Vater. This is a first attempt to get in touch with you. Stay healthy for us. A thousand kisses

From Emil:

Dear Vater, We are still under the impact of the news and very slowly do we dare to believe in it.

From Jewish Community, Berlin

12.8.46 I am deeply sorry to have to give you some news that will hit you very badly. Yesterday, a Dr Johann Zweig appeared in my office and brought me your letter of 14 July. He regretted very much that he is not your father. After checking lists of all rescued Jews in Berlin, I must conclude that there is nobody else with your father's name. My deepest regrets.

12.8.2006:
Dear Grandparents,
It has taken me so long to find you. I am trying to hear you. I have a son, your great-grandson. I called him Sam. He has your face, Grandpa, except he isn't bald.
I love you,
Anna.

Dear Anna,
We wish we had been here for you. We would have loved to meet you, to have held you in our arms, our beautiful grandchild. We are with you always.
Our love,
Your grandparents.

Johann was sixty-five when he was killed, not much older than I am now. This is a death I have lived with all my life.

Why does it matter to me, whether he died in Llublin or Theresienstadt? The letter from Herr Messerschmidt had informed my mother that Johann was taken to Llublin. The Red Cross informed me that Johann had died in Theresienstadt. I hope it was Theresienstadt, for it might have been an 'easier' death. It was a murder either way.

My mother had had her hopes confirmed that her father was, miraculously, still alive. After all, there were survivors from the camps. And her father was strong. The absence of letters from him after he was taken away, was only to be expected, she must have surmised, given the circumstances. After the information from the World Jewish Congress, she started to make enquiries of the British immigration service about bringing her father to England, for these appear in her MI5 files. Could they please send her the relevant documentation? I do not possess their reply.

I can see my mother tearing to shreds the letter of the 12 August 1946, from the Jewish Community (whoever they might have been in Berlin in 1946), and hear her screaming and screaming. The other Johann Zweig was born in the same month of the same year, but he had no children. 'We are so very sorry.'

Certainly, I did not choose a good time to be born. I had been alive for just two years in August 1946. As she fretted over whether her father was alive, did she hold me close, joyfully anticipating telling her father he had a granddaughter, or, distraught, did she push me away? *'Not now, darling, not now.'* My mother could not but have been distracted by her desperate desire for news of her father, and, even more, for good news, knowing all the while how unlikely this was. Did she blame herself in those dark nights of the soul? Did she think, as she went through the chores of looking after me, if only she had stayed and been able to look after him? Did she turn her head away from mine and close her heart?

Cutting herself off from her own and my emotions was, I suspect, the only way she could keep her head above the tides of hope and despair. Or do I look too deep into those months of purgatory for what befell me?

And when her hope crashed into despair, when she discovered that her fears had been right all along, when she thought: how could he have survived, nobody good survived the camps and her father was a good man, did she mourn? Did she weep for her dead father and what now would never be?

Or had she had cried all the tears that she would ever spill? She had wept for her dead uncles in the First World War. She had wept at leaving her sister and her parents, wept when she left her lover in Moscow, and wept when she understood that the Stalinists had probably murdered him. She had wept at the murder of her sister by the Nazis. Perhaps she wept when she was taken away to Holloway prison, though I doubt whether she had any tears left.

By the time I came along, I never knew her to cry. She did not cry when friends died. She did not cry when my dog died. While my father and I sobbed, she laughed. When my father lay fighting for his last breaths, my mother hid away in the relatives' room. 'No point being with him now,' she had declared, dry-eyed. My mother brought me up in a tearless world, for fear that the horror of her pain would spill out over her and me and drown the both of us

This is a strange world to inhabit as a child, where deep emotions do not appear to exist, where the past with all its horrors has also been deleted. My grandfather's death was deleted from my history. She never talked of him. And no, I never asked. But the presence of her murdered family filled my life, not because I knew anything about them, but because I did not.

I did not benefit from my ignorance, from not having any past to call my own. I had no cultural hinterland through which I could understand how I came to be who I am.

I arrived as if the stork had brought me, early one summer's morning, hiding me gently in a warm Oxford garden. And later, as I was growing up, I had no way to understand how my German-speaking parents had come to be shipwrecked on the distant slopes of Durham city.

It is strange never to know anything about your parents except as they are, at that moment, as if they have emerged from the head of Zeus, already grown people. Had my mother been able to look down that long dark tunnel of death, and not keep the past a secret from me, she could have enjoyed her living child.

My sense of insecurity, of never trusting myself to anyone, lies in the intestines of the past. It is only now that I can glimpse the grief that my mother so actively suppressed, along with all other emotions. She found it too difficult to love. I remember my childhood as one long lacunae, as an absence. There was nothing there and I was not there.

Chapter 71

Leon has sent me another attachment. His email warns me:

Only open this when you are ready. It contains information I managed to dig out about your side of the family. Email me if you want me to ring you.

Suddenly, there in black and white are all the details of those who lived and those who died. I stare hard at the computer screen, which appears to be in motion. There had been a large family. My grandmother - how that word still sticks in my mouth - my grandmother was one of twelve siblings. Nazism had blown the family apart. Most had got away and died after the War was over. Not my mother's family. It gives the year of death of both my grandparents. Next to my grandfather's name is a sign. I look it up. Lager: Concentration camp, it reads.

It makes such a difference to see the details. The names become flesh.

Fifty years of keeping my mouth shut and respecting my parents' right to privacy breaks down. I jump up from the computer and, though it is late in the day to see my mother, drive to visit her. It is as if I am possessed. She is dozing in her chair. I wake her up.

'What happened to your parents?' I demand.

Silence.

'Why didn't they try to leave Germany?'

'They had no money.'

'They could have left if they'd had money?'

'Yes.'

'What happened to your mother?'

'She died in a concentration camp.' This is not her usual story of a heart attack.

My mother is holding tightly onto my hand and I feel like scum.

'She didn't, you know. She died a natural death.'

'No.'

'In a hospital.'

'No.' She turns and gazes directly at me, emphatically shaking her head. She cannot hear me. Her mother will always have been murdered. Yet she, who has lied to me all my life about the cause of her mother's death, had, with such a sad irony, been telling me the 'truth'.

'And your father?' I continue.

'I don't want to know.'

'He died in a camp,' I tell her.

'Yes. I don't want to know about it.'

Silence.

We do not share our grief.

I show her the photo of her parents.

'How do you have this,' she breaks into words, 'without my permission?'

I feel as if I have opened up her insides, to feast upon her secrets.

I have learnt more than my mother ever wanted to know: about her sister, her mother's death, and how her father died. I have peered into the box of death and seen their shadows.

I have come to have a grandfather. I have learnt my grandfather's and grandmother's names. It is strange to have a family history. I feel nervous uncovering the tombstones, which have lain so heavy on their memories.

My mother has felt herself to be the guardian of her past, refusing entry to anyone who was not there. But I must carry the legacy now for there is no older generation left.

Some drivers slow down on the motorways when they spot an accident. Do they wonder if they know the victims, or is it some more ghoulish response? An excitement at others suffering, an almost sexual charge at destruction and death?

But I have always prided myself that I was not one of these. I drive past carefully, eyes always straight ahead, not wishing to precipitate another accident, not willing to derive sadistic excitement from the misery of others. But now I wonder at myself.

The holocaust has a greater allure than any car accident. It intrigues in its horror. I cannot leave it alone. Maybe I'm feasting on their lives, using their deaths as a prop, as a way to give my life meaning.

Yet we are not conversing about the six million (or more). We are considering my family: Johann, Rosa. I wish to discover the particularity of their experience. It is the particularity which horrifies.

I know I will never find the answers to my questions. But what if I did? Would the ghosts leave me then?

Chapter 72

I miss Sam. He spent much of the summer with Jaz, before leaving for university. I have done what has to be done, walking the dog, organising the house repairs, clearing up after the builders, visiting my mother, burying my little cat. I want him to be able to hold on to relationships as I have not, but still wait forever on his call.

I remember my beloved son, how I nuzzled his hair when he was a baby, breathing in his smell, I remember the toddler, who, unaware of danger, kept on falling down and getting up, a new injury to be kissed and made better, I remember the young boy, as we held hands, walking together down the street as if nothing could be more natural, I remember the eleven-year-old, telling me stories about his school and his new friends, the proud goalie in his football team: I, watching him from the sidelines, willing him not to be injured, and willing his team to win. I remember the thirteen-year-old, off on his first long camp, both of us knowing he would be back. I remember the fifteen-year old, out every night, but home before it was too late. I remember the eighteen-year-old, kissing me on the cheek as we part at the gates of his new university life.

But you've never before taken your duvet, Sam, the king-sized duvet which lay on your double bed, which I bought you when you were a mere sixteen, so you would know that having girlfriends home was OK.

'How can you sleep here, Sam, when you don't have a duvet?'

'Oh, Mum, I'm not living here any more.'

'What about the holidays, Sam?'

'Well, I'll bring it back at Christmas. Why do you always make a fuss? Chill out. I'm nineteen. Some of my friends have their own children by now.'

I slip into my bedroom, fearing for the loss of the one person whom I have uncritically loved, the child I gave birth to, for whom I became a mother, the child I nourished and adored, whose very life is a triumph against the Nazis.

Chapter 73

Johann Zweig arrived in Theresienstadt on the 10th July 1942. He died on the 1st February 1943.

Shaking, I phone the Red Cross. 'I've got your letter.'

'I'm so sorry,' the female voice tells me.

'Seeing it in black and white makes it real,' I hear myself saying.

'Yes, that often happens. There is something I have to ask you.'

Panic.

'Do you want us to get you a copy of your grandfather's death certificate?'

'Nobody has claimed it already?'

'Nobody has claimed it.'

'My mother has not claimed it?'

'Nobody at all has officially enquired after him or his death certificate, as far as the records show. Many people don't see the point.'

'I want his death certificate.'

'These things can take a bit of time. But the certificate will not tell you anything different from what is enclosed in our letter.'

'Will it include how he officially died?'

'The death certificate does not include cause of death. The certificates for older men might sometimes state something like pneumonia. All it means, I'm afraid, is that the Camp apparatus was efficient at matching the claimed cause of death to the person who had died.'

'Is there any way of finding out?'

'I can make enquiries but what good will this information do you?'

'He succeeded in living there for over six months. Did he starve to death? Or collapse from overwork? Was there any-one there to comfort him?' My voice is rising uncontrollably. I want to know what he felt as he lay dying, whether his faith deserted him. But more than anything, did he die alone?

'I do understand, but I think what you are asking is beyond our remit.'

'I'm sorry. Of course.'

'I do understand how hard this is.'

'My poor mother sent the Red Cross a letter dated 5th February 1943 saying she had just received a letter from her father. But your letter shows that her father had died a few days earlier. She didn't even know that her father was no longer alive.'

'It could take months and months for even Red Cross letters to get through. Many ships never even made it. I'm so sorry. This must be awful for you. But I will see to it that you get your grandfather's death certificate.'

I may not have known my grandfather in life, but, terrified, I claim him in death.

I am glad that I know where you died. But I shall not visit you at Theresienstadt, for it is too late. Did someone hold your hand as you died, Johann, for I fear you died alone? I hope you slipped away, without too much pain, into the arms of your beloved Rosa.

'I want you to know I love you,' says my grandfather. 'But I do not want you to know how I died, for I'm ashamed. Good men do not die as I did.'

Chapter 74

'Why did you have me?'

Sam and I are sitting over a meal at our local pizzeria, a ritual we both enjoy when Sam spends the rare weekend 'up in London'. He no longer calls it 'home'. Sam's query pops out in the silence after we have ordered our food.

'What's brought this one on?' I've been waiting for Sam to ask me this question, yet I do not have an answer.

'You and Frank. You never lived together.'

'No. But having a baby when you aren't living together is possible! It's not a bad thing.'

'It's bad for the child. Two parents are better than one.'

'That's rubbish. There's nothing wrong with one.'

'What did you think you were doing, having a child by yourself? You got it all the wrong way round. People don't first have a child and then see whether their relationship works out. They see whether their relationship works first. You spend a couple of nights together every week, then almost every night, and then, if that works, you move in with each other and get a dog or something, and, if all that works out OK, then you have a child. That might be a functional view of the world but it's what works and it gives the child the greatest stability.' Sam is being analytical, not accusatory. He looks and sounds as if he were a teacher, explaining an obvious point to a particularly obtuse though well-meaning pupil.

I feel faint. 'One-parent families can be as nourishing and give just as much love and stability as two parents,' I remonstrate.

'Not really. Not stability. I have an uncanny memory for the bad bits and there were a lot of those. You had a lot of ups and downs.'

'It would have helped if your dad had been around.'

'Don't change the subject. It's you I'm talking to. I assume you chose to have a child with my dad?'

I nod. But I remember how hard I had found being a single parent. I could not bear it when Sam cried as a baby. I would feel the sobs as if they were mine. His crying tore up my insides. Leave them be, intoned almost all the manuals.

You must not let the child become master of the man. How cruel, I thought (as I still do). I would pick up my sobbing child and hold him tight in my arms. That stopped our tears. But then he got too old for me to still his misery with hugs.

I did not have enough emotional confidence to understand that his upsets would pass and we would both survive. Survival was the last thing I expected of him. When he was little, I checked on him every half hour when he slept; when the school bus returned a few minutes late from an excursion, I just knew there had been an accident and that my son was dead; when the child-minder brought him back an hour late and did not answer her mobile, I considered phoning the police. Of course it would have been easier if Sam's dad has been around.

I had found it hard not to get sucked down into the tempest of Sam's life. My only guiding principle to parenthood was to do the opposite to my parents. This has a limited usefulness. Sam believed every day should be lived to the full, from the moment he was dragged from my womb. No sleeping for him. Such a waste of time and opportunity. Sam wanted it all, from the up to the down and, however much I gave him, I could never give enough. How annoying for him and upsetting for me.

'Or was it that you saw the clock ticking and my dad would have to do?' Sam is enquiring.

What is Sam asking me? 'That wasn't how it was. I wanted Frank's child. You were born out of love.'

'But you'd left it late, hadn't you? Maybe you also thought you wouldn't find anybody better.'

Sam does not sound unkind. He is giving me a clear, clean look, leaning forwards slightly towards me. Has his dad told him this? Informing Sam that he's wrong would not help either of us.

'There wouldn't have been a Sam,' I try.

'Oh, don't give me that argument! It doesn't go anywhere, does it! I'm talking about you. I find it really difficult explaining to my friends why I was born. I think you got it wrong. I'm not accusing you, but being brought up by you was not easy for me.'

'So, what were the bad bits?'

'I don't want to go there. Leave it.' Sam for the first time sounds angry.

What is he telling me? That he was unhappy as a child? That I did it all wrong? That I lost him his father? At least, he hasn't said, 'I wish I'd never been born'. Sam sucks in life like it is oxygen.

I comfort myself. These are not the real questions; Sam wants to sort out his relationship with his one practising parent, when the other is so significantly missing.

Yet I too am confused by how I had managed not to have a child within a stable relationship. I had not lacked for lovers. Although I had many friends who became radical feminists, I could never go along with their underlying belief that the man was almost irrelevant, except for the unfortunate necessity of his sperm. I liked men. I liked their company, their smell, the flirtations, the wonder of sexual pleasure and the warmth of my body afterwards. I had lived with one man, John, and was not against trying again with another. The explanation must lie elsewhere.

I'd watched as my friends had fallen by the wayside into marriage and Mothercare. But having children did not combine with being a revolutionary, was what I'd told myself. Socialists, especially feminist socialists, do not willingly bury themselves in nappies, in Kinder and Küche. Life, comrades, should be lived in the revolutionary struggle. Don't be frivolous. Another push (so to speak) and the revolution will be born.

I'd certainly played my part in the struggle, from anti-racist campaigns to the more mundane but time-consuming union activities at work. Management was child's play compared to the feuding with members of the Communist Party and the Maoists. Later, when I was pregnant, as my body revealed its secret, my colleagues had told me: 'I never thought you'd have a baby.' One man, with whom long ago I'd had a fling, suggested: 'The Virgin Birth?' I had my own ways of keeping silent.

It was Sam's dad, another socialist of avowedly left-wing parents, who had gently and persistently explained to me that it 'really, truly' was possible to be both a socialist and a mother. I need not sacrifice my own life. I should go for what I wanted. Anyway, was it not my duty to contribute to another generation of revolutionaries? Without Frank's persuasion, I would not have had a child.

But I know there are other reasons. I was late in developing a realisation that I had any right to have my own needs, or even control over my own body. I had not dared articulate to anybody, even to myself, how much I wanted a child. Amazing that I managed to have a child at all.

Yet the one time I loved my body was when I was pregnant and, happier every day, watched how, as the baby's body grew, so did mine.

I look across at Sam, as he carefully cuts up his pizza. Sam has had heaped upon him the fears and uncertainties of many generations and I am so glad that he fights back. At least I am there for him. So perhaps there has been some progress after all.

I cannot imagine life without you, Sam. As it is, I feel that death is hiding round every corner, just out of sight, gleefully rubbing its hands as it sees us approach. Yet here you are, Sam, alive as could be, and I'm so deeply grateful.

'Any ideas of what you want to do after university?' I rouse myself to ask. Sam has been chatting to somebody he must know at the next table.

A shrug. 'Don't know. I'd like to get a job campaigning on global warming, but I doubt whether I shall. Probably end up teaching, like you.' A sardonic grin.

'Don't.'

'That's what my dad says. Why did you go into it, if you tell me not to?'

'I didn't want to be compromised in a job that upheld the capitalist system. Even social work is just about applying sticking plaster to gaping wounds and telling the injured and downtrodden that there is no further cause to complain. Education offered a small space to encourage critical thought.'

'And?'

'And I was a good listener and carer for others, while not being listened to or much cared for myself. Perfect qualities for a teacher!'

Sam grins: 'I'd go for the little ones. More hands-on. Universities are awful places. Hardly any face-to-face contact between staff and students. I'd hate to work in a place that was so anonymous.'

My turn to smile. 'Ain't like the good old days! But no point having illusions about primary schools either.'

'I don't have to worry about this yet, Mum.' Sam has ended the conversation. He is checking his watch. 'Could you give me a lift?' he now asks, smiling brightly at me. He has such winning ways when he wants something.

'Where to?'

'Not far. Promise.'

'For you . . .' I laugh, and drive him to his next assignation.

Chapter 75

Seamus and I sit in my local, crushed up into a corner, him with his pint, I, my glass of red. It's crowded and noisy, but warm.

'How's mum?'

'Alive.'

He laughs. 'Good, good. And yourself?'

'Just about the same.'

'The son and heir?'

'Doing well.'

'You make it sound like an insult.'

'He gets good marks without working.'

After establishing that Seamus and his partner, Sinead, together visiting London for the week, are well, we have completed the pleasantries.

Seamus had phoned me a few weeks earlier to tell me that he was coming to Europe for a sabbatical. He would be passing through London and would like to meet.

'Dennis was in Spain,' Seamus continues.

'Excuse me?'

'Did you ever see anything that was sent to your mother from Spain?'

Why is he asking me this?

The postcard had been of a castle in black and white. I had found it, buried deep amongst my father's papers, pushed into the furthest corner of the bookshelves. Nothing of interest here, I had thought. The postcard's legend was in Spanish. The stamp had been removed, as had the signature, which had been heavily scratched out together with the name of the person and address to which the card had been sent. I had tried to decipher the few words, which had been so carelessly scrawled over the writing bit of the card.

Doing well. The pomade seems to be working. Yours always.

I had pushed it into a file with all the other uncategorised bits of paper to and from my parents.

I remembered John retrieving the card. He had got so excited.

'It's a code!' he had exclaimed. 'It must be from Dennis. The 'pomade' refers to POUM.'

POUM, as I'd discovered, when young, from both George Orwell and my parents, was a non-Stalinist Marxist party (often inaccurately referred to as Trotskyite), fighting the fascists in the Spanish Civil war in 1936 and 1937, with a particularly strong working-class base in Catalonia.

'Dennis was telling Louise that POUM was worthy of support,' John had explained.

John and I had looked anxiously at each other. This was not 'on message' for a Soviet spy.

'I wish he'd been right,' I say. I knew the history. POUM had been annihilated by the Stalinists as much as by the Fascists.

'The postcard must have eluded the Spanish fascist security, Stalinist security and MI5,' John had commented. 'Otherwise Louise would never have got it. I haven't found anything else from Dennis.'

I had stared at the 'yours always'. It was not to be. I remember feeling very sick.

Seamus informs me: 'I found a reference to Dennis. He died in a camp in 1948. I don't think he was actually murdered, if you can distinguish that from dying of neglected illnesses and continual ill-treatment.'

Surely this is what I expected. Yet finding out the truth about his death shocks me. Dennis: so dear to my mother, a key to whom she was to become, whose ashes were thrown to the winds, un-honoured, along with a million others, whom I shall never know.

'Do you have a photo of him?' I ask.

Seamus looks startled. 'The only photo of Dennis which I've found was in his secret Russian file. I think he'd been beaten up. His face is swollen.'

'Could I have a copy?' I persist.

Only a momentary hesitation. 'Sure. I'll send you a copy when I get back home.'

'All that time Louise was trying to find out about him, he was still alive. I wonder whether my mother ever really found out what happened to him?'

'Very unlikely. The Russian records are now publicly available but I still found it hard to unearth the information. Freedom of information is more a policy than a practice.'

'She will have guessed about Dennis, but she can't have known the way you know when there is a body or a death certificate.' I feel for her. All those years of wondering. All that pain.

'She was certainly robbed of that.'

'What must she have felt when a past she thought she had long buried suddenly popped up, as if from the dead, when you appeared?'

Seamus gives a grimace. 'She didn't want to talk when I did come to see her.'

'I asked her the other day whether there was one thing she regretted in her life. Her eyes cleared and she told me in that loud clear voice of hers, that she wished she had killed herself. Too many deaths, too few funerals.'

Seamus has got up and is getting ready to go, pulling his tweed cap firmly over his ears, disguising his balding head. He can't have heard what I'd just said. My mother had lived with too many deaths. Murders. Saved herself, but lost her family. Lived with memories that were unbearable to live with. Lost memories that would never be.

It is I who now gather up my family's memories and mark the comings and going of the dead. I've had enough of being invisible in the shadow of history.

PART 3

Chapter 76

I can hear Sam's voice at the other end of the phone, but he sounds far away. 'I've been arrested.'

'Oh!'

I'm allowed one phone call and this is it.'

'What have you done?'

'I'm not allowed to say.'

'Are you OK? Are you hurt?'

'I'm fine, Mum. Would you let my dad know?'

'Of course. Do you have a lawyer?'

'Yes.'

'I'll drive up.'

'Don't. I'm fine.'

'Take care.'

I sit shaking on the sofa downstairs. It feels as if my head is going to explode. I'm scared that Sam is hurt, and scared of all the things I don't yet know about, except to know that this will be no fun. I phone up the police station. A small group have cut their way into an airport where they held a service to commemorate those who have died from global warming. The policeman reassures me: 'They're not your criminal types.'

I send Sam's dad a letter. This is scary but I know it is the right thing to do. If he behaves as normal, he won't reply anyway. I tell him about Sam's arrest. I add: 'Maybe, it's time to be in touch.'

To my surprise, he phones the next day.

'I'm terribly worried.'

'Don't be. He's not going to prison.'

'I think this requires a man's touch.'

'Kill him!' I think, unable to stop myself remembering when I alone had been there for Sam after one of his many near-deadly scrapes. I had coped, single-handed 'as ever', when at nine months and just able to walk, Sam had been rushed into hospital after falling through a friend's broken banisters onto the stone stairs below; when he had just started to climb and jumped from his bedroom cupboard, dislocating his shoulder; when he had broken his arm falling off his bike; when he smashed up his knee; when he almost cut off his thumb; when he was beaten up at school. I'd plenty on which to hang my fears about Sam's continuing survival. And my anger at Frank.

'I'm pleased you're involved but aren't you rather late?' I snarl.

'Another time.'

We agree to meet at the hearing.

It has taken Sam's being charged for us to talk for the first time in thirteen years. 'Meet you in court' takes on a whole new meaning.

Chapter 77

My mother is having a clear moment. 'Did you and Papa get on?' I ask her. She gazes at me with blurred eyes. The staff have dressed her well today in a stripy red and black Breton jumper I once gave her, and an almost matching, extraordinarily long dark skirt, but then any sign of female flesh, even old flesh, appears to be seen here as immoral.

'He was a kind man.'

She has not answered my question.

'Were you always together?' I am angling.

'I wish he hadn't left . . .' She pauses and a furtive look passes over her face, and she adds: ' . . . died.'

'Hadn't left? Did he ever leave you?'

The past presses on her memory. She shakes her head at me but I can see what she is really telling me. Yes, he did but I won't say it because you are his daughter and I don't want to upset you.

'Did you ever leave him?'

'No.' She pauses, then continues: 'Yes. When I went to Russia.'

'Why did you go there?'

'I was interested. I wish I hadn't. Russia was awful.'

'You met up with Dennis?'

'I never knew anybody called Dennis.'

'Dennis. You were in Moscow with Dennis.'

'Oh yes. Dennis. I was very young.'

'What happened to him?'

'They put him into prison. It wasn't my fault.'

'No. Of course not.' I decide against probing this denial.

'Trotskyites!' My mother laughs wildly. 'If they wanted to murder you, they called you a Trotskyite. They kept people in the camps for decades. There was no way out and nobody knew if you were dead or alive.'

'Did Dennis die?'

She glares at me with caged fury, a look I recognise from my childhood. 'I don't know.'

This is ground upon which I dare not tread.

After a moment I ask her: 'How did *you* get out?'

She sits there in silence, then as if a window has suddenly opened, she replies: 'Via Norway.'

'There's no common border. How did you manage that?'

Again she is silent, staring out of the large windows onto the open sky. I ask again.

'I was a delegate to a conference there.'

'Good heavens! What conference?'

'Your father was very worried. He was a lovely man.'

'Yes. Most of the time.'

'Most of the time?'

It is my turn to shake my head. I'm not going there, at least, not for now. She smiles at me, pressing my hand. We have never had a conversation like this before.

Chapter 78

Amongst my father's papers I find a letter that he had written to Susanne, the daughter of Beate. Every Christmas, my family had received a parcel filled with different sorts of marzipan. My father had explained that Beate, from Hamburg, had sent it.

The best bits of Christmas, when I was a child, were these fantastic parcels of marzipan, which arrived from Beate every year. My father would carefully unknot the string, remove the wrapping paper, and there would lie a myriad of glistening bundles of marzipan which he would put round the Christmas tree. Then on Christmas Day, in the afternoon, he would take a marzipan sausage and carefully place it onto a decorative plate, get out a tiny knife, and slice us each a couple of slivers. Our Christmas ritual.

What I never knew was that Beate and her daughter, Susanne, only just survived the camps. Her husband, my father's only cousin, was murdered, along with their son, Freddie. I hadn't even suspected. They had fled to Yugoslavia and lived under the protection of the Partisans, but in the dying days of the war, in 1944, the SS had caught up with them.

I cannot imagine what it took Beate to send those marzipan parcels every year. She had married after Emil had fled Germany, so she may not even have met my father. But, to remember her husband and make life sweeter for her husband's cousin's little girl, she helped us celebrate Christmas by her gift.

How could Anna lack any curiosity about her past? asks my father's letter to Susanne. She's never around long enough for meaningful conversations to take place. At least she'll have enough imagination to work things out for herself.

I sit reading this letter in disbelief and horror.

It is dated shortly before he died. Is this a copy of a letter that my father had written, or had he never sent it? I'm overwhelmed with sadness that my father had wanted to talk

268

to me but that I had not been there for him. *Why did you not say, Father? Tell me now what it is you wanted me to know.*

I continue reading my father's file containing Susanne's papers. I had met Susanne when I had visited New York before going to university, and found her closed and reserved. Did my father send me to meet her in the belief that she would spill the beans? He was mistaken.

Later, I find another of the carefully bundled files of letters to my father. One letter informed my parents of the terrible death of Uncle Hermann in Theresienstadt. My father had occasionally spoken of Uncle Hermann, the man who had nourished him when he was young, giving him the protection of his home. Uncle appeared to be the only person my father had loved as a child.

I discover many tender letters from Hermann to my father in London. In one letter from 1936, he describes burning all correspondence that was not of historical significance, because of considerations:

The steam from this drives our egg–mixing apparatus and made wonderful egg liqueur. Lots of other material, including old inflationary bank notes, has turned our apparatus into a boiler! I'm very happy about this.

In another letter, from 1938, he wrote:

Yesterday afternoon I could admire an absolutely wonderful sea of flowers in the garden so that, wandering from one tree to the next, I forgot all that could sadden me. The very first pear tree on the espalier, the good Louise of Arranches, has to suffer from the shade of the birch trees, but it survives and bears its beautiful and delicious fruits year by year, delighting heart and also stomach.'

He promises that he will send my father some special sausage.

But the letter which touches me the most reads:

If you have prospects of having an addition to the family, I would be very happy for you, your dear parents, and very much so for myself, if I could have your offspring with me, and if possible to care for them.

The letter telling of Hermann's death, sent from Munich, is dated two weeks before I was born.

Uncle was deprived of the joy of knowing his favourite nephew had produced the heir he so much desired. My parents' grief at his death, and joy at my birth, surely became intertwined. It is easy at the best of times to start off laughing and end up weeping. Did my father hold his precious newborn and bury his tears in her soft body? And did this baby draw in sorrow with her first sighs?

I cannot cope and withdraw from the world.

Chapter 79

'Do you have to shout?' Sam glowers at me. We are sitting on either side of Grandma, Sam perched on the side of her chair, me on a stool at her feet.

'She's deaf.'

'The whole room can hear you.'

'I have to shout for her to hear.'

'Everybody thinks we're mad.'

One of the other inmates is indeed grumbling. I turn round to see who it is. The room only holds about eight people, lined up against the three walls. Most are not up to such invective.

'Why isn't she wearing her hearing aid?' Sam asks.

'She pulls it out.'

'Then the staff should put it back.'

'Should we try to talk to her now?'

'How are you, Grandma?' Sam has leant forwards and spoken at a normal pitch into her ear.

'Who are you?'

'I'm your grandson, Sam.'

'No. Not my grandson.'

Sam flushes. 'I'm the son of your daughter.'

She shakes her head at him, eyes gleaming. She knows best. 'How did you two meet?'

I start to giggle. 'He's your grandson.' I'm shouting again. One of the carers comes over and puts his hand gently on my shoulder. 'She's very old,' he reminds me.

'He's not my grandson.'

'How's that?'

She smirks and looking at Sam, appears to be fluttering her eyes at him.

'I'll guess.' I yell. 'You're too young to have a grandson.'

She nods. 'Do you like my daughter?' she asks my son.

My laughter is getting out of control. 'I like my mother very much.' Sam has raised his voice now.

My mother again nods. 'Are you going to get married?'

'No!' we shriek in unison.

'How old are you?'

'Nineteen.'

271

'No! How old is she?' She indicates to Sam that she is talking about me by a toss of her head in my direction.

'How old were you when you had Anna?' Sam is trying hard.

'I was thirty-four.' She remembers that as if it were yesterday.

'And now?'

'I don't know.' She turns to me. 'Do you know how old I am?

'You're ninety-six.' Sometimes I try to avoid the truth but my sensitivity is worn right out.

'Nonsense.'

'This is your daughter.' Sam informs her.

'No,' she laughs at us, shaking her head vehemently.

'I want to go,' I announce.

'Stay,' Sam instructs me. 'At least wait till we've had tea with her.'

Chapter 80

I have picked up Ruben to go for a walk on the Heath with the dog. He has told me he feels little for dogs, but is willing to humour me. The talk is of the past.

The light fades so soon it is as if there has not been time for day, and we drive back to my home in the dark. In the cloak of the night, we turn our bodies towards one another. As if in a dance, he moves his head slowly towards mine and I turn my mouth slowly towards his. The kiss, if it could be called that, was all lips and no tongue. I couldn't say who pulled back first. He has taken hold of my hand and I feel its warmth.

'I haven't groped in a car for a long time.' Ruben sounds both pleased and indignant.

'Come in.'

He enters hesitantly. 'Still messy, but artistic.'

I walk him to the kitchen. But he stands stiffly by the door.

'Why don't you show me your etchings?'

For a moment, I think he is referring to my sculptures.

Taking my clothes off in the bedroom is excruciating. I'm aware of how his skin has started to sag and frightened of his awareness of how I too now droop. I hide beneath the sheets, grateful at concealment. I wonder whether I will remember how to do it. Where does everything go?

'Still lovely after forty years,' he breathes into my ear afterwards. He has learnt to put his arm around the woman at the end of love-making, and my body feels like a part of me in a way I had almost forgotten was possible.

I laugh, content. A few minutes later, he gets up. 'I have to pee. Stay in bed. I'll let myself out.'

And he is gone.

Chapter 81

'I met a man recently who had survived Auschwitz,' I tell Seamus, who is returning to the USA the next morning. He has invited me to a goodbye meal in a German restaurant.

'To remind you of what you're missing,' Seamus had joked over the phone. I stare at my wiener schnitzel and flowery German white wine. I have little appetite.

'I asked this man how many locks he had on his door. He told me four. He seemed so pleased somebody understood enough to be interested in that.'

I notice that Seamus is looking at me puzzled. I persevere: 'My parents needed five, which they had to unlock every time they wanted to get out. Or let me in.'

'How many locks do you have now?' Seamus asks.

'I try *not* to lock my door. But my son hates it. He tells me I'm old enough to have got over my sense of childhood captivity. He double-locks everything. I can't bear it!'

'It seems your hunch was right,' Seamus starts. 'Dennis did reach some sort of Faustian pact. The Russian secret police were suspicious of him and Louise and spied on them. You know: 'a western bourgeois couple'. They were forced to move from place to place. Then they were essentially put under house-arrest. After she left, they sent Dennis to the Spanish Civil war. You know the rest.'

'You mean Louise was let out if they could hold onto Dennis?'

'That sort of thing.'

'He probably hoped he would be able to get out of the USSR that way and go back to Louise via Spain.'

'Maybe. But I don't think he had much choice in the matter. Dennis and your mother were still in touch when he was in Spain. Weren't supposed to be. One condition they both had to sign: no contact after Louise left the USSR. But the secret police intercepted her letters to him, and they weren't very happy. In the Russian notes on Dennis's interrogation, it shows Dennis was repeatedly asked about his association with your mother and the Trotskyites.'

'She didn't understand how real the dangers were; she must have been dangerously naïve.'

'You could call it that. Dennis's interrogators suspected her of being a British spy and a Trotskyite.'

I snort involuntarily: 'The two accusations hardly sit well together.'

'She had close contact with dissidents in the Communist Party.'

'That's hardly the same thing. She always denied being a Trotskyite.'

'The distinction is not my field of interest.'

'Is she responsible for Dennis's death?'

'It's not useful to ask that question. Dennis chose to go to the USSR. She isn't responsible for that. She isn't responsible for the Stalinist purges of 1936. But let's say that she didn't help.'

I seize my chance. 'Do you know how my mother got out of Russia?'

'No. Dennis put Louise on a train at Moscow station but the records don't show where the train was going or who agreed her journey.'

So my poor mother bade her farewells to Dennis amongst the shadows and beggars of Moscow station. I can see her now.

She is leaning out of the window which opens over the door at the end of the compartment. 'Write!' she is shouting, and she is waving the red bandanna which she had been wearing round her neck.

She waits till the train turns a bend and Dennis totally disappears from sight. Then she collapses down into her seat. The seven other people squeezed into the compartment surreptitiously stare at her. Nobody says a word. Foreign speakers do not usually travel on the regional trains, and they are afraid. She gazes unseeing as the endless flat countryside rolls by, and wonders when she will next see Dennis.

'I'd have loved to talk to her. Find out her side.' Seamus tells me.

'She'd have been reopening the gates to hell.'

'Hadn't seen myself recently as the Devil.'

'Maybe somewhere within her, she hoped that Dennis would still be alive?'

'Dennis was so young when he died. Not yet thirty.'

'Once my father died, there was nobody else left who remembered him. It must have been lonely for my mother.'

But Seamus has finished his pint and appears restless.

'I must be going. We'll talk again. Your mother was one amazing woman. Don't be too hard on her - or yourself.'

We shake hands outside the restaurant. I head back home, feeling numb and alone.

So what if Louise had followed her lover to Moscow? So what if she had married Dennis when she was already married to my father? So what if she had contributed to Dennis's death? The young can be foolish. All a person had to do was sneeze at the wrong time to be put to death in Stalinist Russia. Dennis had made the extra mistake of being a spy. 1937 was not a good year to stay alive in Moscow.

But Dennis lies between my mother and me. Always has. Can't be undone. So much easier to keep silent, lock the door, lock up your daughter and keep your mouth locked tight.

Trouble is, when to open up? One word leads to another. Uttering a word can toll the bell for death. Better not to talk at all. Silence has got her tongue.

Chapter 82

Ruben and I are sitting chatting over a delicious lamb stew that I have lovingly prepared, candles working their magic, a bottle of Chateau Neuf du Pape, bestowed by Ruben, already almost drunk. The dog, too, is having a great time, acting as the dustbin to bits of fat and gristle that I toss under the table.

'You are just encouraging him.'

'I've been feeding him off the table for twelve years now and there haven't been any ill effects so far.'

Ruben pulls a face.

'Do you think if we'd had a relationship all along, I would have cared so much about the past?'

'What kind of damned question is that?'

'I've been living in the spell of the past for goodness knows how many years. Sex puts you bang into the present.' I try to grin.

'Is this turning into a conversation about some future you are planning for us to have together?'

'Why did I choose you, Ruben? Was it that I knew at some level that things would never work out between us, that it was safe to fall for you?'

'What did I see in *you*? Some unconscious desire to recreate the persecution experienced by my ancestors. Was that it?'

The stew sits uneaten and congealing on my plate. The dog is in luck.

'I wish we'd had a child together, Ruben. An older brother or sister for Sam.'

Ruben starts to cry. I can see his shoulders shaking. 'A bit late now.'

It ends as it so often does. Ruben bids a hasty goodbye. I have changed the bed sheets for nothing. I crawl alone under my duvet.

Chapter 83

John and I meet for our own annual celebration. We go, as always, to a Mauritian-French fish restaurant that lies almost midway between our two homes. John orders in French. He asks for champagne kir to start, then fish soup to be followed by a lobster in ginger for the two of us. The waiter looks confused. He does not speak French.

'How's the excavation going?' John asks.

'Memory dissolves as it is touched. What do I really know about my family's past? They didn't talk to me about it. I can't catch my parents' experiences.'

A thick eyebrow is raised. 'That was to protect you,' John interjects.

I glower. 'More like to protect themselves. They couldn't talk about their pasts because it was too hurtful.'

'They wanted you to be no different from everybody else. Surely you can see their point of view?'

'Or maybe, they didn't dare tell me anything because they had never resolved the conflicts between themselves over their memories.'

John does not argue, somewhat to my surprise.

'How far can the MI5 - or Stalinist - records about Dennis be trusted? How do I know that my father wasn't insanely jealous about my mother's relationship with Dennis?'

'That's the nature of history. It's always partial, one-sided. The trick is to choose the left side.' John grins. He can be infuriating.

'I would at least have liked their version of history. Their silence was more overpowering than any knowledge could have been. It's hard to have a future without a past.'

'They didn't want you to know the pain they'd been put through.'

'But I had to carry their pain! I had to be the vessel of their trauma. That was their legacy to me. And I became their future.'

'They couldn't help it.'

'Do stop defending them. In my darker moments, I do wonder whether I've lived my life for them or for me.'

'I was very fond of your parents.'

'The thought that I allowed myself to be influenced by their initial dislike of you does not feel good.'

'I don't think this is a fruitful discussion.'

'My parents wanted for so much, who was I to deprive them of the one thing, me, that they were attached to?'

The waiter arrives with a very dead lobster. John looks delighted. I push the dish towards him.

'I don't even know whether what I remember from my own childhood is accurate,' I continue, as John starts to crunch. 'Was I actually unhappy, or do I just I think I was? My mother after all was not simply a depressive, as I supposed for all those years. She was sitting in her bedroom writing plays and poetry. What I remember is her disappearing into her bedroom and occasionally emerging to produce almost edible meals.'

John chuckles. 'Do you remember that chicken, the one that was all burnt up? She was so proud of it.' John prides himself on his culinary skills.

'You remember she threw it at me when I said that chicken was easy to cook?' I continue: 'But it does make it different, doesn't it? She didn't just shut herself away in that room, all depressed and refusing to cook, as I used to believe. Maybe she loved me to bits but just couldn't show it. Maybe I'm expecting her to be like a modern mother, shouting out her love at every hour. Or maybe the massacre of her family made it impossible for her to feel love – or trust - for anybody who was still alive.'

'They did see shadows everywhere.'

'You don't need to tell me. I grew up with whole armies of imaginary enemies camped around my home and ready to attack at any moment.'

'Not entirely imaginary.'

'Do you remember when they thought you were a spy?'

But John demurs. 'They didn't really, you know.'

'Of course they did. My mother did, anyway. She told me that the only reason you would go out with me was to spy on them.'

'That isn't really how it was.'

'She threw you out of the house. You do remember that?'

'She didn't really.'

'Have you forgotten? It was late at night. You had

279

nowhere to go. I had to phone up my ex-boyfriend to ask if you could stay there. I knew then that there must be something wrong with you. And with me for wanting you.'

John shakes his head, regarding his glass of wine, as he twists it slowly in the light.

'She was an exceptional woman.'

'You should have married her yourself!'

'You know I've always had a soft spot for your mother.'

I nod. 'It's amazing she's still with us. Twice at death's door and still going strong. I wonder what drives her to stay alive.'

'She wants to see in the Revolution?' John suggests, smiling.

'Or see me re-married,' I laugh. 'To my mother, a life-long revolutionary,' I declare, and raise my glass. 'I suppose I am proud of her.'

'Rightly.' John pours out the last of the wine, and is regarding the empty bottle with some dismay.

'Why did we break up?' I suddenly ask.

There is a silence. John regards me evenly. 'I loved you.'

'I know you did. You told me often enough. But I could never believe you would stay with me. Do you know that?'

He leans over the table and kisses me carefully on the cheek.

Chapter 84

'Mum, I won't be spending New Year at home.' I listen to Sam's indistinct voice down my mobile.

'That's OK. I didn't think you would.'

'Are you spending it with anyone?'

'Something will come up.'

'How about spending it with Frank?'

'I don't think so.'

'I don't think he's doing anything either.'

'Maybe another time.'

'Did you and Frank want me, Ma?'

That question again. I fumble with my mobile, wishing I could see Sam. I guess he prefers it this way. 'When I met your dad, everything just seemed to fall into place and I wanted to have a baby with him.'

'And Frank?'

'I can't answer for him, sweetheart. We both love you. That's what matters.'

'Got to go. I'll be over soon.'

And the line goes dead.

Do not spend New Year's Eve alone. The ghosts come out and play with your soul.

'She's mine. Jump from the roof,' one whispers *seductively in the ear. 'Cutting your wrists is so much safer,' whispers another. 'What if it doesn't work? What if I get blood poisoning?' The voices still. They sound anxious. 'Get blood poisoning. Stop wasting our time. You said you wanted to die. Be serious now. She's just playing with us. Sorry for herself because she's all alone on New Year's Eve.'*

Johann's voice: 'I must be buried. How can you mourn me when there is no grave?'

Rosa's voice: 'Find my daughter. Find Marthe. How can I rest when I know not where she lies?'

But Uncle does not visit me that night, though I seek his comfort and wisdom. After all, it is a long journey from Theresienstadt.

The wraiths continue: *'You too will be dead soon.'* But I am not ready. I want to have my story first. I get up early and brush my teeth. Even I can manage that. I go out into the dark morning to walk the dog and stare at the many other early walkers. Are we all thinking the same thing? How come you too are up so early on New Year's Day? The light starts to creep up, the base line of the sky turning a greyish purple, the hoar frost on the grass to sparkle as the first rays of the sun break out from the dark.

I visit my mother. Here she sits, propped up in her chair, skin stretched to break, still angry, so angry she refuses to die.

'She will die within the next few days,' the doctor had informed me about a fortnight previously. He told me this as one adult to another, rational beings who are comparing notes. I sat in a chair across the desk to his. I have wrapped my arms around my mother and said my goodbyes.

'How are you today?' I shout in her ear. I have to squeeze in besides her chair.

Silence.

'It's New Year's Day.'

'The Jewish New Year?'

'Roman calendar.' What an extraordinary question. Since when has she cared whether it's the Jewish New Year?

'I hate the Romans.'

'Because they killed Christ?'

'They killed lots of people.'

Is she thinking about Mussolini or Caesar?

'Do you miss your parents?' It's remarkable that I'm able to ask her this. It wrenches my guts.

'Yes.'

''Do you miss your sister?' I continue.

'You mean Marthe?'

I nod.

'No.'

'Do you miss Dennis?'

A shutter flicks open in the pupil of her soul.

'Yes.'

I am taken aback. She has told me the truth. It may be seventy years since they made their farewells on Moscow station, but he is still important to her.

For the first time, I take hold of her hand and cup it between mine. She does not pull it away.

Is she able to lay herself bare as death draws her closer?

My mother has lost too many people. Had her parents encamped alongside her, whispering to her that she had deserted them to their fates in Germany? Was this why she could not speak of them? Did she lie in bed and hear the weeping of her sister next to her ear? Now, I, the parent, give her permission to accept her losses. But they have become my losses too.

Always the same thought: the last time I shall see her alive.

Chapter 85

'. . . as bad as terrorists.'

I turn towards Frank, sitting on the chair squashed up next to mine, at the back of the tiny Magistrates Court. I wriggle so as to avoid hip contact. I had suggested to Frank that we didn't sit next to each other in court. Sam had not seen us together since he was little and this was not the right time to unsettle him. I was anyway unsure whether I wanted to sit next to this man. But such was the competition for the few chairs, such considerations became impractical.

I have dressed up for the occasion in a well-cut (German), purple tweed jacket. Frank, I note, is wearing a rather fetching dark suit. We look the epitome of concerned, middle-class, middle-aged parents.

'Is the Crown Prosecution Service mad?' I hiss into Frank's ear.

Sam, who is standing at the back of the packed defendants, has turned round and is rolling his eyes at me, pointing a finger at his skull, as if he were being shot. The defendants are a moth-eaten looking lot, with more long hair and fair curls than I had seen since the 1960s. I expect the prosecutor to say, 'Off with their heads' at any moment.

'. . . much too serious a matter to be tried at a Magistrates Court,' I hear the Prosecutor proclaim. 'Potentially threatening the safety and lives of air passengers.' Our lawyer is mumbling something.

'All rise,' proclaims the Clerk. We scrape to our feet. We are having an adjournment.

Frank and I escape to the corner pub, quite trendy in its unconverted nineteenth-century, low-ceilinged bleakness. Frank gets us both drinks, himself a pint of the local, me a bottle of sparkling water. I'm feeling cold and had wanted tea, but it's not that sort of pub. We sit opposite each other across the wooden table.

'Thanks for the drink.'

'It's going to be OK,' he informs me.

'Off with *your* head,' I think to myself, unable to stop myself remembering how often I'd have liked his reassurance in the past. I say: 'How come Sam seems so like my father?'

Frank nods sympathetically, wise enough to know he is not expected to voice an opinion.

He says: 'I just want this over with.'

Glower. 'It's not so simple.'

'I know that.'

'Sam takes risks with life and limb as my father did before him. Takes the sins of the world onto his shoulders.'

'I understand.'

'The State has really overreacted in this case. They should have had them up in court within a few weeks, rather than dragging out the case for months and threatening them with a Public Nuisance charge.'

'He's guilty, you know. He did what he is accused of. He has to recognise that. That's why he should plead guilty. He should be properly punished, too.'

'He's right to take a stand against global pollution.'

'It's an easy target, Anna. Do you know anybody who is in favour of global warming? Even the Tories are telling us how green they are.'

'But Sam has helped raise the issue.'

'There are other ways of doing that which mightn't have cost us all so much sleep and anxiety.'

'You know, he is going to be watching our every move together. He'll want to know how his parents are getting on.'

'I understand.'

After all, Sam is his son too; I feel content.

A couple of weeks later, after the case had been adjourned for a few months, Sam phones me up.

'I can't do it.'

'What?'

'My essay. I can't write it. It's taken me a week to write two hundred words and I need two thousand. It's due in two days' time.'

'Slow down. Tell me about it.'

I reassure Sam. He will be fine. I can hear his voice calming down, his panic subsiding.

'Is the trial upsetting you?'

'No.'

'Have you heard anything about when the trial will be?'

'No.'

'Have you talked to any of the other defendants?'

'No.'

'What are you going to plead?'

'I've had enough of your questions. I'm going now.'

I would never have expected that Sam's trial would have upset me so much. It is as if I can only take short gasps of air, unable to pull in the normal two lungfuls. I have no time for thoughts or dreams. I cannot write. I cannot sleep. My head is fit to burst. All I can understand is that I am under attack and have to be prepared.

Aphro tells me everything will be all right. Nothing I can do after all. Have to let Sam get on with his own life, make his own mistakes. He would learn, mark her words. It feels as if she has hit me across the face with a wet fish. What is the matter with these people? Don't they appreciate the resonances for me of my son's arrest? OK, so it's not the SS, the GPU, or even M15. But it is the British state and it is acting against my son. I have to protect him. That is all that matters. My paranoid self is jumping around with glee. *'You see, nothing is safe. Your son is not safe. You are not safe. There is nothing for you to do. Don't you understand this yet? Get used to it.'*

I drive Sam and Jaz up for the last leg of the trial. We set off while it is still dark, stopping briefly when Jaz volunteers to get us all an essential cup of tea.

'I'm really glad about you and Jaz,' I seize the moment and whisper to Sam. 'You're able to sustain a relationship through the ups and the downs. It feels as if somehow the curse of history is broken.'

'Stop it, Mum. It's got nothing to do with you.'

'I think you've done brilliantly.'

'I've never believed in this third generation rubbish.'

'Oh, I don't know. The third generation are supposed to be particularly prone to get angry with their parents.'

'Doesn't fit me at all, then!' Sam grins briefly in my direction.

'Not at all!'

'You can be really annoying,' says Sam.

'But I do try not to keep secrets.'

'You talk a bit too much sometimes.'

'I'm flattered,' I tell him. Jaz arrives with the tea. We gulp it down and start off again. Further conversation will have to wait. Light is starting to stretch out on the horizon.

We all cram ourselves into the Magistrates Court. The defendants have to sit squeezed up against each other on the floor as there is not enough room for chairs. The lawyer stands before the Magistrates Bench, talking so quietly to them, we can hardly hear what he's saying. He keeps handing papers to the Clerk and, as far as I can tell, making references to past cases. Only one of the less serious charges is left against the defendants. The man representing the Crown Prosecution Service who is arguing for the graver charges, ends up looking silly.

The magistrates look down kindly upon the group of protesters. *My son or daughter could be one of them,* I imagine them thinking.

One by one, the defendants are asked to rise, and how they plead. 'Guilty', announces Sam, as do they all. Sam ends up with a conditional discharge.

'I'm proud of you,' I tell Sam as we bump into each other in the hall of the Court.

'I told you,' Sam informs me. 'I told you there was no need to worry.' Yet he looks delighted.

Chapter 86

Sam has survived. I am surprised by the profundity of my relief. That Sam was born at all had been a miracle. He had to shoot the rapids of history just to get conceived. The Nazis did not succeed in wiping us out after all. The sun embraces me in its warmth and light. I love the promise of the new spring. Now Sam, in full voice, carries on the struggle.

And the time has come for me, too, to cut the umbilical cord. It's time to make my own story. The silence is past.